The
ANIMAL
CATCHERS

The ANIMAL CATCHERS

| | | | |

COLIN WILLOCK

DOUBLEDAY & COMPANY, INC.

For Vano

AUTHOR'S NOTE

This book is set in an imaginary African state on the verge of independence. The characters are imaginary, too, though I have met, worked with and admired men like them. Their views about the future of wild animals in emerging Africa are their own. I do not share them. I believe quite simply that the new African nations see clearly the cultural and economic value of keeping their big game on the hoof. I'd like to dedicate this novel to anyone, black or white, who is trying to save what's left of the greatest collection of wild animals the world has ever known.

PART ONE

The lion was lying in a clump of dried grass and he was beginning to be dissatisfied with the situation. His belly was full. The sun had climbed high into the sky and there wasn't enough shade for comfort. Several times he had considered moving, but this would have meant a long lope down to the shelter of the nearest thorn tree. For the moment, desire to sleep overcame discomfort. The smoky lamp in his eyes flickered and went out. He dozed, head on paws. A few minutes later, his head was up again and he was awake, but without panic. His ears had heard something beyond the hissing sound barrier set up by the cicadas; his stomach had felt something strange tremble in the ground.

Soon, he saw them. At first they were just a far-off cloud. Then they became three separate dots, each one trailing its own plume of choking red dust. The lion watched them advance, twisting and weaving their way between boulders and anthills, each vehicle a little to the side of its nearest companion in an attempt to escape its asphyxiating wash. The lion relaxed now that he had placed the intruders in his limited scheme of things. He had seen these creatures before, and, since he had never been hunted by them, knew no reason for fear. If he stayed still they would almost certainly pass by. Then would be as good a time as any to make the effort and seek the shade.

But the three trucks came straight on. The lion heard the first one give a curious growl as it approached the base of the little hill on whose crest he lay. He flicked a speculative ear. Was this growl, perhaps, an offer of aggression? He flattened his belly to the grass. He had no way of knowing that the noise came from the gearbox of one of the most maltreated vehicles in the entire history of locomotion.

The first truck ground its way straight up the little rise and stopped not twenty yards from where the lion was lying. Its motor beat painfully under its battered bonnet like a labouring heart. The truck was an exceptional specimen of ex-W.D. fifteen hundredweight. It had been shipped out to North Africa too late to take part in the eviction of Rommel. Thereafter, by some freak of maladministration, it had lain in vehicle pool after vehicle pool, unwanted, undriven and slowly deteriorating. Its early post-war career had not been much more exciting. Its movement then had been like that of a human derelict well on the slide. It had journeyed wearily from dump to dump, each dump more tired and tatty than the last. Always there was the faint chance of redemption and reprieve but all the time ultimate decay and dissolution only drew nearer. The turning point came unexpectedly in a sale of Government surplus material in Northern Rhodesia. A man bought the truck. He didn't buy it for its tyres: they had collapsed long ago. He certainly wasn't swayed by its accessories: its battery had corroded to green dust and its hood was a shred or two of canvas on a rusted frame. Nor did he fancy it for its engine. This was in pretty poor shape, too, though he knew that a good mechanic could soon make sense of what lay under the bonnet. He bought it because he saw that it had a remarkably low centre of gravity and because its metal flanks had sufficient freeboard to enable him to bolt two stout tree-trunks vertically to each side. And these things, for him, were what counted.

Whatever the truck had missed in the way of glory during the war years, it had more than made up for it in the hands of its present owner. It had been with him now only two years and yet it bore wounds that few of its brothers could have sustained in the service without being pensioned off. From radiator to tailboard it looked as though it had been shot up by small arms fire. Every few feet, something heavier had hit it and left its mark. The edges of its front wings were folded back on themselves like the cauliflowered lobes of a boxer's ears. The nearside cab door had been torn from its hinges. At intervals along its flanks something like armour-piercing cannon shells had punched large holes. Of the two tree-trunks bolted to its starboard side, one had been torn loose at its upper fixings and swayed with every irregularity of the ground. The petrol tank showed a series of weld marks which untidily made good the damage caused by something sharp going violently in at the bottom and coming almost as violently out of the top. As the vehicle panted on to the top of the hill its radiator boiled.

The face of the man at the wheel was almost as marked as the truck he drove. The face was not so much scarred as eroded: eroded by wind, weather and, most of all, by sun. The driver was, in fact, just the right side of fifty, yet he had features that were hard to place in the age scale. They resembled much of the countryside in which he lived and worked—on the surface downright inhospitable and yet in certain tricks of light and mood capable of becoming softer and friendlier. There were certain purely physical resemblances to the African countryside as well. The ridges and wrinkles of this face closely matched the fantastic weather patterning of the sandstone gullies of a thousand dried-up watercourses. The lines round the eyes were caused by screwing up the face against the sun, and by sheer hard looking in a blinding light for something that could make itself featureless in a featureless landscape. The man had been so much exposed to brilliant sunlight that both the troughs and the crests of the wrinkles that covered his face were the same even shade of sepia.

He climbed down from the driver's seat and held up his hand for the two vehicles following him to stop. His body beneath the faded khaki shirt and the clean but anciently spotted khaki slacks also gave impression of extreme weatherbeatenness. He wasn't exactly thin; he was spare. The arm he raised was muscled yet skinny, like a limb of old driftwood rubbed bare of every bit of soft tissue by the sea. He might have been a plainsman from the early West of America. The fair hair, thinning on top but growing thick and wavy down the neck, heightened the impression as did the red sweat rag knotted inside the neck of his shirt.

He dropped his hand, took a pair of battered binoculars from behind the driver's seat and slammed the door of the truck. On its dented panelling was shakily painted:

TED MAXWELL
BIG GAME TRAPPER
KENYA

Maxwell walked round the front of the truck and lifted the

11

bonnet, taking care to stand back from the cloud of steam that gushed out at him. He nodded to one of the Africans sitting huddled in the open body of the truck and the boy leapt down with a five-gallon oil drum filled with water. Maxwell ordered him in Swahili to wait before he poured the water into the boiling radiator. This African, a Kikuyu, had topped up the water level on at least a hundred previous occasions but Maxwell knew that unless he told him this time, and every time, that he must wait for the engine to cool down he would surely pour the water in at once. Maxwell no longer felt any particular rancour about this situation: it was just something you lived with like mosquitoes at night or dust by day. Equally, if the African had poured the water in straight away he would have had no compunction in abandoning him to walk home. Home was six hundred miles away, but then that was the way Maxwell operated.

He watched for a second to see that the message had been received and understood. Only when he saw the boy drop the can, sit down on it and relapse almost immediately into an attitude of semi-coma did he start towards an outcrop of rock that stood some fifty feet higher than the point at which the vehicle rested.

His path took him within thirty yards of the lion. The slight breeze blew steadily from lion to man, so the lion remained wary but comparatively unalarmed. Flattened like a hearth rug, he watched Maxwell climb to the top of the rise and scramble up on the rocks.

As Maxwell made his first stride onto the sloping surface of the outcrop the heat came out to meet him like a leaping antagonist. Used as he was to the sun, the force of it all but knocked him off balance. By his second stride he had forgotten the sensation and stood on top of the highest rock.

Maxwell looked first with his eyes because, on the whole, he trusted them more than binoculars. The plain beneath him danced and sang with the heat of the day. Yellow as the skin of the lion, it stretched away into the distance and far beyond. Just as the lion's skin rippled with the tensed muscles beneath it, so the plain rippled with the sheer muscular power of the sun. The only relief to its yellowness was an occasional rock or bush that looked like a large animal and in some instances was just that. Maxwell searched the horizon and at last seemed to have found what he was after, for he finally put the binoculars to his eyes. Somewhere in that punishing heat haze he had detected a hint of green and the glasses now confirmed this for him.

Still holding the binoculars in his hand, he leapt down from the rock. This time the path he took down the outcrop set him on a different course towards the vehicles. He was upwind of the lion and heading almost straight for it.

As he approached, the lion flattened itself even more, only the tip of its tail moving. Though it was invisible to Maxwell, he stopped dead still ten yards from it and stared at the tall grass ahead of him. The smell of man was now overpoweringly terrifying to the lion. It did not wish to attack and yet it knew that it would be forced to do something. The lion raised himself slightly on his pads the better to spring—or fly. Maxwell saw this movement and, for the first time, saw the lion. He knew instantly that the lion had been forced into an intolerable situation and one which, in a second, would be resolved by attack or flight. There was no question now of his backing away. Any movement might trigger the lion off. There had, however, to be movement to break the deadlock. Without being aware of making the decision, Maxwell raised his hand and hurled his binoculars full at the lion's head. The lion saw the whirling black shape coming and turned his head so that the glasses struck him on the shoulder. But the movement of the head had started a train of action and he followed it blindly. Once turning, he kept turning. He flashed past the stationary trucks and away down the hill towards the thorn trees. Maxwell stood watching him. Then he picked up his binoculars, tried the adjusting screw and examined the lenses. Miraculously, they seemed undamaged. He walked slowly down towards the vehicles. For the first time since they had stopped he spoke to the grey-haired woman who shared the front of the fifteen hundredweight with him.

'See that bloody lion?' he said.

'Yes. But you didn't.'

He ignored the implied criticism. 'Big bastard,' he said almost admiringly. 'Big black-maned bastard.'

The woman, who had a strong, pained face, asked 'See anything else up there?'

'Yes. We're spot on. The river's about fifteen mile up ahead. I told you we were right.'

'Time something was,' said the woman.

13

Maxwell called out. 'Here, Mgulu, you lazy good-for-nothing bastard. Fill that damn radiator.'

The Kikuyu grinned and got off his water drum.

Very shortly afterwards the little column started off again, kicking up its red cloud behind it.

It took them two hours to reach the river. Once they were down the hill, the plain became tussocky, furrowed by soil erosion and runnelled with game tracks. The going was not nearly as flat as it had looked from up top. Maxwell kept the fifteen hundredweight moving at a steady rate, bouncing it from rut-top to rut-top and seldom hitting the troughs. As in a sea-going convoy in which some ships wear the weather better than others, so there was a wide difference in performance between the three units of this party.

Second in line came a jeep. Even though it was weighted down with gear and the two cook boys, the jeep bucked like an impala. Its proper pace in the bush was flat out on good going. On this rough stuff it skittered and jumped as though trying to twist its frame apart at the welds. The girl who drove the jeep was used to this kind of thing but she had her work cut out to hold the wheel.

Behind the jeep, a Mercedes three-tonner wallowed and rolled like a fat old freighter in a North Atlantic gale. She was overloaded and top heavy with it. Roped on her long, flat, open back were two wooden crates big enough to hold a rhino or a young elephant. They had done both in their time and would do so again if they didn't jolt to pieces first. Packed round the crates on top of the safari gear were the remaining eight Africans who made up the outfit. The young man driving the Mercedes was not troubled by the conditions. Driving was something he did as if in his sleep; sometimes he had actually done it in his sleep. His job was to maintain the vehicles and keep them going. At the wheel he regarded himself as another working part that could expect no better treatment than wheels or springs. He was aware that he might have had a more comfortable ride by increasing the speed a bit, but he felt too much sympathy with his vehicle to do so. So he kept the revs down.

The fifteen hundredweight gained consistently on its two companions but, since it boiled twice more and had to stop to refill each time, the convoy arrived more or less together at the greener land that announced the river.

Here the leaves were surprisingly vivid. The going became easier,

14

but the vegetation was more lush and there was more need to change course to avoid bushes and trees.

Once they disturbed three giraffes busy lassoing the tops of acacia thorn trees with their long tongues and dragging the merciless barbs down into their velvet mouths. Maxwell, who had seen this a thousand times, screwed up his eyes in wonder and laughed aloud. 'How the hell they do it beats me,' he said. The woman didn't answer him but looked at him sideways and for a moment her face, too, relaxed. The giraffes took off in fright, accelerating quickly through the trees in a gallop that appeared almost to be done in slow motion. Maxwell gave the fifteen hundredweight some throttle and chased the animals for fifty yards but they were soon doing twenty miles an hour and this was more than he could manage, heavily loaded and in such close country.

The fifteen hundredweight's burst of speed was surprising. In third gear she snarled away with a throaty crackle. This was due to the work of the young man driving the Mercedes lorry. She might boil but he saw to it that when called upon she could certainly go.

As Maxwell slowed down again, the woman beside him said 'Do you mind?'

Maxwell didn't answer.

As they approached a thick belt of scrub Maxwell changed down and set the nose of the truck at the nearest thorn tree. It collapsed without resistance and disappeared under their wheels. In this way they began to cut their way steadily forward. Suddenly one of the boys up top called out '*Tembo.*'

Through the screen Maxwell could only see the foliage jammed against the bonnet. Without anger he said quite quietly '*Where*, you silly bastard?'

The boy answered by banging on the metal roof of the cab. Then the black hand darted down through the roof hatch on the passenger's side, its palm extended to the right. At the thump Maxwell eased his foot off the accelerator, keeping up just enough speed to deal with the bush which the truck was, at that moment, trampling flat. When the hand appeared he swung the wheel in the opposite direction to the pointing fingers. The code of thump and point had been devised to deal with the thunder and chaos of a full-throttle chase. Very often when driving flat out through tall grass in pursuit of a running animal it was impossible for the driver to see a rhino wallow or ant-hill five yards ahead of him. Thump meant stop at once if you can;

the pointing hand indicated an urgent change of course; or, as now, the direction in which imminent peril lay. For all his experience Maxwell had no wish to bump the rear end of an elephant in country that left no room for a speedy exit. Elephants were the one animal for whom he had great respect. They could gang up on you. They were brave and intelligent. Moreover they had a weapon that could be more terrible than their sheer bulk or thrusting tusks. They had a trunk that could tap a man on the top of his skull and drive his head down into his shoulders. This trunk could also pluck a man off the truck. This had happened to Maxwell's head roper, Nguru, on a previous catching expedition. The man had escaped by quick thinking. While the elephant still held him the African had whipped off his bush shirt and stuffed it into the elephant's mouth. The beast had been surprised into dropping him and Nguru had managed to crawl back under the wheels of the stationary truck. Others whom Maxwell had seen caught by elephants had not been so quick or so lucky. Twice he had watched an elephant pick up a man, toss him four or five times and then kneel on him just to make sure.

It was Nguru who had given the alarm now. Maxwell knew this, knew his head boy's dread of elephants, but knew, too, that he would not have dared to call for a sudden stop unless there was good reason.

The truck emerged from the bushes into a small clearing to find itself faced by a large cow elephant flapping its ears, flinging its trunk about and squealing with fury. Beyond her the foliage bobbed and thrashed with life.

'*Totos*,' Maxwell said. 'They've got babies around.'

A second later six adult elephants came out at the run. As they turned their trunks towards the truck, Maxwell marvelled at the speed and silence with which they moved. Beside them, and often beneath them, ran a party of small calves dodging the huge legs and feet and squealing like children in delighted terror. The big cow who had made a couple of false charges now offered a more determined threat, bashing the front of the truck with one tusk and whipping her trunk about over the bonnet. Maxwell shouted to the boys up top 'Scream at her.' At the same time he pressed the horn button. The elephant checked. Above, Nguru thrust a long thick bamboo lassoing pole at her. The elephant caught it and flung it far over her shoulder. By now the herd of adults and *totos* had run a hundred yards into open country. They paused in their own dust cloud and looked back towards the truck.

With a final trumpet, the big cow turned. As she did so her flank caught the front of the truck and lifted its front wheels off the ground. Then, ears still flapping, tail erect, trunk waving, she retreated at a dignified trot to join the herd. Maxwell let out his breath. Tensions gone, the boys were roaring with laughter and banging the sides of the truck.

Maxwell turned to the woman beside him who seemed unmoved by the encounter. 'You've got to hand it to 'em,' he said. 'They've got bags of guts.'

It didn't even occur to the woman that he might have been referring to the Africans who had driven the elephant off with their shouting. She had been married to Maxwell for eighteen years.

They stopped half a mile from the river bank. Maxwell halted the fifteen hundredweight and climbed out on the bonnet. The jeep pulled up alongside. The girl driving it was in her early twenties, tall, with a slight figure, small-breasted beneath her bush shirt. She wore her brown hair short and was innocent of make-up, her features coated with dust. She had a small nose, firm mouth, widely spaced eyes, well-modelled cheek bones and chin. If she'd lived in London, Paris or New York she'd have been rated a beauty, but grooming might have spoilt her. She was nevertheless striking in her own rather masculine way. A quality of beauty came through her habitually sullen expression. She glanced up at Maxwell on the bonnet without particular interest. 'If you're looking for a camp site,' she volunteered, 'it's half a mile back. Big tree. Lots of shade.'

The Mercedes came lurching up from the opposite direction. Ron Webb, the young man who drove it, had cut his own path during the last short stretch of the journey. He climbed down and walked over towards the jeep.

'I've just passed the best place. Small stream running in. Shade. The lot.'

'Where?' the girl asked without looking at him.

Webb pointed towards the river.

'Stuff it,' the girl said. 'You'd get eaten alive down there at night. The mosquitoes are just waiting for suckers like you.'

'Okay,' said Webb. 'Okay. I suppose you've got it all worked out.'

The girl jerked a thumb over her shoulder without looking round. 'Certainly. The best site's back there. Half a mile.'

'God almighty. Where's the water?' said Webb.

'Look, boy scout. I know you've only just left school . . .'

'They don't teach you how to find camp sites in school. I knew those sort of things while you were still wetting your nappies.'

They bickered on with what seemed on the girl's side to be real animosity and even contempt. Their voices rose in pitch and intensity.

Maxwell climbed down off the bonnet. He didn't even look at them. 'We'll camp right here,' he said. 'Tell the cook boys,' he ordered the girl, 'to get cracking on the far side of that tree. We'll have the living tent right under it. Hey, Ron. Make camp and start 'em in cutting wood for a *boma*. Tons of it, right here.'

No one argued with these decisions. Webb got into the Mercedes. The girl pressed the jeep's starter button and drove off towards the big tree.

The woman remained seated in the front of the fifteen hundred-weight long after everyone else had dismounted. She sat there watching everything that went on with a sharp eye. She sat rigid and straight, much as she had done during the rough ride over the plain. The cook boys had unpacked their oven equipment and the fly-sheet of the living tent had been rigged under the tree before anyone took notice of her. Then, when a fair degree of order had been established on the camp site, Nguru approached the truck.

'Ready, memsahib?' he asked.

She nodded. 'Took your time, didn't you?'

Nguru grinned at her. He had heard her grumble in this way often and recognized that there was no real weight behind the words. He unlatched the door of the cab, and, reaching inside, swiftly undid a canvas strap, rather like an aircraft safety belt, that was looped round the woman's waist. Then he slipped a sinewy arm under her knees and lifted her swiftly and easily out of the truck. Her legs, hidden in khaki slacks, hung like dried sticks. They were lacking in flesh and insignificant in weight. They were, in fact, lifeless.

Nguru carried her across the beaten brown earth to the shelter of the fly-sheet. He called angrily to the Kikuyu, Mgulu, who came after a few seconds pushing a ramshackle wheel-chair. Nguru lowered her gently into it.

'*Chai*. Tea,' she ordered. 'Where's the damn tea?'

Nguru explained. The cook boys were away chopping wood. They hadn't had time to brew up yet.

18

'Chopping wood,' she said in swift stinging Swahili. 'Why aren't they carrying firewood with them?'

She dug fiercely at the wheels of the chair with bronzed arms that were as vital as her legs were derelict. The chair leapt into motion and bumped away over the uneven ground in the direction of the makeshift kitchen. Nguru ducked quickly out from under the fly-sheet and made off in the opposite direction.

As she relentlessly propelled the chair she muttered to herself 'I suppose they think that because I'm a bloody cripple . . .' Then she saw her husband walking towards her. Ted Maxwell held a *panga* in one hand. In the other was a long straight young tree trunk he had just cut as an additional tent pole.

'Can't *you* get some action?' she complained. 'Tea's not ready.'

Maxwell stopped and looked at the small, hot, grey-haired woman in the wheel-chair. His face was without expression and this made the woman all the more furious because she was certain that he was unaware of her and impervious to her discomfort. In truth he was far from unaware. As he looked at her his mind was filled with a thought that was never far from his consciousness when his wife was around. 'How the hell,' he was thinking, 'can this woman be ten years younger than I am?' But he knew the answer only too well and this fact made him more determinedly expressionless.

'*Chai*. I want some tea,' she yapped at him.

Maxwell came to the surface. 'Oh, tea,' he said, 'sure.' As he caught sight of the two cook boys returning with armfuls of brushwood, he called out mildly enough '*Chai*, you flippin' layabouts. *Chai*. Chopchop.'

By the time all the tents had been pitched and the trucks unloaded, it was early afternoon. The sun struck down on the camp like a blow from a copper hammer. They had drunk the tea from chipped enamelled pint mugs and now they sat beneath the fly-sheet round a battered barrack-room table. Webb had pulled his bush hat over his eyes and showed signs of dozing off.

'Well,' said the girl, 'if *he*'s going to take a nap, I'm going to have a kip, too.'

She got up to go to her tent, a small bivouac affair that stood a little way apart from the rest of the camp. When she'd walked only a few yards, Maxwell said quietly 'He's not going to sleep. No one is. We've got work to do.'

The girl shrugged and walked on. Maxwell watched her stroll across the clearing and throw herself down on her camp bed. He turned to Webb. 'Time you were starting work on that *boma*, son.'

Webb dropped his chin lower on his chest as if he had fallen into an even deeper sleep. Maxwell addressed the back of Webb's hat. This was now balanced between his forehead and his shirt and completely covered his features.

'Fifteen yards by ten should be plenty. Build it well in the shade,' Maxwell murmured.

To his wife he said 'Sit here out of the sun for a bit but see they make us a decent meal by six.'

Maxwell went to the tent that he shared with his wife. His glance took in the fact that the boys had done the job of setting up home properly. The two low safari beds were spaced as far apart as the walls of the tent allowed. Above them the mosquito nets hung from hooks in the ridge pole, their ends knotted so that they should be out of the way during the daytime. A small calibre rifle stood in an improvised rack by Maxwell's bed. On top of a tin trunk was laid a freshly and spotlessly laundered shirt and slacks and beside them a dented wash bowl full of muddy water. He took the bowl outside, put it on top of a crate and buried his head in it until the water sluiced and sploshed over the curly hairs at the back of his neck. He stayed submerged, snorting and snuffling, for several seconds and then stood upright and shook himself like a dog. He dashed the water from his eyes, wrang out his hair and shook his hands to dry them. This done, he crossed the open space in the centre of the camp towards the vehicles. The jeep was barely one hundred yards away. By the time he reached it his skin, if not his hair, was dry.

Maxwell climbed into the jeep, being careful not to touch the metal of the bodywork. Before he sat down behind the wheel he turned the rubber cushion over so that he had something bearably cool to sit on. Then he started her up and buzzed the accelerator once or twice. He let in the clutch so that dust spurted from beneath the heavy duty tyres and, accelerating fast, swung the jeep in a wide careering circle right round the camp. The heat-saturated air rushed past his face in an exhilarating stream. The sensation was so enjoyable that he decided to make a second circuit. As he approached the Mercedes lorry for the second time, Ron Webb, wide awake now and with hat squarely in place, was chivvying Nguru to get the boys aboard. Nguru, Maxwell noticed, carried his *panga* ready for work. He slowed. 'Build the *boma* in the shade,' he yelled to Webb.

Webb called out 'When you aiming to start catching?'

'Tonight, maybe. Don't know,' Maxwell yelled back, and then spurted away again. This time he headed for the girl's tent, changing down fast and braking to a sliding stop alongside.

'Jen.'

'Stop beating up my jeep.'

'Well come and drive it yourself.'

'Why?'

'I want to make a recce.'

'Me drive?'

'Yes. I want to looksee.'

'Okay. Give me a second.'

'Come on. You can do one in the bush.'

Maxwell climbed out of the driving-seat and swung into the back of the jeep. This was open and empty except for a rudimentary metal framework at the front. These metal uprights were not unlike hood supports but they were stouter since they were intended to prevent a lassoer from being pitched out when the jeep was doing forty miles an hour across country. Maxwell stood leaning on this framework until the girl wriggled out of the tent and took the wheel.

'Head towards the river,' Maxwell told her.

The girl drove as fast as the terrain would allow: about fifteen miles per hour. Handling the jeep on this ground was something like sailing a small boat in a short, nasty sea. You had to feel the next impact before it came and then slide the vehicle down and through the worst of the bumps and up and over again. Soon they were among trees and scrubby bushes and here progress became slower and more circuitous. At the sound of the engine, small, brilliantly coloured birds erupted from the trees like fireballs from a battery of Roman candles. There were scarlet-breasted sunbirds, long-beaked, green-shot, and not much bigger than wrens; carmine bee-eaters, flashes of red, iridescent green, light blue and white that made you catch your breath each time they flew; grey-headed kingfishers, drab when at rest, yet in the act of opening their wings exploding into colours that almost hurt the eye.

The girl's eyes were bright with the pleasure of anticipated action. Normally she was almost impervious to the natural wonders of

Africa, but now the promise of a new adventure made her look at every fresh manifestation of life as if it was newly minted and this was the beginning of the world. Maxwell, too, had lost his expressionless imperturbability. Once when a family of warthog trotted across their bows with absurd dignity, their tails erect like wireless antennae, he shouted out 'Mind that silly little bugger.'

The smallest warthog who was on the tail of the column had lost sight of the stern of the slightly larger warthog ahead of him. Flummoxed, perplexed, but defiant, he had stopped in the track of the oncoming jeep and dared it to attack. The girl trod on the brakes but, at the last moment, the baby lost its nerve and darted off into the bush squeaking and snuffling. The girl turned, still laughing, and looked up at Maxwell. For a second, in the spontaneity and identical quality of their reaction to the warthog, their laughter met and fused. Then they were moving again, lost in a sea of bush that cut off their view of the surrounding world as the branches crunched and smashed beneath their wheels. Above them arched tall trees in which Maxwell occasionally caught a glimpse of a leaping monkey. Then they emerged from the narrow forest belt into the sun and ahead of them lay the river.

Four hundred yards of flats separated them from the river itself. They had come out on high ground. The girl stopped the jeep without consulting Maxwell for she recognized the place as a natural vantage point.

The forest lay only ten yards behind them yet they had burst out into a world that might have been a hundred miles from its green dark edge. On the flats a magnificent water buck, dark-coated, tall-horned, stood like the Monarch of the Glen amid his harem of shaggy hornless wives. He was poised for flight but his females munched the rich river grasses feeling secure in his patronage. There were reed buck, smaller and greyer than the water buck, the males with short forward-pointing horns, the females less assured the intruders meant them no harm. They bounded a few yards, then stood again looking towards the jeep. Far to the left, a herd of elephants wallowed in a papyrus swamp. A cow squirted two calves with water and swished some mud back playfully over herself. Further out in the river two big old bulls pulled the spikey heads from a floating island of papyrus, their trunks feeling sensitively for the most succulent morsels and rejecting the rest. It seemed impossible that such large creatures could remain above the surface in the midst of the morass, yet when they moved to find new feeding they lifted their feet from the muddy bottom of the river as effortlessly as figure skaters and surged forward with the power of battleships.

The birds here were quite different from those they had met on the plain and in the forest area. In the marshy grass towards the river's edge marabou storks strutted, long-legged, bald-headed and nakedly obscene of face. Everywhere along the river, pied kingfishers hovered watching for fish fry and repeatedly diving to the attack. Only rarely did they complete the dive for the fish often sensed their presence and dived first. When this happened the black and white birds checked just above the surface, stood off, and climbed away to hover again.

But the most spectacular bird of the river dominated the scene not so much by its appearance as by its cry. It made a tingling, whistling, shrieking sound, liquid and penetrating, incredibly lonely and poignant. The cry was everywhere, as if the blue bowl of the sky was an amplifier that picked the call up from no matter what direction, magnified it and flung it direct at any pair of ears ready to receive it. Often it was hard to spot the bird that called. The girl pointed high above the river. Maxwell looked and saw two large broad-winged, bronze birds circling. White-headed and short-tailed, they flung their heads back in flight so that their whole bodies contorted and strained with the frenzy of an orgasm, and this spasm produced the cry, the cry of the fish eagle.

These fish eagles were the coloraturas of the river and they had a continuous bass accompaniment scored for bassoon, tuba, and sousaphone. This took the form of a series of stertorous grunts, sometimes performed by two or three instrumentalists, sometimes by a lone virtuoso who took the theme and repeated it on a single rasping note that ended on a great wheezing bellow, and just occasionally by the massed brass bands of the entire waterway. The nearest group of these musicians stood half-submerged on a sand-bar that jutted into the river close to where the jeep had stopped. A rival orchestra basked in the shallows on the opposite bank, while smaller combinations were dotted all over the surface of the river. In the main it was these quintets, quartets, trios, duets and even soloists who were responsible for the more interesting variations. It was hard to see how they produced such cavernous noises while still remaining afloat, for, while they grunted, only the pink tops of their ears, eyebrows and nostrils appeared above the surface. Often, having given out a crescendo of bellowing snorts, the performer scuttled himself on his final stupendous note and disappeared under the muddy water with scarcely a swirl. When he eventually surfaced again he invariably blew the accumulated water out of his instrument in a fine spray, with a noise like the release of air brakes on an Underground train.

Maxwell took in these creatures with a sweep of his arm. 'They were right about the hippo,' he told the girl. 'There are bloody hundreds of 'em.'

She was standing on the driving-seat now, looking towards the river.

'I don't see many *totos*,' she complained.

'Ah, they'd be pretty hard to spot from this distance. They're probably afloat in the middle of the pack. There's one.'

Maxwell pointed to a group of four hippos lying inert, their backs just above the surface, close to the far bank. Three were the usual one and a half tonners. The fourth was about a third the length of the others.

The girl said 'Well he's not much use to us on that side of the river.'

'Too big, anyway. I'm after real *totos*.'

'P'raps they've sold us a dud. Just like them.'

'No. Not them. They want us to deliver our end of the bargain. They know I won't start 'til I've got our cut. Besides, where there's this many hippos, there must be bags of calves.'

'Well, all I can see is adults. I bet they've sold us a dud and you've dragged us all this bloody awful way for nothing. And that would be just about the last straw.'

Maxwell took no notice of this outburst. He had taken up his glasses and was examining the hippo herds more closely.

At last he said 'Come on. Let's see what sort of catching country we've got.'

'You think this thing can swim?'

'It won't have to. When we come back tonight the hippos will be ashore having their dinner. Now come on, let's get going. Though watch how you go on this stuff. It could be soft.'

The girl eased the jeep down the bank onto the top of the flats. Here the going was firm. They were on packed sand washed down by the rains. She built up the speed gradually until they were doing twenty-five miles per hour, snaking in between fallen trees and round boulders. Once they surprised a big croc who took off for the river at a stiff-legged, galloping run, its body raised well clear of the ground. It launched itself like a torpedo and entered the water with hardly a splash.

The diversion took the girl's eye off her driving for a second and the jeep ran onto softer ground on the marsh edge, slowing and slewing crazily. Maxwell, who had nearly been pitched out by the sudden stop, didn't yell at the girl but simply watched her whip the vehicle into four-wheel drive before it had time to think of settling. With a spurt of mud and a writhing heave they were out. It was a neat and accomplished piece of driving but Maxwell said nothing about this either.

When they were moving more cautiously on firm ground again the girl remarked, rather as though she'd just carried out a valuable and essential test, 'Well, we won't be able to catch near the river, that's certain.'

'We won't have to. Here, this is the lot we want. Hold it.'

About twenty hippos were waddling fast out of a reed bed at the end of a dry watercourse. With them were eight calves, three hardly bigger than full-grown pigs. 'Those are ours,' said Maxwell.

'Will they stick around?'

'Should do. I reckon this is their home. Go down into the river bed but don't go too close to them.'

The girl drove the jeep slowly down the ravine on a gradient of one in three. This time she controlled the thing as a skilful rider might hold a horse on a steep mountainside. They slid the last few feet onto the hard sand of the river bed.

'This is the ideal place,' Maxwell said. 'Just look at those tracks.'

During the rainy season the river bed would quickly become a torrent. Now it was a deep sandy cutting with a hard level surface. Imprinted on this were the tracks of baboon, antelope of many sorts, leopard, lion, elephant, and hippo.

Maxwell told the girl 'The hippos use this as a main road to their grazing grounds.' The herd complete with calves was now well out in mid-stream. Maxwell waved towards them. 'We'll come back for those later. Meantime, Jen, if you follow this river bed it should get us a fair way back to camp.'

They roared up the dried out watercourse, jinking and swerving to avoid obstacles. Maxwell's spirit soared at the prospect of getting somewhere at last. Even the girl was smiling again.

Supper was sausages and beans. Zakari, the second cook boy, produced three plates of the mixture, holding one in each hand and one balanced on each forearm. He grinned happily in anticipation of the pleasure he was about to give his customers. Maxwell sat at the table with the girl. Ron Webb came out of his tent rubbing mosquito cream onto his arm.

'What's for grub?' he shouted.

Zakari grinned more widely. 'Sausage and bean,' he said in clipped, far from perfect English.

Without looking up, Maxwell asked him 'Where's memsahib?'

Zakari answered him in Swahili. She had decided to eat in her tent. Maxwell nodded and picked up his fork as the tin plate landed in front of him and clattered to a standstill.

Webb rubbed his hands and said to the cook 'Sausage and bean, eh? More than one bloody sausage and more than one bloody bean, I hope.'

Zakari slid his plateful in front of him. Maxwell was already eating but the girl looked at hers as if it was a swimming bath full of extremely cold water and she had to brace herself before jumping. Webb attacked his long before the plate had stopped spinning. A second later he leapt to his feet as though he had shovelled a handful of hornets into his mouth. He spat the food out in a great spray beyond the fly-sheet.

'Christ,' he shouted, 'Ker-rist.'

Zakari had already retreated fast in the direction of the cook's lines, but now halted as if he'd received a spear in the back. Webb shouted at him in a jet of words that consisted of a smattering of Swahili stuck together with the present participle of a choice selection of Anglo-Saxon four-letter verbs.

Maxwell, who was still eating, asked 'Something the matter, Ron?'

'Matter. Can't you taste anything? Those dumb bastards have fried the effing beans and boiled the effing sausages. I'll kill that bloody Zakari.' And Webb seized a knife from the table and began to chase after the cook, but Zakari was already retreating through the bush like an impala. After a few seconds Webb came back.

'Can't you do something about that bastard?'

The girl, who was fastidiously and slowly eating hers, said venomously 'I'd be obliged if you'd moderate your effing language.'

'Boiled sausages and fried beans! The first time we get a change from dried buffalo meat they have to . . .'

26

Maxwell said 'But they *always* boil the bloody sausages and fry the perishing beans. It's the only way they know. You have to tell 'em how to do it right every time.'

'Dumb bastards.'

'Dumb?' said Maxwell. 'The lot we've got here are direct from the Stone Age. They didn't have tinned dogs in those days. They just tore a hunk off a dinosaur.'

Webb said 'Well, I'm tired of eating dinosaur, too. So I reckon, Ted, it's time you laid into those bastards.'

The discussion now went forward on predictable lines, for the ground had been gone over many times before. All present knew that no amount of threatening or violence could make any difference and that the food would go on just the same unless they wanted to cook the stuff themselves. They had got to the stage of deciding this might not be such a bad thing when Obuji, the other cook, approached the table cautiously holding four plates of tinned peaches well in front of him. He knew this was sound tactics since no one, no matter how goaded, would contemplate physical violence until he had safely delivered his cargo. Then would be the time to consider the swiftest means of flight. It gave him some satisfaction that, although he was condemned to go into the firing line, he had at least had the pleasure of hitting his assistant hard over the head with a length of firewood before Zakari had fled.

He put the plates down at arm's length and dug his bare toes into the hard ground to give him every possible purchase for rapid take-off. The situation was the more ominous because neither of the *bwanas* had said anything. He dropped the last plate, Webb's, and prepared to retire at speed. But at the last minute Maxwell's voice, still very quiet, caught him round the throat like a lasso.

Obuji knew a master of abuse when he met one; he had met a good many. Despite the fact that he could feel the skin being peeled off himself layer by layer, and although he half feared that Maxwell meant it when he said that he would abandon him and his fellow cook one thousand miles from home, among unfriendly people and wild animals whom he hated and feared, without pay, food or water, here in the bush—and indeed thought Maxwell perfectly capable of doing so—he could not but admire the fluency of the invective. He waited for the pay-off that would come as surely as a ritualistic incantation at the end of a long tribal ceremony, and hoped that he would be alive, or at least with a whole skin, to hear it. Here it came now

. . . kickyourbloodyarse. Obuji had never thought deeply about it, but he had heard this phrase so often that he imagined it to be one word.

He grinned. He was alive.

'And hurry up with the *chai*,' added Webb.

This was the release signal. He had survived. Webb he did not worry about, but Maxwell could put the fear of whatever gods he had into him.

Five minutes later both Obuji and Zakari approached the table again with steaming pint mugs. Zakari kept in the background but he knew that once the fire had been drawn he was unlikely to be the victim of any further assault, for, to the *bwanas*, the cooks were as one and their failing hideous and indivisible. One could take the blame for both.

This time when they put their load down on the table Maxwell said simply 'Zakari, you damned idiot, ask the memsahib to come. Tell her we've got to get going in an hour.'

Directly Nancy Maxwell's wheel-chair, driven by her piston-like arm strokes, had stopped at the place left for her at the table, the conference began. Maxwell described in low, unexcited tones the dried river bed and the herd of hippo they had seen there.

'How many *totos*?' Webb asked.

'Eight our size. Maybe more. Anyway, lots more along the river.'

'We'll get a dozen,' Webb said.

'The deal,' Maxwell reminded him, 'was for six.'

'Oh, hell. We're not dealing with *our* Game Department.'

'No. We're dealing with *their* National Park.'

'But just look at their bloody record.'

Nancy Maxwell said 'Their Park record is pretty good.'

Webb gestured extravagantly. 'Yes, but look at their Colonial record.'

'I didn't make the deal with their Colonial Office, or their Foreign Office, or any other bloody office. I made it with the Parcs Nationaux.'

Webb, feeling all the insecurity that was only thinly covered by his cocksure attitude, just had to follow through somehow. The girl's silence during his outburst made his unsuccessful plea for a bit of fast dealing seem worse. 'Supposing they die?'

'Who?'

'The *totos*. We've never tried catching hippo before.'

'We'll know within a day or two how they're making out. If any of them look shaky we'll give 'em back to mum and try again.'

'We haven't all that time.'

'No,' agreed Maxwell, 'we haven't. But if everything goes fairly well we'll have enough time to get our hippos and then do the Parks' job for them.'

'Since when did things ever go fairly well?'

'Never,' agreed Maxwell.

'And the rains are about a month off. Once they break we won't be able to move even if we can still catch.' Webb fancied that he had unexpectedly broken through and had the far more experienced opposition on the run. He went on 'And God knows what's going to happen politically in their bloody country.'

'Oh, shut up,' said the girl. 'That applies to any African territory.'

Maxwell let Webb and the girl bat the ball back and forth for a short rally. Then he said decisively 'We take exactly six.'

Nancy Maxwell said 'Six baby hippos crated and delivered at the coast at £500 apiece. That's what we contracted for and that's the lot, and it's not too bad.'

Webb said petulantly 'And in return they get six animals worth £10,000 a pair.'

Nancy Maxwell told him 'Aren't you forgetting that the animals were theirs in the first place? They're just paying us to shift 'em.'

Maxwell turned toward Webb slowly, as if it hadn't been worth facing him directly before. 'Look, sonny,' he said mildly, 'you let me worry about the flippin' animals and Nance take care of the money and you look after the trucks, handle the lasso and build a few *bomas*. That should keep you busy. Finished that *boma* yet?'

'All but one side.'

'Well, you'd better find some way of closing that side up pretty smartly because in a couple of hours I'll be bringing in the first of our six hippos. *Six*,' he repeated.

'Okay. The boys will never finish it in the dark unless I stay to see they do.'

'No. I want you up top in the truck with Nguru, lassoing.'

'Then the *boma* won't get finished until tomorrow morning.'

'Try dragging the crates up to the open side. And leave it big enough for six. *Six*,' Maxwell repeated. 'That's the deal. Six.'

Night came like the sudden dipping of the house lights in a theatre.

One minute everything and everybody was in full visual contact; the next a soft, total darkness had fallen. No matter how many times this was experienced, the senses were sharpened by it. Perhaps because of the stupefying, hostile heat of the day one's being rushed out to greet the night. Awareness of the night scents and the night sounds was instant, and the moment that the lights had gone down and the night orchestra was tuning up, attention turned at once to the stage, and the stage was the sky. The spectacle to be presented this night and every night was the stars. Ice-cold and numberless they were so close that one could reach up and touch them.

As the moment of complete night arrived they stopped arguing. This silence was not matched beyond the circle of light from the hurricane lamp which Zakari had brought to the table. Towards the river the bull-frogs were beginning their intermittent rattle. A hyena jibbered close to the camp and a mosquito whined like a jet-fighter far beyond the range of normal sight.

Maxwell said 'Plenty of moon to catch by.'

'What's the drill?' asked Webb.

'Well, I'll admit that hippo aren't something we've tried before, so we'll stick to the usual routine for a start. Did you get the lassos ready?'

Webb nodded.

'How many do you hope to catch tonight?' the girl asked.

'Maybe none,' Maxwell told her. 'We're learning with hippo. But it might be so easy we get all six. They're pretty stupid creatures.'

'Ever tried annoying a young hippo's mum?' Webb asked.

Maxwell nodded. 'Sure. No mums are quite stupid when it comes to sticking up for their *totos*, so be prepared for anything.'

The girl asked 'Do we catch from the jeep?'

'No. The fifteen hundredweight.'

'Hell,' Webb said, 'we've handled full-grown giraffe from the jeep.'

'Giraffe can kick,' agreed Maxwell, 'but they haven't got a ton and a half to argue the toss with. So we'll make the first run from the fifteen hundredweight.'

The girl said 'Well, don't think I'm staying *here*.'

'You're not. We want your headlights to rope by. After the first catch we'll see how we go. Okay, Ron? When you've taken care of that *boma* we'll be moving.'

Maxwell, Jen and Webb got up from the table.

Nancy Maxwell watched Maxwell and the girl walk out of the

lamplight towards the vehicle lines. When they had vanished she spun her wheel-chair round and propelled it towards her tent where Obuji was lighting the lamp and putting down the mosquito nets.

Half an hour later they drove out of camp, Maxwell led in the fifteen hundredweight. The excitement and high spirits that always overtook the Africans before a catch found outlet in a stomping chant. Since the six boys couldn't dance in the swaying back of the truck they treated the metal sides like drums and thumped them while Nguru played a piping accompaniment on a whistle made of reed buck horn. The words of the song pointed out to all and sundry that they were fearless hunters who went out to catch a giant hippopotamus with a piece of string. While he played, Nguru held his lasso pole steady against the roof of the cab with the prehensile toes of his left foot.

Ron Webb leant against the cab beside him, holding onto the other pole. He snorted at the words of the song. His contempt for Africans was never really hidden. He wondered how many of the singers would sing so fearlessly if the piece of string broke and the giant hippopotamus turned on them. Nguru could be relied upon, but the other brave hunters would, he guessed, run for it at the first sign of trouble. At the thought of an angry herd of hippo steaming around in the dark his own guts gave a little flip. Often this sensation was pleasurable. Tonight he found it disagreeable. They were trying something for the first time. He was surprised and dismayed to realize that he was just a bit scared. If he had been a more imaginative young man he would have known that this was a healthy sign and by no means a mark of cowardice.

Maxwell smoked as he drove. He had long since passed being apprehensive. He was now totally relaxed. He smiled at the row the boys were making. 'Dumb bastards,' he thought, 'but then they can't really help it. They're just made that way. Poor dumb black bastards. But not Nguru. He has something more than the rest. So perhaps in a thousand years, or a thousand thousand years, there's hope for the whole black lot of them. But it will take at least that long.'

A serval cat leapt across the truck's path, looking like a tabby three sizes too big. It stared at the cyclopean eye of the fifteen hundredweight (the other had been put out by an angry elephant), its own eyes becoming topaz jewels. Then it was gone.

The girl drove the jeep in the rear. She was alone in the front of

31

the vehicle. Behind, leaning against the metal frame, were two more African roping hands. They waved and shouted to their friends in front and caught up snatches of the song. Jen saw Webb tilt his bush hat over his eyes as if to shut out the sight of the cavorting Africans, and disliked him for it. She, too, felt the same thrill of the hunt which at this moment possessed the boys. She tried her headlights and swung the wheel so that the two beams painted a swathe of bright green across the darkened trees. It said something for Webb that he could keep the lights in service and correctly levelled after the buffeting they had received since leaving base. But she immediately dismissed any feeling of admiration she had for this efficiency.

When they came close to the river bed Maxwell called up through the roof hatch 'Ron. Tell them to belt up now. Tell Jen no lights until we see where they are.'

Webb bawled at the boys and signalled to the girl to kill her lights. The Africans stood silent now, facing the front, their grins put away. As the singing died they could all hear the distant sound of hippo grunts.

The trucks found an easy way down into the river bed. Maxwell followed the tracks made by the jeep during the afternoon. Now they kept meeting animals. First a leopard, then some buffalo moving late from the river, a rhino who stamped a forefoot as if about to charge this weird night visitant and then, full of some strange, dark fear, rushed off up the bank into the bush. Maxwell did what was for him a very rare thing. He laughed out loud at the pleasure of it all. He half turned towards the passenger seat as if to share with someone who sat there the pure joy he felt in tasting the quality of the night and everything in it. He had driven this route a few hours before with the girl. With a rare flash of self-knowledge he realized that it wasn't the shadow of the girl to whom he had turned. A girl, but not that girl. Jen, he knew, would be wound up with the excitement of the coming catch. She wouldn't even begin to sense what the African night held for him. His wife, however, would have done: would have done, though she might not now. He thought of the bitter, old woman's face which had been beside him through the long drive to camp that day, and for two days before that, the face which would be there on many other days to come. Was he to blame that she was a cripple who had to be strapped in against the truck's jolting?

'*Kiboko.*' An African voice called from up top.

He saw the black bulk of the hippo on a bend of the river ahead.

The animal paused and trotted away unconcerned. He held up his hand for the jeep behind him to stop, and then signalled it up alongside.

'Jen, I want you to give us your lights all the time. Stay clear. A big hippo will wallop that thing flat. Try not to get between the herd and the water. We'll approach them nice and slowly with the lights on. Try to dazzle them. I'll go for the first calf I see and cut him out. When you see we've picked one, give us all the light you can. Ron?'

'Yes.'

'Try to get the rope on in the usual way. Tell Nguru to watch out for mum.'

'Don't worry. We'll watch.'

'Remember that it's dark.'

'We'll remember.'

'Good. Let's go then.'

Maxwell and Jen switched their lights full on and together they moved abreast down the river bed which was beginning to widen out onto the sand flats at the mouth. Once round the bend they saw the hippo ahead in a bunch. One stood slap in their path, its eyes glowing in the glare of their headlights like luminous pink dinner plates. The girl had taken the jeep out on the flank a little now, swinging it so that the lights moved across the herd.

The hippo were still undecided what to do.

'There's one,' Webb shouted.

Maxwell had put his foot down. Surprise was half the battle. Hippo could move when they wanted to. The thing to do was break them up and get in amongst them before they knew what had happened. The engine of the truck whined as it accelerated fast in second. Webb felt his stomach muscles tighten as they always did at the sound. He was leaning forward with his belly against the cold metal of the cab. His backside was wedged against a wooden crossbar put there to prevent the two catchers from falling backwards. Nguru crouched on his left in the same attitude. Each held his twelve-foot bamboo catching pole ahead and to the side like a lance. From each pole hung a noose of inch sisal rope. The noose was fixed to the end of the pole by an open fork of soft wire through which the rope ran. Behind the wire the running part of the noose was twisted twice round the bamboo and the slip-knot itself was secured further along the pole by insulating tape that would break away at the first shock impact. The rest of the rope was piled in loose coils in the lorry, the ends being finally tied, one each side, to one of the tree-trunks bolted to the truck.

Maxwell was driving slowly by daytime standards but even so it was all his crew could do to stay on their feet as they pitched across the river bed in a straight line for the target.

The hippos broke and ran when the truck was nearly among them. Webb felt the truck touch a hippo's stern. He was excitedly aware of the great rumps flashing and thrashing along just below him. He caught their river smell. The truck was galloping neck and neck with a big frightened beast which was making flat out for the river. Several times Webb could have slipped the noose of the lasso over the big hippo's head and he had a wild impulse to do so to see what happened. Certainly there was no calf in sight and as far as he could judge they were alone, away from the herd, and running with this single adult.

'Watch it,' Maxwell shouted.

Webb felt the truck turn and the speed increase. The radiator hit the big animal almost a gentle, pushing blow on the buttock, sufficient to shift her off her line without damaging her. As she swerved away to the right, Webb saw the calf who had been running all the time at her right flank, hidden by her body. The calf checked when he sensed that his mother had deserted him and Maxwell overshot so that Webb missed his chance. He dabbed with the lasso pole and hit the ground. The pole splintered and the next second they overran, the front wheels of the fifteen hundredweight hitting soft ground as they slithered to a stop.

Maxwell shouted 'Everyone out and push like hell.'

They jumped down and threw themselves at the front of the truck but she remained obstinately bogged.

Finally Jen drove the jeep up behind and waited for Nguru to hitch on a tow-rope. Half an hour later they were out on firm soil again.

'Okay,' said Maxwell, 'we'll have a blow for ten minutes and then we'll go after them on the flats.'

Despite the commotion, the hippo did not seem unduly put out. Some returned to the water, but, before long, the habit of centuries became too strong for them. Night was the time they came ashore to feed because night was a safe time. This one bewildering assault by the monster that roared and threw strips of daylight at them was alarming but not something that could long deflect them from the need to fill their stomachs with two or three hundred pounds of grass. Before the catchers had finished their cigarettes, most of the herd was back on dry land. Only the cow whose side had been bumped remained well out in the stream, her calf snuffling and snorting gratefully beside her.

Maxwell told the others 'We'll give this lot a rest and try our luck further along. Jen. Get round the far side of the next herd and dazzle them while we come up from the rear—only don't shine your lights on us. You'd better start now.'

The girl vaulted into the driving-seat as a man might have done. The engine started and she was away, barely waiting for the two Africans to jump up behind.

Maxwell gave her a good start, then followed slowly. Behind the cab Webb, armed with a spare pole, watched Jen's tail-light recede and then disappear as she turned beyond the herd. As the jeep made the half circle so that it faced them on the far side of the next group of hippos, he saw that she was driving on sidelights only, waiting for the fifteen hundredweight to close. Webb couldn't help admiring the instinctively right way she worked and yet it didn't please him. She might as well have been a man.

Webb had signed on with Maxwell six months ago as an apprentice, aiming at the end of three years to qualify for his own trapping licence. Maxwell had introduced him to Jen on the first day. 'My ward, Jen Stewart,' he had said. Webb had looked at the girl and whistled inwardly. Some starry night, he had assured himself, he would roll over her gleefully on a blanket in the bush and she would love it. But Webb's conceit had been totally misplaced. She had barely so much as spoken a friendly word to him, let alone made an encouraging sign. Nor had Maxwell ever amplified his original introduction—'My ward.' Webb wondered bitterly how far guardianship should be taken or was entitled to go, but the only person who could throw light on any of these matters, apart from the two concerned, was Nancy Maxwell, and she, poor bitch, certainly wasn't the one to ask.

They were close to the herd now. Maxwell flicked his one good headlight once, briefly, and the jeep's lights instantly came blinding across the sand flats. The jeep swept round slowly so that the beams moved across the foreground like a pair of traversing searchlights. They revealed eight or ten hippo well away from the water and then they stopped, pinpointing a very small calf on the landward fringe of the group. The little animal stood bewildered until Maxwell was nearly on top of it and then it broke into a belly-to-ground, split-legged run. It was a sitter for roping. Webb lowered the pole and slipped the noose over its head. The calf ran forward as Maxwell braked. Webb pulled back on the pole to tighten the noose and felt the insulating tape break free. He dropped the pole and went for the rope, taking up the slack and making a quick double turn round the foremost tree-trunk on his side. The truck had stopped now and the baby was jerking and straining at the lasso. Webb took a quick look round for trouble but could see no furious mother getting ready to charge. Out of the corner of his eye he saw that the jeep had moved round between the rest of the herd and the catching truck ready to stand off any attempt at rescue. That girl had plenty of courage.

'Tie him,' Webb yelled to Nguru.

Maxwell was, however, already out of the driver's seat and running towards the floundering calf with a short length of rope in his hands.

The terrified baby saw him coming and backed away fast. When the *toto* reached the maximum distance that the head rope allowed him, he shook his head once and was suddenly free. The young hippo couldn't quite believe his luck. He stood looking as Maxwell dived for his feet in a flying tackle. Maxwell got one hand on a leg, even slipped the rope round it in a quick, tight turn but then the hippo had gone, this time for good.

After several minutes of inspired cursing and a pause for a cigarette, they tried again with another calf from the same bunch. This time the animals were far wilder and took off as soon as they heard the truck coming. All the same, Webb got his lasso on a slightly larger calf quite easily and then bawled for Nguru to cross the floor of the truck and put his rope on, too. Webb, Maxwell, and as many of the boys as could grab a portion of young hippo were over the side at once, but by the time they were ready to try roping the feet of the struggling animal, the calf had mysteriously slipped both head ropes and had pulled a foot free from the one binding which Maxwell had managed to secure.

They ran after the galloping *toto* in the darkness until it dived into a thornbush and stood with just a portion of its leathery back-side exposed to view.

'Come on, we've got him,' shouted Maxwell. They pounded after the hippo but, when they were nearly up to the bush, the jeep hooted urgently and they heard its motor start to rev as it spurted forward.

Webb shouted 'Look out. Here comes Mum!'

The jeep came weaving in, trying to head off a charging female hippo. Its efforts distracted the mother long enough for the roping party to split up, some running to bushes behind which they hoped the hippo would not see them, but the majority doubling in a half circle back to the truck. The hippo came on at full bore, and, either seeing or sensing where her child was hiding, ignored the lot of them. She stuck her great blunt nose into the bush, shoving the youngster right through it and out on the other side and then galloped with him at her side towards the river.

The party regrouped by the catching truck.

'Nice going, Jen,' Maxwell said. 'That old girl wasn't any too pleased.'

'Thanks,' said Webb.

'You're welcome,' said the girl. She smiled at him. Her normally withdrawn face was lit with the excitement of the last few seconds. Webb, imagining that the smile was for him, added 'You were bloody quick.'

The girl said disinterestedly 'I'll do the same for you sometime.'

Webb pushed his hat on the back of his head so that his fair curly hair fell over his forehead, a pose which he knew some people found charming. 'I thought you did it for me that time.'

'I didn't single you out for rescue separately,' said the girl. 'In fact I didn't even see you. Just the hippo. Why didn't you brave lads catch the *toto*, by the way?'

Webb felt for a crushing reply but Maxwell got in first. 'These damned things,' he said, 'beat anything I've ever seen. To begin with they're the wrong shape. How did it strike you they got out of the head rope, Ron?'

'I dunno. Just kind of pulled. It slipped off, like it was going downhill. There was nothing to stop it, not even a pair of ears. I reckon you've hit it. They're the wrong shape for roping.'

'Same thing with the feet. Twice I had a nice tight turn but the foot seemed sort of wedge-shaped, as though it was tapering towards the hoof, so that when the *toto* wriggled the rope just slipped off automatically.'

'Notice the way that one dived for a bush and just stood there?'

'We'd have had him if it hadn't been for his devoted mother.'

'Yes, and she'd have had us if it hadn't been for our devoted Jen,' said Webb.

The girl turned impatiently towards Maxwell. 'I thought I heard you saying back in camp that you'd be bringing in the first calf in a few hours.'

'You're right, Jen. It's getting late,' said Maxwell. 'There'll be some more ashore further along. Let's have another try. This time, Ron, you stay up top and keep the head rope really tight while we grab him.'

But the pattern of the next catch was an exact repeat of the last. The baby ducked out of its rope halter like a powerful dog backing away from a loose-fitting collar. Once free, it ran for the nearest bush and buried itself. This time they caught up with it and were beginning to pull it free when they were scattered by a headlong charge from the mother, a charge that nearly demolished one of the boys. As it was he was knocked flying by the hippo's flank as she turned. Panic was all over his fat round face as he lay on the ground. 'Get up and see if you're alive,' was all Maxwell said. He turned away without waiting to check if the boy had any broken bones.

Maxwell held a conference. 'Seems to me,' he said, 'there's only one way to catch these little bastards and that's by chasing them into a bush and grabbing them. But that means that we've just got to keep mum at bay. Now here's how we'll try it. For a start we'll chase and lasso as usual. That will slow the *toto* up and drive mother away. Ron and Nguru, you take all the boys including Jen's two and follow the little brute when he goes to ground in the shrubbery. I'll stay with the catching truck and, together, Jen and I will drive the mother off. You'll still have to watch it though. These hippo seem pretty maternal. And when you do catch up with the *toto*, cover him in rope. It's the only hope you've got of holding him.'

So, at last, when it was nearly light, they caught their first baby hippo on the edge of the dry river bed. The mother charged but Maxwell drove the fifteen hundredweight straight at her, praying as he did so that she would check before he had to hit her. It was not damage to the truck that was worrying him. The African ropers had no doubt that he considered animals before vehicles and vehicles before people. They were slightly reassured in this pessimistic view since he appeared to place the interests of his catch before either black *or* white human beings. Luckily, the hippo did check. She turned back into the darkness, giving the roping party enough time to catch the baby who had buried himself in a bush exactly like his predecessors. Swathed in ropes, some of which had slipped by the time they had all four feet tied, he was hoisted by eight Africans into the back of the fifteen hundredweight. Once he was there, four boys sat on his flanks, while Webb squatted on his head, but not before Maxwell had seen that the hippo was comfortably cradled on straw-filled sacks.

Then, dead-beat, they drove their solitary catch back to camp and turned him loose in the improvised *boma.*

When they turned in after making sure the young hippo was safe there was very little night left. Ron Webb was ready to drop as he crawled beneath his mosquito net, yet he was too churned up by the excitements of the night to sleep easily or at once. The first time he woke, the stars were still faint in the sky and he was aware that someone was moving about the camp. He searched the open ground from under the open brailing of his tent and saw the figure of Maxwell climbing down from the log wall of the *boma.* He had a bucket in his hand. Maxwell put the bucket down and walked quietly back to his tent.

A second time Webb woke with the same sensation. The dawn chorus had begun in the bush. Maxwell was standing still as a statue by the *boma,* just looking at the hippo. Webb could see the glow of his cigarette but there was no other movement. After a few minutes Maxwell turned away and walked towards his tent again. As he approached the lines he noticed Webb propped up on his elbow watching him. Maxwell said conversationally, as though they had only been talking on this subject a few minutes previously, 'Little bastard's okay, I think. He had a bit of a sulk first thing. Had me worried, but I reckon he should be all right now with luck. He won't feed yet. That's the battle: to get him to feed. But I sloshed him with water. He thought that was fine.'

Aware that Webb had dropped off to sleep again before he finished the last sentence, he turned away. As he walked to his tent he spat in the dust. The gesture was partly caused by the fact that a loose shred of tobacco had detached itself from his hand-rolled cigarette but it was also a comment on Webb's disinterest.

For Maxwell, catching was only a small part of the battle. Making them live after they were caught was the real fight and one into which he was prepared to put every ounce.

With the exception of Maxwell who was down at the *boma* early tempting the young hippo to feed, they slept as late as the sun would allow them. The hippo calf had refused all offerings, grunting and charging the walls of its pen each time Maxwell tried it with a different kind of grass. About ten o'clock he persuaded it to drink from a muddy pool of water the boys had made in a corner of the enclosure. Partly satisfied with this progress, he strolled over to Webb's tent and rolled him off his safari bed with a dusty, plimsolled foot.

'Hey, what the hell?'

'Time you were fixing the rest of that *boma*. I wanted to get him to feed before the boys start banging and bumping round him. But no luck. He's drinking a bit though. If I had got him to feed,' Maxwell explained, 'I'd have got you out earlier.'

'Thanks.'

'That's all right. Women and *totos* first here.'

'And that includes hippos?'

'What else?'

'What's for breakfast?'

'Pawpaws.'

'Well, at least they can't boil *them*.'

'No? Well, get that *boma* finished by midday. I want him to settle down, then we'll try him on some river grasses. If he's not feeding by tomorrow morning we'll have to find a substitute for hippo milk.'

'Think a little chum might cheer him up?'

'Might do but it's probably his mother he wants.'

'He's welcome.'

'We ought to get one or two more tonight. Then we shall see what a little company does for him.'

The extra company did a lot for the original calf and none of it was good. That second night they caught one calf after a series of confused skirmishes in which the escorting vehicles were unable to hold off the attacks of the adult hippos. More by luck than anything else, no one was hurt, but three hippo calves escaped. Eventually they caught one considerably larger than the first baby. When they turned him into the now completed *boma* he charged his smaller relative and kept battering him against the log walls. Maxwell, Nguru and Webb took turns in trying to keep them apart with poles but by dawn it was clear that unless the smaller animal was given complete protection soon, then that would be the end of him.

40

Maxwell ordered 'Get him out and crate him.'

The girl, disturbed by the noise, had left her tent and was sitting in faded pink pyjamas on an upturned five-gallon oil drum. 'Going to keep him in the crate?'

'No. Going to turn him loose.'

'Oh, for Pete's sake,' said the girl. 'After all that.'

'Yes, Jen. After all that.'

'Well, I think you're nuts.'

'Maybe,' Maxwell said, 'but back he goes to mum.'

'Why crate him? Why not just let him go here?'

'In his state of health?' Maxwell sounded outraged. 'A lion or even a leopard would get him if he didn't die of shock first.'

'So what. There are plenty more where he came from.'

'True enough,' agreed Maxwell, 'but back he goes.'

'Well,' said the girl, 'you're mad all right.'

Nancy Maxwell now appeared round the angle of the *boma* in her wheel-chair.

The girl didn't see her. Jen stormed on 'No wonder this half-baked outfit never makes its keep. Just so long as it's run by a flaming philanthropist. We could make our bloody fortune at this game if only someone with a bit of brain . . .'

The wheel-chair pushed its way between Maxwell and the girl. Nancy Maxwell ignored Jen and turned to Nguru and Webb. 'You heard what Ted said,' she ordered. 'Crate him.'

So they took the baby back and released him close to the river's edge. Maxwell prised the lid off the crate and pushed the *toto* out into the swamp. He stood there dazed for several minutes and then made a wild plunge into the water.

Maxwell watched him snort, flick his small pink ears and then scuttle himself ears first, nose last, in the manner of all freeborn hippos.

'He might make it now,' he said.

'Sure,' said Webb. 'But what about us?'

'We've still got one.'

'And if *he* doesn't want to eat.'

'I've got a feeling he will.'

That night they gave the hippo a rest. Maxwell declared that the animals must be given time to settle down before they were chivvied again. Webb agreed with him but with one difference: he felt it was the catchers who needed the rest. This thought, he was quite certain, had not entered Maxwell's calculations. Maxwell outlined a new plan.

It was now quite certain, he had stressed, that the mother and possibly some of the other adults were going to charge once the baby had been separated from the herd. The problem was to keep them at bay. Noise frightened them. So did lights. The trouble was that two vehicles was not sufficient to cut off their attacks. There was always one unguarded side. He now proposed that they should use the Mercedes as well. Nguru would take charge of the catching and roping. Because it would waste petrol and slow down the speed of the operation if the big lorry had to drive to the river each night, they would leave it down there, under a tree, during the day. If hyenas showed any signs of wanting to eat the tyres, then they would have to leave a boy to guard it and that, Maxwell concluded, would suit the lazy bastard as he would have nothing to do but sleep all day.

Morale picked up a little after a good night's sleep. Even Maxwell spent a few hours in bed, for his prediction about the second calf, now alone in the *boma*, had been correct. It had started to feed greedily on any grass offered to it. He set Webb to building an extra wing to the *boma*.

The first night operation carried out on the three-vehicle plan went far better than anyone expected. Only one charge was pressed home and this was when Webb, cut off by soft ground, was unable to close the gap with the Mercedes. However, they caught three calves, two very young indeed, and the third, the biggest to date.

There had been a good deal of grousing about enlarging the *boma* but now the expansion paid off. The two very small calves were released together in the smaller pen. The big *boma* was shared by the two senior members. Apart from a preliminary butt or two there was no repetition of the battering and ramming that had endangered the first catch. Moreover, after a sulky start, both babies started to feed. Maxwell thought it a fair bet that the biggest hippo would soon follow the lead of its greedy stablemate, but he hung around the *boma* tempting it with titbits to make sure.

It was on the second night of the three-truck operation that it happened.

They had caught their fifth calf quite easily and without a hint of opposition. For once no charge developed.

'One more to go,' Maxwell said, 'then we've got our lot.'

Webb said without much conviction but simply because he felt that pride demanded that he say it 'Now we've got 'em taped, it seems a pity not to grab another couple.'

Maxwell told him 'Son, you've *never* got animals taped. We've just been lucky, that's all. Besides we haven't caught our sixth calf yet.'

The jeep was approaching in the darkness. While the last calf was being loaded the girl had taken the jeep up the river bank to reconnoitre for the next herd. Now she pulled up alongside the catching truck where Maxwell and Webb stood smoking.

'About a mile further up,' she said. 'A place we've never tried before. There's a big lot of them with at least three calves in amongst some scrubby bushes. They're well back from the river and on real hard going. It should be a snip. We can come at them from three sides.'

Maxwell threw away his cigarette. 'Fine, Jen. You lead. Where's the best ground?'

'It's wide open down towards the river. Inland, where the hippo are grazing, it's far closer.'

'Okay. When we get to the place you turn off and take the open ground. When we rope they'll panic towards the river. Let 'em go through but don't allow mum to come back at us. We'll make the catch from the side we're on now. That means that we'll have to give you time, Ron, to get round opposite me. Once the stampede has taken place, both of you close in on me and form a box round the calf.'

They had never tried catching this far along the river before and the country was new to them. Here was fine hippo grazing interspersed with bushes that became more dense as they went along. The tops of the bushes were about the same height as a hippo's back. The girl had done a good job in spotting the herd at all. Now she waved her hand to show that they were approaching the catching ground and almost immediately swung off left towards the river. Maxwell checked, knowing that the herd must be immediately ahead, and signalled Webb past him. He watched the Mercedes move out to the right and begin to make a wide sweep round to get beyond the hippo. Maxwell waited four minutes for Webb to reach his position and then put on his lights and rushed the bushes.

He hadn't gone fifty yards before he realized that he was in the middle of a far bigger herd than Jen had reported. Everywhere were glistening backs and gleaming eyes. What had seemed to be bushes now broke into a run. He swung the wheel about searching for a calf. One jinked across his bows running with its mother. Maxwell swerved and accelerated, coming between the two of them so that the calf was on the left of the truck. He yelled 'Now' and saw that Nguru had been quick enough to cross the truck and get his lasso round the baby's head.

Out on the flank the girl saw the first burst of hippos break from the bushes and rush for the river. She was surprised and slightly shocked to see that there were not ten but about forty of them. She let them go careering by and then, seconds later, when she judged they had run well clear of the catch, went in at full bore to close with the now stationary fifteen hundredweight.

As soon as he was down on the ground and running for the roped and struggling calf, Maxwell sensed that the situation was dangerously confused. The thick bushes were the trouble. The calf had gone safely to ground in one of these and the roping party were struggling with it, but somewhere among the bushes and between the three trucks were other hippos trapped and mad with fright. He saw the first one come and managed to throw himself clear. The animal travelling at about fifteen miles per hour hit the catching truck just in front of the cab, tearing off what remained of the driver's door, flinging the bonnet cover ten feet into the air, the main impact falling on the off-side front wheel. The whole truck swung round through a quarter circle and rocked on its springs. The hippo had gone.

Two more animals who had been trapped in the ring of trucks followed the first one's lead and the bushes became silent. Only the calf, now well roped, remained.

In the jeep, the girl's attention had been held by the scene in her lights. She heard the clang of hippo on metal and saw the fifteen hundredweight heave with the impact. Suddenly she was aware that the very thing she had been put there to stop was now happening. From outside the ring the mother of the calf was coming back.

She had begun to accelerate with the idea of facing off the charge when the hippo hit her. This slight turn saved her from a full, head-on charge. The animal struck the jeep a glancing blow just in front of the passenger's seat.

She heard metal crumpling and felt the jeep lift and sail briefly through the air. Then she was in free flight herself, clear of the driver's seat.

She saw the jeep fall, bouncing on two wheels, to collapse on its side. She fell in the grass, feeling the breath driven from her body. The hippo's hoof passed within a foot of her chest. At first she thought that it was this that had crushed the air from her lungs. When Maxwell picked her up in his arms saying 'Jen. Jen. For God's sake, Jen,' she could tell from his face that the hippo hadn't touched her. When at last her breath returned to her in aching gulps she was very sick.

Maxwell was saying 'Well, that bastard certainly wrote off the jeep.'

One headlamp of the jeep still glared. It looked out of the bent framework wall-eyed and pointed up into the sky at forty-five degrees. The vehicle lay on its side. The fifteen hundredweight's one good light had been extinguished. Webb drove the Mercedes up and illuminated the scene.

The jeep was barely worth examining. Maxwell looked at the wreckage as cursorily as a doctor might check for life in the body of a man who had fallen from a twenty-storey window. The jeep was no longer a going concern. The hippo had flattened the whole of one side and the body was so out of true that the frame resembled an orange crate on which an eighteen-stone man had sat. The near-side front wheel was at least eighteen inches to the rear of its fellow.

The fifteen hundredweight had, by comparison, merely fallen off the roof of a normal house. Webb wriggled under the body and reported that, as far as he could tell, the frame did not seem to be greatly bent but that the front axle had been shifted forward on the side of collision and the steering linkage ruptured and track rod bent. Water the colour of blood was pouring from a fractured vein in the radiator and there seemed some likelihood that the engine had been shifted on its bearers. In any case the truck was undriveable. There was nothing to do but leave the wreckage and get back to camp.

The girl had climbed into the front seat of the big lorry and was smoking a cigarette in sharp grateful puffs. Maxwell jumped up behind with the boys and they all packed themselves in round the hippo crate.

The baby hippo seemed sprightly enough. 'Well, you caused enough trouble, mate,' Maxwell told him. The hippo snorted. When they were all up, Maxwell banged on the roof of the cab and Webb moved off. Webb was surprised to find Jen conversational, even friendly. The accident had smashed her normal, sulky, withdrawn quality. She grabbed at his arm as he held the wheel, almost like a girl on a date being companionable though not yet amorous, and cuddling up to her boy in anticipation or perhaps recollection of some treat. The gesture had a great deal of innocence about it. It was a young, almost childish movement. Webb was displeased by the little-girl quality of her excitement but reflected that it was infinitely better than her usual rude, even insulting, indifference.

'Wasn't that something, Ron? *Wasn't* that something?'

He thought 'That's better and better. She's actually being human.' He took his hand off the wheel and tilted his hat back so that the fair hair fell forward.

She gabbled on 'Did you see the way she came in? Was I *lucky*? I just saw her coming out of the corner of my eye and got going. If I hadn't turned three-quarters on towards her, well then—*boosh!*'

'Well then *boosh* is about it,' he agreed. 'Ever had a close one like that before?'

She shook her head. 'Have you?'

'No. You forget I'm fairly new to it. But it often crosses my mind.'

'Never crosses mine,' said the girl. 'Besides I've been around catchers ever since I can remember. My dad was a catcher. One of the first. Of course, I only just remember him. He used to be partners with Maxwell.'

'I didn't know. What happened?'

'Dad got a bug one safari up in the Karamoja. No antibiotics then so he pegged out.'

'Where's your mum?'

'She died before that. Pneumonia.'

'And Maxwell adopted you?'

'Yes. I'm legally his ward.'

'Because he was fond of your dad?'

'I suppose so, though I've been told he was fonder of my mum. I can just remember him fighting like hell with Dad.'

Webb sensed that she was beginning to tighten again. He wanted to keep her relaxed and friendly so he said 'That old hippo certainly meant trouble.'

'*Boosh*,' said the girl happily, almost sleepily, as if the adventure had made her muzzy, even drunk, with too much violence.

'By the way,' Webb asked, 'whatever happened to Mrs Maxwell? I've never found out. Did she get a bug like your dad?'

'No,' said the girl. 'She was flung out of a catching truck—*boosh*— fifteen years ago and she's never walked since.'

Ahead now were the fires of the camp.

This night, as always, Nancy Maxwell was seated in her wheel-chair, waiting to greet them as they reached camp. She took in the situation, saw them all in the one truck, saw, too, that there were no other vehicles following. She sat as if taking a salute while the Mercedes trundled past her. She watched it pull over to the *boma* and then back up to the entrance. She made no attempt to follow it. Maxwell jumped down and gave orders to the boys to start uncrating and releasing the one hippo. Only when this operation was in hand to his satisfaction did he approach his wife.

'Trouble?' she said.

'Yes.'

'How bad?'

'Pretty bad. The jeep's a write-off and the catching truck's in a bloody bad way.'

'Oh *those*,' she said. 'What about the crews? What about Jen and young Webb?'

'Jen got thrown clear when the second hippo hit the jeep. I imagine she's shaken up a bit but she's okay.'

'Shaken up a bit,' Nancy Maxwell repeated slowly.

The girl herself came up at that moment. She limped but she was smiling fixedly.

Nancy Maxwell said 'I told you that you'd catch it one day. You seem to have been damn lucky.'

'I've got a sore backside and my ribs ache a bit if that's anything.'

'That's nothing.'

'I must have hit the ground a fair wallop.'

'I can imagine,' Nancy Maxwell said dryly. 'Now let's hope you pack it in.'

'Pack it in? *Pack* it in?' The girl's voice was shrill. 'What on earth for?'

Nancy Maxwell looked at the almost feverish light in the girl's eyes and thought 'Tomorrow or maybe tonight the reaction will hit her and she'll want to have a good cry. But not now. She's drunk with it and don't pretend you can't remember what that felt like yourself, because you can.' Aloud she said waspishly 'What for? What for? you silly little cow. Because you don't want to end up no good from the waist down to man or beast, and particularly man, like me.'

The girl felt embarrassed as she always did on the rare occasions when Nancy Maxwell referred to her own paralysis, so she caught the handle of the wheel-chair and started to push it towards the mess tent. 'Come on, Nance,' she shouted, 'I want a stiff drink.'

'I can imagine. But thanks all the same, I'll be there just as soon if you don't push me.'

The camp was usually a dry one. Tea—great pints of sweet army tea—was the standard stimulant in exhaustion and constant pallia-tive against dehydration. Shandy was drunk occasionally, but storage space on long safaris was so limited that supplies were usually spent within the first two or three days of leaving civilization. Only in ex-ceptional circumstances were spirits drunk. Tonight all, except Nancy Maxwell who called for tea, had at least two fingers of Scotch at the bottom of their chipped tin mugs.

Immediately the girl sat down in the camp-chair at the table she felt a slump setting in, but the whisky had the effect of damming the release of tension that her body and mind now ached for. She burned up brightly again as the spirit reached her empty stomach, and she talked fast, compulsively, spilling out the story of the few seconds of packed action out there on the sand flats. Webb suddenly felt too tired to talk and Maxwell had no intention, anyway. At the moment he had nothing useful to say. He watched the girl and noticed a trickle of dried blood on her temple. The rosette of a bruise was ap-pearing on her left bicep. He saw vividly the moment in which she had hit the ground and the image was confused with that of another figure falling and turning from the speed of the truck, seeming to bounce and roll for a horribly long time and then lying with legs doubled beneath its body and the face open to the sky, eyes closed and a trickle of blood from the nostril, or was it the temple? The face was at first his wife's and then tiredness blurred it until it became Jen's. The two images were, as so often, intermingled like those on a twice exposed film.

Nancy Maxwell was saying 'There's nothing more any of you can do tonight. We've got our six hippos: that's something. And we've still got the big lorry to get them to the coast. The rest of it is some-thing we'll sort out when everyone's had some sleep. You're lucky you're all in one piece,' she added, without any sense of bitterness or self-pity. Her strength lay in times of crisis. She knew this and the rest of them knew it, too. Legs weren't essential when it came to telling a disorganized camp how to pull itself together. She called out 'Goodnight' to them cheerfully and pushed her wheel-chair towards her tent.

Webb drank another whisky and then said that he would turn in, too. Maxwell and the girl sat on listening to the night sounds and feeling the cooler air coming up from the river. The girl's eyes were bright as if with fever. The nerves and muscles in Maxwell's wrists and stomach still felt like springs under compression. The girl was repeating for the tenth time how she had felt when the hippo charged. As she spoke she plucked at the neck of her bush shirt and a button came off with the fierceness of her gesture. It rolled, a small white wheel, across the table and spun round to stop in front of Maxwell. Knowing that her eyes were on him he forced himself to look up. He did not want to meet her stare. Instead, although he did not want this either, he found himself looking at the opened shirt neck and the lighter patch of skin it revealed. He got out of his chair and started after his wife. Then he checked and changed direction towards the *boma*.

The young hippo was quiet among its companions. He offered it a handful of reeds through the log walls of the compound and it champed on them happily. Normally this would have delighted him but the unresolved tangle that the near disaster had made of his nerves left him unmoved by its co-operation. He wondered what the hell had come over him. It was not like him to feel reaction from a close call. But he knew that the feeling was not for himself but for the girl and, in a more complicated way, for his wife.

The girl was coming. He watched her walk past the *boma* towards the bush. Her stride was stiff, like a sleep-walker's. After a second he threw down the grass he was holding and followed.

Jen was standing facing him in a small clearing enclosed by short bushes. She was not looking at him but up at the trees. The moonlight now picked on the white spot where her shirt had sprung apart. Almost reluctantly and as if he had no free will, Maxwell approached her and put his hand softly on the blood mark on her face.

The girl still did not look at him but placed her right hand under his loose torn shirt, running the fingers round and up his spine. The gentleness was all in those two gestures. Then the girl moaned and pulled him down into the grass. Their love-making was short, violent, without a caress, but utterly releasing. Afterwards the girl lay in the grass and turned her face away. On his back, Maxwell stared up at the stars.

After a time he was aware that the girl was asleep. He looked at her face, quiet now. He buttoned her shirt, lifted her and carried her quietly round behind the trees until he reached her tent. He laid her under her net and put a blanket over her. She woke briefly and said cryptically 'Not often.'

'No,' he repeated quietly. 'Not often. But tonight . . .'

'Yes,' she said.

When he got to his tent his wife was lying on her side looking out towards the *boma*.

'Hippo's settling down,' he told her.

'Oh,' she said, 'then that's a good thing. I hope that girl is all right.'

'She'll be all right.'

'Of course.'

'She's sleeping now.'

'Oh, then that's a good thing. Time you got some. You look like, well you look like you had a hell of a night.'

Now the knot had gone from his muscles and he knew that he, too, would sleep deeply. In his dream he saw his wife running towards him but when she got close the face was Jen's.

The girl woke early to the soothing murmur of laughing doves and the pure fluting whistle of a bush shrike. The morning felt so clean and innocent that she could hardly bear it. She flung off her blanket and looked disgustedly at her soiled, torn shirt and the khaki trousers in which she had slept. The buttons were still undone. Her body, stiff with bruises, was nevertheless purged of the strain of the night before. Her mind, however, felt bruised and almost an insult to offer to the bright daylight. She rummaged frantically in her tin trunk for clean clothes and a towel, and then ran with them through the bush to the stream that trickled at low water level down towards the river. Four hundred yards from the camp there was a shallow pool. A small party of oribi were drinking there, their delicate front legs splayed apart to enable them to reach the water, their soft dark eyes flicking from side to side to warn them in this defenceless attitude of approaching danger. The wind was towards the girl and she moved softly so that the little antelope did not spot her until she was fifty yards from them. Then they took off like huge golden grasshoppers, leaping through the bush, legs and belly in one continuous line as they soared out of sight, the moment of their touching the ground so fleeting that they were almost flying.

The slots made by their hooves were fresh in the sand of the creek. The water was clouded by their drinking, but at the moment it seemed more desirable than anything she could think of. She tore off her clothes and hurled them into the water, then she threw herself into the deepest part of the pool, rubbing her body with her hands as if trying to remove a stain. After a minute or two she became calmer and, standing up, began to soap her breasts and thighs obsessively. She washed her face and her hair and lay down again, letting the current run over her. At last she got up, walked to her towel and rubbed her body until it glowed. The bruises on her arm, legs and beneath her ribs were darkening now. She prodded them with a finger-tip and the sharp pain emphasized a returning feeling of cleanness. She did not go back into the water to fetch her soiled clothes but instead stood on the sand and lifted them with a bare foot, flicking the sodden bundle out into the current. She watched it whirl away like a corpse. Only then did she put on her clean shirt and trousers, pick up her towel and walk back to camp.

Maxwell had risen shortly after her. His ablutions were shorter. He stripped off under the fly-sheet and then, behind a tree, up-ended a five-gallon drum of cold water, bit by bit, over his head, pausing to snort and splutter and rub the drops out of his eyes. He put on his dirty working shirt and trousers over his wet body, then he went off to find Webb.

Webb was still asleep.

Maxwell flipped some water from his dripping hair at him. 'Growing boys need a lot of sleep,' he said, 'but this is ridiculous. We've got work to do.'

Webb sat up, dazed.

'Work?'

'Yes, you're the mechanic around here. We've got two wounded trucks.'

'Christ,' said Webb. 'Ker-rist. Last night. . . .'

'You've got it.'

'I was so damn sound asleep.' Webb was already dressing. Trucks were his line and his pride, the thing he was good at. 'Nguru,' he shouted. The situation and the mechanical challenge was becoming more and more appealing to him as he staggered out of the clinging clouds of sleep. 'Nguru.' Webb knew that he had no real chance of contacting the head boy, but growing exuberance made him want just to shout for someone. Surprisingly Nguru turned up.

'Working party on the Merc,' ordered Webb.

'How many men, *bwana?*'

'The lot.'

'Hey, steady on,' said Maxwell, 'we want some bloody breakfast when we get back.'

'Everyone except the cooks, then,' said Webb. 'And Nguru. We want ropes, block and tackle, planks.'

When Nguru had gone Maxwell said 'You sound bloody cheerful. Anyone would think the whole show hadn't just gone up the pipe.'

'Has it?'

'Well, hasn't it?'

'I dunno,' said Webb, 'until I have a look at the wreckage. Anyway we've got our six hippo.'

'That,' said Maxwell, 'is probably the easiest part of this operation.'

When the Mercedes had driven out of camp with its shouting, stamping working party, the girl went down to the mess tent to get a cup of coffee and eat her breakfast.

Nancy Maxwell was already seated at the table eating hers. She looked at the girl closely and saw that the pent-up look had gone from her.

'Feeling okay, now?'

'Sure. Feel fine this morning.'

'Been swimming?'

'Just felt I needed a good wash.'

Nancy Maxwell nodded. 'Yes.' She said it as if she meant it. She added, 'Not afraid of *bilharzia?*'

'No. Why should I be?'

'I should think that stream's okay. Plenty of flow. No villages about. Still it's always a bit of a risk.'

'I know. But I wanted that bath badly.'

Nancy Maxwell looked at the girl and held her with her eyes. The girl returned her glance levelly at first. Suddenly the crippled woman asked 'What was he like?'

The girl flushed beneath her dark tan. 'What do you mean?'

'Ted.'

'I don't know what you're talking about.'

'He used to be pretty damn good, or so I remember.'

52

The girl said sullenly 'I don't know how the hell you can talk like that.'

'No. Well let's just say that I have, or rather had, first-hand knowledge.'

'It's disgusting that you can sit here and talk to me like this.'

'Yes?' said Nancy Maxwell. 'Well, I suppose you could say that, though I don't really see on what grounds, but just remember one thing, Jen. I'm in no state to stop you hiring the hall but God help you, dearie, if you ever get the idea that you own it.'

'If you only knew,' said the girl.

'But I do. He's a hell of a great man. I can't blame you, even if you are damn nearly his daughter. Ted's got his needs and who am I to stop him?'

The two vehicles lay among the bushes like something left behind on a battlefield. About the jeep there could be no doubt. Webb, as the mechanic of the party, did not even consider it worth a close examination. Together, Maxwell and he walked round it, noticing details that had been hidden from them by the darkness, the windscreen splintered and opaque and the driving-seat torn from its anchorage and lolling crookedly inside. Webb said at last 'Some of it may come in useful for spares. The engine should be okay, and the rear axle. Spare wheels are always useful items.'

'You haven't seen this one,' Maxwell told him. He kicked the nearside front wheel close to where the hippo had struck. The rim was distorted and the tyre, now flat, lay twisted round it.

'We'd better salvage what's left,' Webb said. Maxwell nodded. 'The best thing would be to heave the whole boiling onto the back of the Merc.'

'Fine. Go ahead, if you think it's going to help.'

Webb called Nguru and gave him instructions to lift the remains of the jeep onto the lorry and stow it well forward.

'Now for the real trouble,' said Maxwell grimly.

They advanced cautiously on the fifteen hundredweight as if afraid of what they might find. Webb peered into the engine. 'How about trying to start her?' Maxwell suggested.

'Not much good in that. The petrol pipes to the carburettor are fractured, which means that the engine must have shifted some. But I'm not so worried about that. It's the steering I'm thinking about.'

'Too true. Well, let's know the worst.'

On his back, Webb wriggled under the truck. Meanwhile Maxwell smoked, watching the boys hoist the jeep onto the lorry, not interfering with Webb or offering advice. At last Webb surfaced. 'It's a major workshop job,' he said.

'Nearest decent workshop's four hundred miles from here, and then they might not have the parts. Can't you fix her up?'

'This,' said Webb, 'is the way I see it. The engine bearers have shifted, front axle's bent, stub axle may be cracked, radiator's damaged, track rods are broken, frame's out of true, one front wheel is distorted, and one brake drum's smashed. . . .'

'Brakes. We never needed brakes yet.'

'No, but you'll need the rest of the gear. If you hope to go on catching, that is.'

'I do. Can't you patch her up?'

'Some,' said Webb. 'Some. I might just about get her going. But she'll be no damn use for catching. In fact I doubt if I can even make her driveable. To find out how bad she really is I'll have to drag her back to camp.'

'Okay. Go ahead. What's the drill?'

'She won't steer so we'll rig a kind of shear legs in the back of the Merc with planks and rope and then we'll lift her front end up as if we're a garage breakdown service.'

'Son,' said Maxwell, 'at times you're a bloody pain in the neck. At others I'm fairly glad you came along.'

Five hours had gone by before they sat down to the breakfast Maxwell had promised himself before leaving camp. The meal became a battle conference. First there was a lot of hot air. Webb generated most of it. This, he felt, was his hour. On this and every other safari he had been very much the junior member but now, when the whole operation seemed to have come to a dead halt, he alone was the man to get it on the road again. Ted Maxwell might be wonderful, in fact was wonderful, with wild animals, but he did not have the sort of sympathy and understanding that was necessary to persuade maltreated internal combustion engines and their tortured components to keep going in impossible conditions. He, Ron Webb, had that rare gift. So now he talked self-importantly and at length about what might happen to the transmission and the crown wheel and the half-shafts if the catching truck were driven too hard after he had succeeded in patching it up sufficiently to get it going again.

That morning the girl had caught a chameleon. In the middle of Webb's lecture she produced it from a box and placed it on the table in front of her. The little dragon-like creature immediately began a see-sawing dance, rocking backwards and forwards like the moving piston of a small steam-engine. Webb looked at the girl with fury but went on into a further series of codicils and parentheses about the probable effects of harsh treatment on the pressure plates of the clutch. Jen saw Webb glaring at the chameleon and said sweetly, 'They do it to pretend they're waving about like the leaves of a tree.'

Webb was distracted sufficiently to say 'Oh, for Christ's sake' before launching into an estimate of the probable damage to the radiator.

Nancy Maxwell now judged that enough was enough. Her tone stopped Webb where the chameleon had failed. 'All I wanted to know,' she said, 'is—can you get the damn thing going again?'

'Going, yes.'

'How long will it take you?'

'With good luck, forty-eight hours. With bad luck, three or four days. With very bad luck, never. Thank God we've got plenty of gas for the welder.'

'Then there are two ways to tackle things,' Nancy Maxwell said. 'Either way you start work on the truck immediately and with all the labour you want. The first alternative is we send the Merc off now to the coast with all six hippos and the rest of us sit tight here until it gets back. It should be back within the week, by which time Ron will have the fifteen hundredweight ready and we'll all break camp and move to Makole together.'

'Makole?' Jen asked.

Maxwell spoke for the first time since they had sat down. 'Sure, that's where we get the griff for the rest of the operation.'

Webb felt he had lost control of the conversation. 'For God's sake,' he said, 'we've got all our hippos.'

'Sure,' said Maxwell mildly, 'that's why we have to carry out the rest of the deal. I've already explained that.'

'But *now*. Surely things are different now,' Webb argued. 'We can't catch with the transport the way it is, and here we are with several thousand quids' worth of hippos.'

The girl had lifted the chameleon onto her arm. 'Look,' she said, 'he caught a fly.' The creature obligingly flicked out six inches of sticky tongue and caught a second one.

55

'Oh, for God's sake,' Webb told her.

'For once I agree with Webb,' she said. 'For one little time in our lives we've got a chance of making some money. After all it isn't our fault if we haven't got the transport to do their job for them any more.'

Nancy Maxwell went on as if no one had spoken since her last remarks. 'Alternative number two is for us all to stay in camp here until the fifteen hundredweight is going again and then move out either to Makole or the coast together.' She looked at Maxwell.

Maxwell stood up. 'Well, I'll tell you the way it is, mates,' he said quietly. 'Those damn hippo calves aren't ready to travel. They haven't settled down yet. That's point one. Point two is that if they do travel all squeezed up in the Merc they won't arrive at the other end, at least not alive. Keeping animals alive is my business, and that's what I'm going to do.'

He sat down again.

'Well, all I ask,' Jen complained, 'is that when we do get going we take 'em straight through to the coast and collect our money. I'm sick of wearing the same stinking three pairs of slacks and shirts. After that we can worry about catching white rhinos for the Parcs Nationaux—if, mind you, there are any Parcs Nationaux, or white rhinos, left by that time.'

Maxwell didn't stand up this time. Instead he scooped the chameleon off the girl's arm and slipped it quickly back into the box, closing the lid on it. 'Mates,' he said, 'sodding awful as it may seem I'm going to make a speech. As you may have guessed, I'm not in this business entirely for the gold. I intend to catch those rhino and shift 'em, and if you want to know why, though you might not understand, it's because moving them into a park is about the only chance the poor buggers have got of staying alive in this part of Africa. The whole species is in danger of being wiped out and to my way of thinking that would be a disaster, for no one can replace 'em. I think this place is bloody marvellous. I've lived in it all my life. And everything that makes it what it is is damn soon going to disappear. Soon there won't be a bloody animal left. That's why I'm going to shift those rhino, even if it costs me every penny of the few thousand those hippo are worth, and no one is going to get a damn bean from this trip until we have shifted 'em, so how about pulling your bloody socks up and making that truck work, meantime I'll do my best to get those hippo in good enough shape to travel. Now let's have some *chai*. Zakari, you lazy bastard, *chai*.'

The girl said 'You really do like animals better than humans.'

'Sometimes, yes, I think they are more important.'

'Well,' she said, taking the chameleon out of the box, 'I suppose that's not surprising, really. There are times when I reckon you belong up in the trees yourself.'

When they lay on their camp-beds that night Nancy Maxwell suddenly said to her husband 'That was a fine speech you made about saving the rhinos.'

Maxwell was flat on his back, smoking. He went on looking up at the low roof of the tent. He didn't answer her but she could tell by the way his cigarette paused in its regular pattern of glow and fade that he was listening.

'Do you think you carried them both along with you?' she asked.

'Oh hell,' he said, 'how can I tell? They signed on for the same job as I did. What about you?'

'You forget I'm married to you. Besides, what else can I do except come along for the ride? What about young Webb?'

'He'll come just so long as there's a puncture to mend. He beefs a bit but he can't help it.'

'Be nice if he could be paid, though, wouldn't it?'

'I suppose so, but then I never make a damn thing out of these safaris why should he worry? He's learning the job.'

'And the girl? What about Jen?'

'She'll come. She's got to. She's my ward.'

'Your *what?*'

'Okay,' Maxwell said quietly. 'So you know. Do you object so much? What else do you expect me to do all my life? Turn into a bloody nun?'

'Get your sexes right,' she said. 'Monk.'

Maxwell sat up on one elbow and threw his cigarette out into the darkness. It arched like a tired tracer bullet and struck a tiny coruscation of sparks where it hit the ground. He sat looking out after it.

'In some ways she's so damn much like you . . .' he began and stopped.

'*Were*,' she supplied. 'Like I was.'

'Yes, if you like.'

'I don't like, but I haven't much choice.'

'What is this, suddenly?' he said tiredly. 'The third degree? And why just now?'

'Just now because of the state that girl was in today.'

'So now all of a sudden you're vitally concerned for Jen?'

'No, Ted. I'm vitally concerned for all three of us. I know that what happened last night doesn't happen very often. But it's happened two or three times before.'

'Look,' he said. 'You have to believe me. I had no intention last night. It was just something that happened after the accident. She was keyed up. She needed someone.'

'And you?'

'Okay. I was the same. In the old days after a bit of excitement there was always you.'

'I remember,' she said bitterly.

'If it had been anyone else but Jen who nearly bought it last night I wouldn't have felt so damn strung up.'

'All right. I accept that. But now leave her alone.'

'That goes for her, too.'

'I agree. But it's for you to put a stop to it. That girl's been around you since her old man died. She bloody nearly takes you for her father. You're about the one thing she has any feeling for and then you come along and put her on her back just for a bash.'

'Don't be bloody ridiculous.'

'You don't even behave as if you like her. And she's getting to hate your very guts, too.'

'Like?' he said. 'I don't know about like her. I admire her. She's got the guts of a man. More than many men. And she drives like a bloody angel. As for the rest, I don't know about it. I used to be responsible for her, but she's a big girl now. It's so damn complicated, Nance . . .' It was the first time he had used her name in the entire conversation. 'Nance, I just have to ask you to believe this. She's the nearest I can get to you . . . It's as if it's you but all the time I know it isn't. She doesn't think about things like you do . . . like you still do. Jen wouldn't know why the hell I want to move those bloody rhino. She doesn't feel about this place, the bush, Africa, like you and I do. It's just thrills for her. When the thrills run out she's got no further interest.'

'Then send her back to Kenya, when we get to Makole.'

'I can't. I need her to drive.'

'Drive? Drive what?'

'We'll get transport in Makole.'

'With what? Using what for money?'

'I dunno. I'll persuade Alex Richie and his Parcs people maybe.'

'Maybe. It'll be a miracle if you do, but make it a double miracle. Get a driver at the same time and send her back home.'

'You don't have to worry for yourself,' he said.

'I know. And anyway I'm not. Not all that much. I just think you're going to damage her, and you, but most of all her. If you want a woman around, get an African woman. I wouldn't care.'

'I need her to drive,' he said again. 'She drives damn near as well as you did.'

'Yes, and look where that got me.'

There was rarely any physical contact between them these days. Even when it came to lifting her from her strapped-in position in the truck, Nguru did it. Now he reached out across the tent and put his hand on hers. She made no movement in response so he let it remain there and soon he could tell from her breathing that she was asleep.

When he was certain that she slept, he took his hand away but he couldn't sleep himself. Fifteen years ago, when the accident had happened, they had been catching young giraffe. They had been married then three years. Giraffe chasing was always an exhilarating affair because of the speed at which the animals moved. You needed a vehicle that could do well over forty on rough going. You tried to choose level country on which to make your catch, but level is a comparative term. There are always pot-holes, hidden game trails and small anthills to be considered.

Maxwell had found Nancy in the Highlands of Kenya. She was a farmer's daughter who knew nothing of game trapping but a great deal, both instinctively and by upbringing, about animals. He found her beautiful in a relaxed, undramatic manner. He sensed that she had a good business head on her and knew how to handle Africans. He married her and took her on a safari immediately, confident that she would supply the element of management and planning that his own haphazard nature lacked. If he had been an analytical man he would have realized that the main reason he married her was because he hoped she would take over the bookkeeping and commissariat side of his business and leave him entirely free to live the life he loved best which was simply catching animals. It had never entered his head that she would find the same deep-rooted delight in the bush and in the heart of Africa itself which he continually experienced without ever being fully conscious that he did so, so, when he found her fascinated and transformed by everything that happened around her in her strange new life, it was unexpected. Though in those early days she did show some talent and interest in organization and planning, and in trying to make sense of the precarious finances of his enterprise, she seemed unwilling to employ these qualities. The reason was that she saw her husband, seven years older than herself, as immensely strong and experienced and she wished to think of him in this way. She was unwilling to withdraw from him any portion of the sheer masterful maleness which she pictured him possessing.

Maxwell, no great believer in the softer values, had hoped for a pleasing manager who would satisfy him in bed and not get in his hair too much at other times. Instead he had found qualities in his wife which he had hitherto only met in men like himself. Nancy Maxwell took to catching with a verve that he would never have believed possible in any woman. Her farm training had given her a feel for country and a pair of wrists that could make a vehicle behave like an obedient horse. She had a sense of timing that he had found in very few of his catching colleagues and no one had greater skill at getting up with antelope and zebra in a light vehicle. Then came the day when he agreed to let her have a go at the giraffe.

Maxwell had just had an order from a German zoo for five young giraffes and he had got permission from the Kenya Game Department to make his catch.

They were using a hotted-up jeep, the only vehicle fast enough to bring the lassoer within roping distance. The procedure was to cruise among the thorn trees until a bunch of giraffe with at least one calf was sighted. Then they approached as close as possible without alarming the herd. When the animals stampeded, they went after them at full throttle and cut out the calf running at full speed alongside until the rope was safely on. The early part of the chase was always the hottest, particularly if the calf ran with the adults and refused to be separated.

Early that morning, within sight of Kilimanjaro, they had sighted six giraffes, four adults and two calves. The animals were down in a small hollow. The herd bolted when the jeep was still two hundred yards off. Normally Maxwell might have left them or made a second approach, but the calf was just the right size and his wife's shout of 'let's have him' decided him. He yelled down to her to go after them and prepared to hang on to the roping pole and steel framework of the jeep.

The ground was no different from the plains country they had been catching on for several days. In fact it appeared to be even more level. The speedometer needle touched forty-eight miles per hour at the precise moment that the off-side front wheel hit the tree stump hidden in the grass. Maxwell felt himself flung outward as the truck spun. The framework stopped him from going overboard, but, as he hung plastered against the jeep by centrifugal force, he saw Nancy's body leave the driving-seat and spin through the air as if caught on slow-motion film.

With the driver's foot removed from the accelerator the jeep had stopped fairly quickly. But it had seemed an age, for, while it was slowing down, he had to watch his wife roll and bounce like a bale of straw.

He drove her out to Nairobi at once. She was unconscious all the way. At one time he thought that she had died. Within two days the doctors told him that it was almost certain she would never walk again. As if that was not enough, she had a fracture of the skull.

When she came out of hospital six months later Maxwell was away catching in the Congo, so she went to live on her father's farm until he returned. As soon as his safari was over, Maxwell drove as fast as he could to Kenya. He found a woman whose entire make-up seemed to have changed. She had aged not only in mind but in looks. He now seemed immeasurably the younger of the two.

Her father begged him to take her with him on his next trip. She had become morose and at times, he feared, almost suicidal. He thought that life in the bush, however much it pained her, would be better for her than sitting around helplessly on a veranda. She accepted the idea without enthusiasm but also without hostility.

In the fourteen years since then the lower half of her body had not moved. The wound in her mind had largely healed but the scar tissue that had formed over it had changed the mind itself. The strength of purpose and organizational ability which Maxwell had originally sensed in her had now broken through. The moroseness, however, remained. She was never gay again, but she was often and in many ways stronger than he was. She realized that she had always known this.

The girl was lying awake, too. As Nancy Maxwell had forecast, she was feeling reaction from the near-disaster of the previous night. It would not have been so bad had she been able to carry on driving that day, but there was nothing left for her to drive. With the lack of balance that was part of her nature she did not see how there could ever be a jeep for her to drive again. Habitually she alternated between elation and despair. She was now at the lowest point of the downswing. There was no doubt in her mind that this was the end of the track for the Maxwell outfit. She could not see them ever recovering from their present catastrophe. More personally she felt that this was the end of a journey for her. The feeling of sheer spiritual dirtiness which had overtaken her when she had awakened that morning and rushed to the stream had now returned with full and horrifying force. It pressed on her as if the single sheet that covered her under the mosquito netting was a heavy layer of soiled and filthy bed-clothes. She sat up and pushed the net back, slipping her feet into the plimsolls that lay turned soles uppermost against the nocturnal wanderings of scorpions. She laced up the shoes and slid under the tent brailing. The night was soft and scented and its complete purity only accentuated her mood. A lion coughed somewhere not too far away, possibly because it scented the delectable young hippo meat in the *boma*. She continued walking towards the *boma* just the same. Lions in the night did not unduly concern her. She had been snatched from her mother's shoulders by a lioness when she was four years old and, though she had barely any real recollection of the incident, she felt that she could never have any deep fear of lions again.

The lioness had been a semi-tame one that ran around her father's camp, as, from time to time, did many animals that had been found orphaned in the bush and reared for the fun of it. She had been told the story many times so that she could no longer decide what she actually remembered and what had been planted in her mind by her parents and by Maxwell.

She had been running towards her mother who, she thought she remembered, was wearing a flowered dress. She fancied that she could actually see that dress in her mind's eye but this was possibly part of the memory graft, for she had been told many times that in spite of the life her mother led she had always remained extremely feminine. From such photographs as she now had, it was clear that her mother had been a beautiful woman with the most delicate and gentle face. She had, apparently, seldom accepted the slacks and shirt worn by most women in the bush. Whenever possible she had put on a dress. And so perhaps the flowered dress of that particular day was something Jen only imagined that she remembered.

Her mother had caught her by the hands as she ran towards her and had swung her upwards in one easy, athletic motion, letting her go, catching her again and lifting her over her head until the little girl stood on her shoulders. It was then that the lioness, who was a young one and was allowed to run free round the camp, sprang from the grass like a cat after a bird and took the child with a forepaw, almost on the instant she touched her mother's shoulders. Perhaps the lioness meant no harm to her. More likely the sudden movement had triggered off a hunting instinct which hand-rearing had largely suppressed. The lioness dropped Jen on the ground and then picked her up in her mouth and ran with her fifty yards into the bush. Whatever else was falsely remembered, the recollection of the smell of the lioness and the feeling of being carried along was her very own.

She had played with the lioness many times and so, at first, she was not frightened. This was just another game. It was only when the journey went on and on and the pain of the teeth in her shoulder became sharp that she cried out. The lioness, in surprise, dropped her. She lay on the ground looking up at the moist red tongue and the amber eyes and even then it did not occur to her that the creature might conceivably hurt her. Then her mother ran between them and the lioness turned tail and loped off into the bush. To this day she carried the marks the teeth and claws had made in her shoulder.

After it was all over she remembered that there had been one of the towering rows that were a feature of life in her father's camp, and certainly no one had told her about this. The row, which was between her father and Ted Maxwell, had frightened her far more than the lion. She remembered her mother crying bitterly and that the argument had centred round whether the lioness should be destroyed or not. Her father had insisted that it should live and Maxwell had stormed at him, telling him that he had no consideration for his wife. Her father in return had taunted Maxwell that he had far too much consideration. Jen did not, of course, recall this storm thunder-clap by thunder-clap, but certain phrases and expressions and even attitudes, especially when it had seemed that the two men were going to come to blows, stuck with her as vividly as did the smell of the lioness's mouth. What she had learned in later years left her in no doubt that

Maxwell *had* had too much consideration for her mother and had in all probability at some time been her lover. This was the basis of all the arguments and dissensions that shook and sometimes split the partnership between her father and Maxwell. The only reason they stayed together was that between them they formed an ideal and unsurpassable catching team.

On this occasion she had tried to tell them all that there was nothing to fight about because she was not hurt. Her father had pushed her aside as if she had nothing to do with the whole affair and then flung out of the tent. Jen remembered Maxwell comforting her mother and putting his arms round her. Afterwards he took his rifle and shot the lioness and next day they were all catching again as if nothing had happened.

It was a year later that her mother contracted pneumonia and died during one of their brief spells in Nairobi. Jen remembered the terrible pain of her death and the sense of this intense softness and warmth being withdrawn from her.

She turned more to Maxwell than to her father in the months that followed. He had a sympathy with children just as he had with animals and she felt instinctively that he had been nearer to her mother than had her father. Her father tried to find time for her in and around the camp but she became rather like one of the half-tame chimpanzees or cheetahs that ran around most of the time. Whenever possible she rode in the truck with Maxwell and helped him with the animals.

When her father died a year later on a trapping expedition in the remote Karamoja region of northern Uganda, Maxwell had recently left the partnership after one of their periodical bust-ups. A game warden going south to Kampala had passed on the news of her father's death in the bush and within two days Maxwell had arrived and taken charge of the camp and of her. Immediately afterwards he had become her guardian. Her father's death left little impression on her. For the time being it had seemed enough that Maxwell was there to look after her.

Jen was six when Maxwell married. Her first reaction had been one of wild, unbelieving jealousy that had found relief in black, bottomless sulks. Maxwell's attitude to her did not change. He treated her, as always, like an engaging *toto*, a small animal running around loose that needed feeding and humouring and slapping down hard when it stepped across some line quite incomprehensible to it. She was enraged to find that her sulks did not affect him nearly as much as those put on by some animal he had captured. Knowing the concern which he showed when a creature he had caught refused to feed, she decided to go on a hunger strike. Maxwell laughed and took no notice. Her child mind had failed to realize the difference: Maxwell was certain that she would not starve herself to death whereas with an elephant calf, he never knew. After a day of fasting, she caught up with the realities of the situation and ate ravenously. She was doubly infuriated to know that Maxwell had not even noticed that she had decided *not* to starve to death.

In those early days, Nancy Maxwell was pleasant to her rather than doting. She accepted that this odd, pretty child was a responsibility with which her husband had landed himself. She did not exactly become a mother to Jen though she chased her round and organized her far more than Maxwell on his own had ever done. Nancy did not really approve of the unbroken, waif-like way the girl was allowed to carry on, but she felt disinclined greatly to interfere. There was too much else that was new and exciting in her life just then. Besides, she meant to have a family of her own and she was hoarding her maternal instincts for Maxwell's children.

The thing that hurt Jen most after Maxwell's marriage was not that his attitude to her had drastically changed—it hadn't—but that he himself had changed in the company of his wife, and of her alone. Jen had never known him give out any real warmth to another adult, except on that one occasion when he had put his arms round her own mother, but now he radiated warmth to his bride, not in any overt or demonstrative way, but in some low-voltage current her child mind instinctively and subtly trapped. This was what she hated.

This feeling of hers couldn't and didn't last with any intensity beyond the first six months of their marriage. Maxwell and Nancy— she had come to call her this without dislike or self-consciousness— were so obviously pleased with each other that it was impossible not to become drawn into their pleasure to some extent. The atmosphere of each safari became more carefree and Jen benefited from and enjoyed the new lightness in the air and in Maxwell. Nancy still left her pretty much to herself, beyond seeing that she was reasonably dressed and fed and clean. But apart from casually suggesting once or twice that she really should go to school, she allowed Jen to continue her existence as a slightly fey, semi-human wild creature.

When the accident happened, Jen, then eight years old, was appalled at her first reaction. This was quite simply a hope that Nancy would die and that, new atmosphere or not, she and Maxwell and the rest of the camp would return to the state they had been in before Nancy came along. But Nancy did not die. While she lay in hospital they went to try to catch gorillas in the Congo for a film company, and Jen still remembered this safari as one of the bitterest patches of her life. Maxwell barely bothered with her or with any other human thing. He became obsessed with the problems of the catch to such an extent that she barely saw him. He might, she had told him once when in a rage at something he had failed to do for her, just as well go and live with the gorillas. He had replied without irony that this was pretty well what he intended to do since that was the only way of learning their habits. She began to pray then for Nancy to get well and come back.

When Nancy did come back in her wheel-chair and steel braces there was little of the previous lightness left about the camp. As the months went by and Maxwell got used to a crippled, morose wife, Jen found that she, too, had a new force to deal with, or rather to be dealt with by. Deprived of any chance of having children of her own, Nancy Maxwell now began to take a fierce, determined interest in her and her behaviour. The attitude she produced was not exactly motherly but it had a measure of affection as well as of despair in it.

She began to try to teach Jen to read and write and for this Jen was grateful. When Jen was ten, Nancy insisted that she be sent away to school. School lasted, on and off, for six years with breaks of freedom and runnings away in between. When she turned sixteen she was back in the bush, full-time, and she had by then the makings of a beauty. The few photographs in her possession told her that the beauty had much in common with her dead mother's dark good looks.

School and contact with teen-agers had given her a taste for thrills. The word 'kicks' had not yet come into general usage but the principle was the same. She craved for kicks. School had also partly unsettled her for the simple life. She had never consciously felt the joy which many seemed to experience in living in the African wild. She had been too much with it and with animals since she was a baby. She accepted the outdoor life without particular pleasure and certainly without the inner satisfaction which Maxwell, for example, seemed to derive from it. At the same time she had loathed school because it had deprived her of the lack of discipline and absence of responsibility which safari life with a catching camp had offered. So she arrived back with Maxwell disgruntled, bored, and restless with the restlessness of her age. There was no opportunity for kicks until one day Maxwell let her drive the jeep in pursuit of a buffalo calf.

From the age of ten she had been allowed to drive trucks about the camp and sometimes along the rough bush tracks. She had never done any bush-bashing or animal chasing. On this occasion, they weren't trying to catch the young buffalo. They were just testing the jeep after an overhaul. The going was level and the calf should have proved an easy quarry who would quickly become exhausted. It didn't turn out like that at all. The mother of this particular calf was a good one and she stuck with her baby, shielding him from the growling monster that pursued him. Jen stuck, too, sliding the truck into every twist and turn of the two animals, neatly swerving to avoid a charge by the old cow and eventually running the *toto* off without even grazing him. Maxwell was impressed.

From then on Jen drove increasingly, though not yet on the bigger and more dangerous catches. Though Maxwell was never fulsome in her praise, or even went out of his way to speak to her more than usual, she knew that in some way their relationship was changing and becoming closer. Whenever she thought about it Jen admitted to herself that she admired Maxwell enormously.

Jen had petted around with boys during her days at school. It had been entirely experimental and not particularly exciting. She had no views for or against virginity. She just accepted the fact that sooner or later she was likely to give it away. She did so at the age of eighteen during one of their infrequent returns to base in Kenya. The recipient was almost the first young man who had asked her in so many—or rather, so few—words, for he had simply said in the middle of what had started out as a perfectly ordinary petting session 'How about it, Jen? You can't hold back now.' In fact she could have done so quite easily, but this, she felt, was a kick that had to be experienced sooner or later and why not sooner?

Some months before, Nancy Maxwell, seeing the way her mind and her figure were developing, had given her one good word of sound, if not quite motherly, advice. 'When it happens,' she had said, 'for God's sake make sure the feller's got something. You don't want to get saddled with a baby.' So Jen had asked the young man quite straightforwardly 'Have you got something?' He had, and that was that.

The experience did not appal or disgust her—it was rather painful, but she imagined from what she had heard that this was something which would decrease with time. On the other hand it was by no means wild ecstasy. In fact, so far as kicks went, it was not nearly so good as chasing an eland flat out in a jeep. She never saw the young man again.

Jen certainly did not feel that she had parted with anything vital. Any change in her status was purely technical. She had, however, decided that there would have to be a better reason before she experimented again. On the whole she was not sorry that she had tried it.

After this, her relationship with Maxwell changed still more without either of them willing it, trying to influence it, or even being conscious of it. Nor was the change apparent in anything they did. She saw him now as a father who had the advantage of being not a father. He undoubtedly saw in her a close physical resemblance to her mother. In the way she drove and in the fierceness of joy she got from the chase she reminded him, too, of his wife before the crash crippled her. Her casual sexual experience had turned her into a fully-fledged woman and this had probably activated whatever chemistry was at work. Nevertheless nothing happened until Jen was twenty-two.

Life in the camp about that time often became extremely trying, largely as a result of Nancy Maxwell's irritability. These moods came and went, and, at the pit of one of them, the Maxwells had a flaring row, the culmination of which was that Ted had pushed the wheelchair violently from him so that it ran forward, struck a tent-peg and overturned with his wife in it. Leaving her there obviously unhurt but screaming and cursing, he had walked off without really knowing what he was doing or where he was going and had got into a truck. Jen, who had heard the quarrel, was already in the driving-seat because she had wanted to escape on her own. When he sat down beside her she had started the engine and driven away and out of camp onto the top of a hill. There she had stopped the engine and turned to him not knowing what she should do or say to comfort him. That was the first time they had made love. It had been far more satisfying than her encounter in Nairobi. It had released emotional tension in both of them but it had been release rather than anything deeper.

68

When they had finished he had touched her face and said 'You're well over twenty-one now. You're a big girl. You're on your own.'

She had nodded and driven back to camp and the next day things had been pretty much as usual all round.

It had only happened twice more before the night of the hippo, each time after an incident which had left their nerves strung up. It had become increasingly satisfactory physically but she did not crave to repeat it, for it had also in some way become increasingly disturbing. This last time, after the hippo had demolished her jeep, it had left this terrible feeling of near disgust which she could neither place nor analyse.

Now, in the cool of the night, with the feeling deep on her, she walked down towards the *boma* to try to rinse her mind and body of the oppression.

Webb was so tired that sleep should have been easy. But he lay in his tent, exhausted, seeing tortured nuts and bent bolts pass in front of his smarting eyes. For fourteen hours, all through the hottest part of the day, he had sweated and wrestled with the shattered body of the truck. First he had made the boys dig an inspection pit as big as a small swimming-bath. Then he had ordered them to drag the catching truck over it. Only then had he given the casualty his full professional scrutiny.

Webb was not particularly imaginative. If he had been so he might have compared himself to a skilful surgeon who refused to make a move towards the body on the table until every detail of the operating theatre was exactly to his requirements, though it would have been more accurate in this case to say that he was working in an advanced dressing-station. He had a surgeon's dispassionate regard for each mechanical case he was called upon to tackle. Once the casualty had been given to him to put right he was completely cut off from any personal problems the accident might cause for Maxwell, himself, or anyone else. Now, the crashed vehicle was not the cause of a personal crisis, or a financial crisis for the catching camp or for any single member of it. It was an interesting and complex mechanical problem which he alone had a chance of solving.

Webb was that extraordinary, but not uncommon phenomenon: a youth in tune with *things*. Just as some gardeners can make things grow, so Ron Webb could make things go. He had always been able to do so. His blunt fingers had a feel for smooth metal surfaces, for getting the best out of tired steel, for gauging the correct viscosity of motor oil, for making a perfect weld under far from ideal conditions. He could not have designed anything wonderfully original but he could improvise from the impossible.

Webb was now twenty-three. He was the son of a small-time salesman from Nairobi. His mother had been a showgirl who had met her husband during a wartime ENSA tour. The marriage had been a disaster. It had split up when the boy was only five years old and the mother had returned to her native England. Webb had been left in his father's care, but, since his father was almost always touring the country in a broken-down saloon car, selling agricultural machinery, the care had been minimal. So had schooling. Webb had been sent to school largely to get him out of his father's hair. Holidays and every free moment had been spent tinkering with his father's wares and in the workshops of the company for which his father, from time to time, worked. By the age of twelve he had transferred his attentions to his father's own car which returned from its frequent sales trips over the merciless African roads in a barely mobile state. To his old man's surprise, his son had restored the thing to a reasonable state of health.

At this stage, the school had begun to complain about Webb's total lack of application and, indeed, interest. By fifteen it was quite plain that school and Webb were getting nowhere. So, this time to get him out of the schoolmaster's hair and to extricate him before he was expelled for general idleness and rebellion, Webb senior brought his son home and, not knowing what to do next, took him round the country with him. This educated Webb far quicker than school had done. It also provided Webb senior with a first-class mechanic. In the end, as was inevitable, Webb rebelled against what he rightly saw as his father's exploitation of his growing talents, and quit. He did so on the Congo border in the south of Uganda after a particularly shattering mechanical breakdown and an equally shattering filial breakup. Father and son had nearly come to blows over the fact that Webb was being paid nothing for his services and now, at the age of seventeen, was expected to dismantle a groggy differential by the roadside in blinding heat while Webb senior retired to the comfort and cool of a rest-house five miles away. Characteristically, after the dust had subsided and they had decided not to hit each other, Webb had watched his father hitch a lift into the nearest town and had quietly got out his set of beloved ring-spanners and had wriggled

70

under the rear end of the stricken jalopy. Quite apart from any family issues involved, the problem of just how many teeth the crown-wheel might have lost had begun to intrigue him.

Three days later, his father was able to drive his car away to his next point of sale, but without his son in the passenger's seat. Ron Webb had scrounged a differential from a broken-down model of the same make, but earlier vintage, found in the scrap-yard of a ramshackle Belgian transport company across the border. After a modification or two he had made it do service in the defunct family car. His father had thanked his son loftily, offered him two pounds, which he was certain he would accept, and had been, to his surprise, turned down. The Belgian transport company had given Ron Webb a job as mechanical supervisor on the strength of their belief that if he could make his father's car go then no mechanical problem could ever subsequently defeat him. They paid him three-quarters of the minimum rate for the job and the boy, never having earned money in his life before, jumped at it as if it was a fortune. He told his father this, whereupon his old man cursed him for a no-good ingrate during three consecutive rich minutes, climbed in his repaired vehicle and roared off without another word towards his next inevitable, and now possibly final, breakdown.

Webb stuck it with the Belgians for six months and then took a journey on one of their lorries going north into Uganda, with no intention of coming back. His only luggage, apart from a change of clothing, was his wallet of ring-spanners and the bit of money he had saved.

In Nairobi he had got a job at only slightly under the proper rate, servicing the vehicles for an Indian bus company. He was busy there one day when Ted Maxwell drove his catching truck in for a welding job. It was like showing a diagnostician some rare form of a disease he had never before encountered. Webb was fascinated by the dilapidation of the thing and did far more than just weld up the gashes. After this, whenever Maxwell returned from a safari, he brought his tired transport to Webb for his personal attention, and as a private contract for which Webb rarely got paid, at least in full.

It was largely to atone for this debt that Maxwell eventually asked Webb whether he would like to come on a trip with the catchers. His keep, Maxwell stressed, would be free; but, as Webb was expected to supply his own tent and bedding, keep was not excessive.

The excitement of the thing got Webb from the start. Moreover he was not entirely unshrewd. He could see that, properly managed, there might be money in trapping game. Others who weren't so vitally interested in the animals and their welfare as was Maxwell had made more than a go of it. Some of the more commercial outfits had done very well with film companies. Webb had a considerable streak of vanity. Good-looking in a boyish way, he saw himself running a catching outfit in whose immaculately maintained vehicles he personally drove film stars on rewarding safaris. That had been the dream.

He had got back from his first trip with Maxwell still nursing the dream, but unwilling to do anything about it just yet. After that Maxwell had come and gone at intervals, each time returning with trucks covered in elephant dents and rhino holes. The trouble, Webb realized, was that before his dream could become reality he must serve his apprenticeship and qualify for his trapping licence. That meant three years working for Maxwell for almost nothing.

One day when he was especially fed up with the Indians and their bus company, he asked Maxwell to take him on. Maxwell agreed, offering him keep, a small wage, and a smaller share of the profits on each trip. Webb was a long way still from escorting glamorous film stars into the bush, but from the start he enjoyed the life, though he got a bit tired of Maxwell's intense attitude towards his animal charges and his apparent disinterest in his human fellow workers. Still there were always automotive conundrums to be solved and they, certainly, had lost none of their appeal.

On this night he lay on his bed reviewing a plan for bracing the shifted front axle of the catching truck with steel cable borrowed from the winch gear. As he reviewed the possibilities he heard someone walking softly up from the *boma* towards his tent. Webb looked out under the flap of his tent and saw Jen standing looking down at him.

Neither spoke. The girl just continued to look at him. Then suddenly she smiled and fingered the top button of her shirt neck. Webb started forward a little on his bed. There was, he thought, no mistaking the implication of the gesture. But, seeing the movement, the girl smiled again and turned on her heel. She walked quickly away across the clearing, her hips moving with a slight exaggeration of their usual, almost masculine, gait. Webb lay back and watched her. 'You strange bitch,' he thought to himself. 'I wonder what would happen if I tried? She'd probably bite me half to death. And yet I really believe she wanted me to.'

They were at work again by six next morning. By breakfast time Webb had reached a definite decision: he could, and would, persuade the truck to move again, and what's more it would make the two-day journey across the bush to Makole. Two days, he reflected, for a healthy vehicle, but possibly twice as long for a cripple. He had reached this conclusion as the boys had heaved the engine clear of the frame on a block and tackle rigged from an acacia tree. It had been impossible to pull the engine out on the first day because he had had to cut through a great deal of bent metal. Now that the engine was clear he had plans for mounting it afresh, sealing off the more vitally damaged parts of the radiator and organizing some very approximate steering. The winch cable idea was a key part of this plan. As he walked across to breakfast the boys were unwinding its twisted, rusted coil from the winch drum.

He told Maxwell what he had decided.

Maxwell nodded and asked 'When will she go?'

'Fercrisake,' said Webb.

'Never mind him. I'm more worried about them hippos.'

'Not about us by any chance?'

Maxwell looked at Webb in genuine amazement. 'You're living and breathing aren't you?'

'Certainly,' Webb said with heavy sarcasm, 'but not much else.'

'There ain't much else.'

Nancy Maxwell looked up from her breakfast. 'Ain't,' she said. 'For God's sake you don't have to talk like that. You can say aren't, can't you?'

'There aren't anything else,' said Maxwell. 'Sounds bloody silly.'

'Fercrisake,' she said, mocking Webb.

All this took place, apparently, with complete lack of humour, but anyone who worked and lived with the camp would have recognized this exchange as a sign of reasonably high spirits. They were all cheered by Webb's diagnosis and report on the truck. No one doubted that he would do what he promised.

After a long silence Maxwell asked 'What kind of load will she pull?'

'She'll just about manage herself and the driver.'

'She'll have to do better than that.'

'All right, then, one or two bods and maybe the safari gear but she'll boil a hell of a lot.'

'Always did.'

'Yes, but now you'll have to fill her up every mile instead of every two.'

'She'll have to take at least one hippo—the biggest.'

'Do me a favour,' said Webb.

'I am. I could have said two.'

'Be pretty cramped for the five poor little bastards in the Merc,' Nancy Maxwell said. 'Won't they kick each other to pieces?'

'It's a risk,' agreed Maxwell, 'but not if we make special crates with separate compartments. That's why I wanted sonny Jim here to tell us how long we've got before we move out.'

'Long enough to build twenty crates,' Webb told him.

'Tomorrow night?'

'Don't be funny, Ted.'

'I'm not. Time's running out.'

'Have your crates ready by the night after and we might just get away. Unless we have any complications.'

'Don't have 'em then,' Maxwell told him.

To Webb's surprise the girl brought him a mug of hot tea just before midday. He was too grateful for the refreshment to make one of his usual cracks.

'How's it going?' she asked.

'So-so. Got the radiator off. I reckon we can seal off the damaged part. I might have to find a way of giving her more water to play with. Maybe we can make a sort of extra reservoir for her with an oil drum. I could lash it on the front down low and connect it by a length of hose.'

This was about the longest speech he had ever succeeded in making to her without losing his audience. But there was a bigger surprise to come for she now said 'Is there anything I can do to lend a hand?'

'*What?*' he shouted.

He had not meant to goad her and the disbelief in his exclamation had been spontaneous. He just could not imagine that she had said what he had heard her say. He saw that he had made her furious but even so she did not immediately put the shutters down. At any other

74

time she would have snarled at him and turned away. Instead she said 'You don't have to be so bloody rude.'

He climbed up out of the inspection pit and wiped his hands on some cotton waste. 'Hang on a mo,' he said, 'I didn't mean it that way at all. It was just that this is pretty damn dirty work and I'm not sure that there's anything you *could* do.'

She stood staring at him. 'That wasn't it at all. You just couldn't believe I'd offer to help you.'

'Well maybe a bit of that,' he admitted. 'I could certainly use some help. These characters,' he jerked a thumb at the Africans, 'try, but you've got to watch 'em all the time. If you want to help, why don't you help Ted? He's got quite a handful cutting those crates down to size, let alone making fresh ones. You could hold a nail or bash with a hammer, okay, but I dunno about this lot. I'd like you to help no end,' he added, 'but surely, Ted . . .'

'To hell with Ted. Let him build his own crates.'

Webb looked at her closely. There was something odd here but whatever it was he couldn't analyse it. Her face remained expressionless but determined.

'Well, if you say so.'

'I do say so. To hell with Ted. I offered to help you.'

'Okay,' said Webb, accepting it at last. 'But what can you do? You can't weld or lift weights.'

'No. But I could stay up top here while you're down below in the pit and see they did what you told them. If you told me what you wanted done, I could supervise it for you while you were on something else. I do recognize one end of a truck from the other, you know.'

Webb believed her offer was genuine now, though he was at a loss to understand her change of attitude. 'You're hired,' he told her and put his arm round her shoulder.

She moved away. 'Your hands are dirty,' she said coldly.

Webb took his arm away quickly. He had just enough imagination to reflect that at any other time she might have said 'Keep your dirty hands off me.'

When they broke for a snatched lunch Maxwell said 'I could use an extra hand with the crates, Jen.'

'Well get one of the boys then.'

'No. I want someone to take charge of building while I'm chasing up some more timber.'

'Sorry. I'm helping Ron.'

Maxwell looked at her, puzzled. 'What the hell can *you* do to a truck?'

Nancy Maxwell said 'Let her alone. I'll come out and look after your crates.'

'But she's more damn use to me.'

Jen said 'You've often told me that I'm a big girl now. I can do what I damn well please.'

'Not in my camp, you can't.'

'Pack that in, Jen,' Nancy Maxwell said. 'It's my job to plan who does what and I say you'll go and join Webb there. I'll help Ted.'

When Webb and the girl had left the table, Maxwell said to his wife 'What's got into that damn girl, and you?'

'I told you she'd had enough of you and I told you you ought to leave her alone. It's far better for her if she hangs around Webb.'

'She don't like Webb.'

'No, and at the moment she doesn't go much on you. Now come on, Ted. You've got work to do.'

The next morning the sky clouded up into great meringues of cumulus and at midday there was a short thunderstorm. Enough rain fell in ten minutes to fill the inspection pit until the water slopped over the top of Webb's gym shoes. Webb let the rain stream on him, washing dirt and dust down from the truck in a cocoa-coloured stream. He had the operation well in hand and he didn't see any reason to stop for a little rain. Dirty or not, the water was deliciously refreshing after the claustrophobic heat of the last few days. The engine had been lowered onto the new plates he had drilled to receive it. He had improvised some rubber mountings from lozenges cut from an old ripped tyre. He was coaxing one of the bearer bolts through the frame and into these rubbers as the storm broke. When he had at last wheedled it through without burring a single thread he shouted to one of the boys for the appropriate spanner. The boys, however, had all taken cover. He swore at great length in a coruscating spatter of Anglo-Saxon, bawling for them to come. The girl answered him. He had forgotten about her. Since yesterday afternoon she had hung around, sometimes making herself useful but most of the time just being there, sitting silent and absorbed in the cab. He was reasonably sure that she hadn't attached herself to him for his own sake, but his vanity was such that it didn't allow him altogether to exclude this possibility.

A hand reached the spanner down to him. He was not quite ready for it. He was busy closing the end of a split-pin with pliers, so he kept the hand waiting, thinking it belonged to one of the Africans. When he looked up, ready at last to take the spanner, he saw that the hand was the girl's and that the water was streaming down it. He was too involved with the job to bother about the fact that she must by now be wet through. But his mind did find time to register briefly that her shirt must be plastered to her, and that this would be worth seeing. Tackle things in order of importance, he told himself, so he took the spanner and shouted 'Thanks' and then went to work on the nut. It took a few minutes to complete the job. When he looked up again her feet were still in the same place on the edge of the pit. He pulled himself up by the partly dismantled front axle and swung out of the pit. The pleasure of returning to daylight from the cramped conditions in which he had been working and the exhilaration stung out of him by the full force of the rain momentarily put the girl from his mind. He stood facing away from her for a second and ripped off his dirty shirt, letting the rain beat on his body. It was a good strong body with a deep wide chest and narrow hips. The rain plastered the sandy hairs to his chest and he ran his hands up, catching its fall, collecting it and whooshing it up into his face. Then he turned, grinning, and faced the girl. She was standing, watching him and, he thought, not viewing him with displeasure. He looked full at her breasts which were stuck to her shirt much as he had once seen an Italian film star in a publicity picture bathing in shirt and slacks somewhere on the Riviera. He threw his shirt away with a whoop of joy. Out of the corner of his eye he saw Maxwell running for cover across the clearing. They were both in full view to Maxwell when the girl did what was to Webb an utterly surprising thing. With a quick movement she tore her own shirt off, too, and stood there naked from the waist up for a full second. Then she ran her hands up from her waist as Webb had done, scooping the water and cupping each breast. Webb saw Maxwell stop to look at her and then run on. In that instant the girl ran too, leaving her discarded shirt on the ground.

Ten minutes later when they all met in the mess tent she was dried, in clean clothes and silent. No one passed any remark on the incident.

Jen did not come to help him that afternoon. The rain disappeared into the earth as if it had never been. For a few burning hours in mid-afternoon the bush smelt as if it had been scrubbed clean. You could almost hear the new grass fighting to get out of its roots. Then the heat clamped down again, the sky cleared and the storm fell into true perspective. It became no more than its real life-size, a hint that the rains proper lay some two or three weeks over the horizon. Nevertheless, this hint was enough to give everyone a push on. By nightfall, Webb had the engine back and running. He had also sealed the damaged radiator and fixed the hose extensions for its additional reservoir. Maxwell had finished four of his new crates and the timber lay cut for the remainder.

They turned in, dead beat, but were at it again by six the next morning. When they broke for breakfast at eight, Webb had lashed on his makeshift water container and had run the engine sufficiently long to ensure there were no leaks. The sound of the fifteen hundred-weight snarling away raised everyone's hopes, so that they began to feel ready for anything.

When Webb had announced that, with reasonable luck, he would be able to try the truck out by late afternoon, Maxwell said 'Fine. Then we'll pull out tonight.'

'Tonight!' Webb and the girl cried together.

'What's wrong with tonight?'

'Simply that you've got a hundred and twenty miles to do before you hit a track and it's not much of a track when you get there.'

'So?'

'So that's a hundred and twenty miles across the bush in the pitch darkness.'

'So?'

'So it may not be too easy to find the way,' said Webb.

'Ted'll find the way,' said Nancy Maxwell.

'Well, then what about my truck?'

'What's the thing you're most worried about with the truck?' she asked.

'Well, that we'll hit something and bust up the steering again or that she'll overheat and knock out her bearings.'

'You're liable to hit a rock or something in daylight, aren't you?'

'It could happen,' agreed Webb, 'but it's not so likely as at night.'

Maxwell sat calmly eating his pineapple. As far as he was concerned the issue was clear-cut and decided. He saw no reason to intervene.

This discussion was just something that had to be got out of their systems.

Nancy said 'In that case you'll drive in convoy close on Ted's tail in the Merc and let him guide you so that you *don't* hit things. Now over-heating, that's a real danger in the daytime. There isn't enough water in the district to keep that radiator filled up in the heat of the day. But at night it will be cool.'

'Cool for us, too,' said the girl.

Maxwell said gruffly 'To hell with your home comforts. It's the hippos who need it cool. Jammed up in those crates the poor little buggers could pack it in long before we get to Makole.'

'Too bad,' said the girl. 'All I'm interested in is that we get them there alive and collect the money for them.'

'From what I saw yesterday,' said Maxwell, 'you'd never need to starve. You'd find a way of earning a living.'

The girl rose slowly, picked up her mug and threw the coffee deliberately at Maxwell. The liquid hit him full in the chest. It had lost a fair amount of heat but it was still uncomfortably warm. He didn't even take his feet down from the chair on which they were propped. 'Bitch,' was all he said.

When Jen saw that he wasn't going to do anything about it, she started round the table towards him but Nancy Maxwell shot her wheel-chair forward suddenly and blocked her way. Jen struck the chair and stumbled.

Unconcerned, Maxwell went on talking to Webb. 'I'll want the smallest of the hippos in a separate crate on the fifteen hundred-weight. We'll load them all by five this afternoon and we'll pull out by six-thirty. . . .' He paused, but scarcely looked up when the girl got to her feet and ran, sobbing, towards her tent.

'Watch her, Ron,' Maxwell said, 'and watch yourself with her, son.' Then he, too, rose and went into his tent to put on a clean shirt.

They moved out not at six-thirty but at eight. There had been last-minute hitches all round. First there had been trouble assembling the steering linkage. One of the welds had prohibited freedom of movement on the track-rod so Webb had to break this down and make another and, in his opinion, not so successful, join. But the main difficulty had been stowing all the gear onto the two trucks, for the fifteen hundredweight with hippo and crate aboard was not in shape to stand much additional weight. Eventually they compromised by loading the damaged vehicle with the lighter camping gear and relying on the Mercedes to take the remaining five hippo and all the Africans. Even so they had to abandon one or two of the less useful and more termite-proof items of gear, simply leaving them where they stood. These included the wrecked and partly stripped jeep, a cooking stove and one steel chest full of odds and ends. Maxwell had little hope that they would return to collect them or that they would still be there if he succeeded in doing so. Some itinerant tribesmen were bound to come across them and think them of value, if only for melting down to make spear heads. Any spare space on either truck was taken up by water containers for the hippos and the fifteen hundredweight.

Maxwell drove the Mercedes with his wife beside him. The girl and Webb shared the catching truck.

The late start had one advantage. The temperature had dropped quite considerably so that it was at least five miles before the truck boiled. This was, in fact, a rather better performance than Webb had dared to hope for since progress was extremely slow and had necessarily to be made in low gear. Every jolt and jar had been agony to him. His nerves seemed to run down through the shuddering steering column to every one of his painfully careful welds. When they hit a rock, he felt the shock to his jury-rigged front axle almost as if it was his own sinews that were being pulled. He flashed his one good headlight as a signal to the Mercedes that he had to stop. Maxwell swung down from the cab and came strolling back.

'What's up?' he asked.

'Tea's ready,' Webb told him. He pointed to the steaming radiator. A deep-throated bubbling came from the intestines of the engine.

'How long will she take to cool down?'

'Ten minutes. But she'll boil again much quicker next time.'

'What gear were you in?'

'Second most of the time.'

'Well try her in third.'

'It'll knock the living daylights out of the steering.'

'Maybe. But we can't stop every two miles—and that's what it's going to be like if you stick in second now she's good and hot. I want to be on that track by eight tomorrow morning.'

'Okay. But I don't think we'll be with you.'

'You've got one hippo. I've got five.'

'Oh, sure. We're expendable.'

'Well try and keep up. We'll notch the speed up a bit and see how she goes.'

'Okay, but I think it will kill her.'

When they moved off again Maxwell increased the pace by about four miles per hour. This was just enough for Webb to hold the truck in third most of the time. Every now and again he had to change down into second, however. Once when they fell suddenly into a mongoose hole he felt the axle shift appreciably, but the steel cables binding it held.

They made five miles again before rusty water started to spit back onto the screen. Webb felt for the light switch and began to flick it. At once there was a flare under the dashboard and the cab was filled with smoke and a stench of burning rubber. Webb darted his hand under the instrument panel and quickly ripped out the red-hot wires. The lights went out and the engine stopped. He made sure that the fire was out and then took time to examine his fingers. He found that the skin of his forefinger and thumb was burnt raw in a searing line where he had grasped the wires.

Maxwell came walking back. 'Same again?' he asked.

'Same again only different this time.'

'Smells bloody awful,' Maxwell said.

'Just been on fire, that's all.'

'Any damage?'

'To the truck?' asked Webb.

'What else?'

'What else?' Webb echoed.

'Can you fix her up?'

'Probably fix the ignition but we won't have any lights.'

'Plenty of starlight soon,' Maxwell told him. 'Must see how the hippo are getting on.'

'Yes. Don't forget *them*,' Webb said with heavy sarcasm. He got out a grease gun from under his seat and smeared some of the contents across the smarting burns on his hand.

All this time the girl had said nothing.

It was a quarter to ten when they got going again. By then they had covered barely ten miles. Webb calculated that if they did as well, or as badly, as this they would still be only half-way to the track by the morning. The same thought was passing through Maxwell's mind. There seemed to him to be two alternatives. First, to leave Webb to make his own way and come back for him once he had unloaded his own five hippos at Makole. Second, attempt half the journey to the head of the track this night and carry on again the next evening. If he pressed on alone to Makole, then he still had three hundred miles to do once he reached the track. Always provided he could find somewhere to uncrate and leave his five baby hippos safely in Makole, it would be at least two days before he could reach Webb again. He did not doubt Webb's and the girl's ability to survive in the bush for that time, but he did have serious misgivings about the stamina of the *toto*. It was the smallest and least self-reliant of them all. As it was, he was pretty certain he would have to build a fresh *boma* at Makole to hold his hippos before he went back for Webb. They would need room after the cramped conditions of the journey. Building another *boma* would take at least a day. Webb's hippo would probably flake out in the meanwhile. He did not intend to lose that baby hippo.

When they stopped for the sixth time at three a.m. Maxwell poked his head into the cab of the fifteen hundredweight. 'Change of plan,' he announced.

Webb sat waiting and said nothing. 'About ten miles ahead,' Maxwell told him, 'and about five miles to the east of the way we're heading, there's a big wallow. I'm going to make for it. We'll spend the day there and move on tomorrow night. It'll give the hippos a break. Plenty of shade and water.'

'Bully for them,' Webb said as Maxwell walked off.

For the first time he noticed that the girl was sound asleep. In fact, she had been asleep for the past hour. Neither the joltings nor the sudden quiet of the stopping had wakened her. Webb took his bush jacket off, easing it over his swollen right hand and put it round the girl's shoulders. He didn't feel all that protective towards her. There was, however, something pathetic about her face in sleep that briefly touched him.

As it was getting light Maxwell recognized the outcrop he had been looking for and signalled that he was swinging out towards the east. Soon the ground began to slip away and Webb sensed that Maxwell, as usual, when it came to finding his way in the wilderness, was right. They would soon see the water. The truck did not boil on the way down but he found himself wondering and worrying about how it would behave on the up-gradient that coming night. If only he didn't have that damned hippo aboard. He would dearly have liked to tip it off and leave it to take its chance for the day under a tree, but his tired mind realized that the excursion to the waterhole was not intended as a respite for him, or for his truck: it was strictly for the benefit of the hippos.

The wallow was about two hundred yards long and fringed with reeds at the side nearest to their approach. The far bank was flat mud that had been baked hard by the sun as the water level had dropped after the rains. There were some scrubby bushes on this flat and beyond them a group of tall trees. Webb's spirits rose slightly at the thought of a cool rest in the shade of those trees. In another few minutes he would stop the panting truck beneath them.

But it was further to the far bank than it looked, for the going on the near-side was soft and treacherous and they had to make several back-tracks away from the water before they found a firm route. There were several adult hippos already in the wallow and a croc ran down the bank ahead of the lorries. A party of twenty flamingoes ran stiff-legged to take off. They flew down the lake, each a long pencil streak of elegance against the sky, to wheel and glide back to land almost precisely where they had first become airborne. The end of their flight was as absurd as its beginning. Their long, knobbly-jointed legs trotted through the water in double-quick time to absorb the momentum of their landing. Webb gave them barely a glance. He kept his eyes glued to Maxwell's tailboard as it weaved its way between the pot-holes and the soft patches. Once, Maxwell jinked so suddenly that Webb was caught unawares. He swore, expecting to feel the truck sink in a suddenly revealed quagmire. He swore the more fiercely when he saw why Maxwell had turned so quickly. A monitor lizard was busy excavating and gobbling crocodile eggs while the female croc was away at the water. In his anger Webb drove as close to the big lizard's tail as he could without actually squashing it, but the monitor took no notice. It was too preoccupied with tucking away its feast before the avenging croc returned. As the rear wheels cleared it, the monitor flicked its forked tongue and began on another egg.

They pulled up at last, but not by the trees. Maxwell led the trucks down to the waterside and stopped the Mercedes as close to the edge of the wallow as he dared.

Webb sat there, waiting for it. It came.

'First thing we're going to do,' Maxwell announced, 'is to get the hippo crates off. Then I want them down on the edge of the water so that the bottom part of each crate is in the drink. Then I want a tarpaulin rigged over the lot. On poles. That'll keep 'em reasonably cool. We'll slosh 'em with water as well throughout the day. Now come on. For Christ's sake. Chop chop, Nguru.'

Nguru got down, grinning as usual. He began to roust the sleepy boys from the crevices between the crates into which they had managed to jam themselves. Some had even slept soundly there. Without enthusiasm they began to lower the tailboard of the Mercedes.

Webb sat for a few minutes summoning up the energy he needed to tear himself free from the sweat-soaked seat to which he felt immovably stuck.

Maxwell came over to the cab. His face did not particularly show the strain of the night march. It was lined and solemn but no more harassed-looking than usual. He said quietly 'Get a bloody wriggle on.' He peered into the cab. As he did so the girl stirred and put her arm round Webb sleepily. She snuggled up against him. When he saw the movement, Maxwell turned abruptly and walked away from the truck. Webb looked down at the girl's arm. She seemed to be still asleep, but he was reasonably sure that she was awake. He disengaged her and began to dismount and shake the stiffness out of his own limbs.

It was six by the time all the hippos were unloaded at the water's edge and the tarpaulin shelter rigged above their heads. All things considered, their cramped and disturbed night had not done them much harm. One of the smaller *totos* on the Mercedes appeared slightly exhausted but he perked up when he smelt the water into which his crate was being pushed. He lay down ecstatically with his heavy lower jaw awash. When Webb returned to the truck after supervising the unloading, the girl had already gone. He saw her in the distance, beneath the trees, standing close to Nancy Maxwell who, from her wheel-chair, was already chivvying the cook boys around. He climbed back into the cab, started the now practically cold engine, listened to its rumbling for a few seconds and registered that the night's exertions did not seem to have produced any additional mechanical complications. Then he drove to a tree standing a little apart from the main body of the temporary camp, dragged a blanket from under the seat and lay down in the shadow of the truck. Within three minutes he was sound asleep. His last waking impression was a distant view of Maxwell throwing a bucket of water over one of the hippos.

The girl woke him with breakfast long after most of the camp had eaten. At first he did not register what was happening to him at all. He simply felt something shaking at his chest and imagined it was an animal. He opened his eyes in fright and dimly saw that the thing that had awakened him was a foot. He was about to let rip a stream of abuse at this outrageous piece of familiarity on the part of one of the cooks when he noticed that the foot was white. His eyes followed the leg that owned the foot and found the girl staring down at him, as expressionless as the face of the most disinterested tea-shop waitress. He wondered why she had bothered to bring him breakfast at all if that was the way she felt. Then he saw Maxwell beyond by the mess table and heard him call for *chai*.

'Thanks,' Webb said to the girl and sat up.

'Anything else you want?' Jen's voice was loud enough for Maxwell to hear.

'Well, now. That looks about the lot thanks.'

'Jen, how about some *chai*?' Maxwell called.

The girl set down Webb's bread and jam carefully and then, without turning, walked away from the truck and the mess tent where Maxwell sat.

'Well,' Webb said to himself, 'you *are* a bitch. Damned if I know what you mean or why I'm getting the treatment, but as long as it's going I might as well have it.'

The heat in the low-lying land surrounding the wallow was stupe-fying. It made the day seem forty-eight hours long. Normally, when stuck in a spot like this, the catchers would have let a little air into their lives by taking the jeep and racing round the countryside look-ing for game. But now there was no jeep and no one felt like driving the Mercedes just for the fun of it. Anyway, there was no spare petrol.

Webb spent the rest of the morning and part of the afternoon checking the truck. He replaced the burnt-out wiring and got his one good headlamp working.

In the late afternoon Maxwell took a foraging party of four Africans out on the Mercedes to cut grass and reeds to feed the ani-mals during the night's march. Then they all ate a hurried meal, struck what remained of the camp and prepared to load the hippo crates all over again.

They put Webb's hippo on first. Directly all the other gear was aboard the catching truck, Maxwell told Webb: 'You push off first.

Give you time to climb the hill to the outcrop without thrashing her too much. We'll meet there in about an hour. Think you can find the way?'

'Do me a favour,' said Webb.

'Okay, an hour then. Take Jen.'

But Jen was already seated in the cab.

Webb pressed the starter and began to feel the heaviness of the day drop away as the engine caught. He eased into bottom gear and pulled slowly out of the soft sand by the water, accelerating happily and snapping into top as they bowled along the flat shore.

'That's the only good bit of going we'll have all the way to Makole,' he said. The girl had stuck her head out of the cab and was enjoying the sensation of movement after the smothering torpor of the day. She made no sign that she had heard him.

Webb found the track round the end of the lake fairly easily, but as soon as he began to climb, pathfinding became more difficult. The country here was thick, bushy scrub and it was impossible to see the morning's tracks. The truck soon boiled and, while they were waiting for it to cool, dusk began to fall. The early evening was heavy with scent and the closeness of the surrounding bushes gave the spot an enclosed and secret air so that Webb soon became unbearably conscious of the girl. At last he let his hand slip down the side of his seat so that it brushed along her arm. The arm felt as warm and downy as a peach in the sun.

'For Christ's sake,' said the girl. 'If you want to paw me, why don't you?'

Webb turned towards her and grabbed her clumsily.

'Oh my God,' she said. 'Just pretend I'm a bloody piston ring or one of those damn things you waste your technique on. Your trouble is you're all look and leer. When it comes to it you go on as if you're chasing a hippo. Here.' She sidled up to him putting her mouth on his and parting his lips with her tongue.

They stayed like this for nearly half a minute. Webb made no further move. He was scared of the girl's scorn and, out of real inexperience, did not know what she expected him to do next, if anything. The girl left her tongue between his lips but remained utterly, almost insultingly, passive. The tip of her tongue felt cold to him, inanimate, and certainly not exciting any more. At last, Webb retreated for breath.

'Jen,' he said. 'I didn't expect . . .'

'Well, don't,' she snapped. 'Just don't expect. Come on, I'm fed up. Let's get moving.'

'But . . .'

'I said let's go.'

'Next time,' he pleaded, 'next time I won't be so clumsy.'

'What next time?' she said.

'I don't get you at all. You go on as if . . . I don't get you.'

'Very likely not,' she said. 'Let's move on.'

It was nearly dark now. Furious with himself and with the girl, Webb filled the radiator and then climbed on the roof to get his bearings. It was impossible either to see the lake behind or the outcrop somewhere ahead. All around was identical-looking scrub. Webb switched on his single headlamp. It gave one burst of light and then the bulb blew.

Webb was now in a spot and knew it. Twistings and turnings through the scrub had left him with no very clear idea in which direction the outcrop lay. For a moment he considered staying where he was and waiting for Maxwell to overtake him. But in this close country there was no guarantee that he would see Maxwell's lights as he went by. The thing that finally made him decide to push on towards the outcrop was the certainty that he would have to face the girl's scorn if he stayed. He started his engine and moved off with more confidence than he felt.

'I suppose you know where you're going,' the girl said.

'Watch me,' he said.

Half an hour later the girl spoke again. 'I'm watching you. That outcrop should be pretty close now, if we *are* heading for it.'

In the growing starlight, Webb thought he saw the big lorry's tracks. He stopped and climbed down to examine them. There was no mistaking whose they were. They were freshly made. He had been circling.

'Looks like our tyre marks,' the girl told him. 'We're lost.'

'Looks like it,' he admitted.

'What are you going to do?'

'Get a bearing from the stars.'

'Fine. That'll tell us where north is, but where's the outcrop? We could drive around all night.'

'You're right,' Webb admitted. 'But we can't just stay put.'

'Oh, I don't know. They'll have to come and find us.'

'Without our lights they'd never spot us.'

'We could build a fire.'

'Sure, but let's get on the highest piece of ground around here first.' He made it sound as though the fire was his idca.

Ahead was a slight rise. Webb eased the truck up it, watching anxiously for rocks. When he reached the top his heart gave a leap. Below and far to the left he could see the gash made in the night by Maxwell's headlights.

The girl said 'Pity. I was just beginning to look forward to a cosy session round the old camp-fire.'

Webb stopped the engine.

'Aren't you going down after them?'

'Not until they stop moving. When they stop they'll be at the out-crop. We can take a bearing on it by the stars. If we just chase off we could easily lose them once we get down off this hill.'

'Clever boy.'

The distant lorry stopped at last. It was, Webb judged, at least three miles away. He took every possible bearing from the stars and from such natural features as he could make out, then they set off.

'Sorry,' he said to the girl, 'I'm afraid I've made a balls-up of that.'

'Oh that's all right.'

'Never thought I could get lost.'

'You're not so bad when you're not so damned cocky,' the girl told him.

When they reached the Mercedes, Maxwell was sitting in the cab smoking. He barely looked up. Webb drove alongside. 'Sorry,' he said, 'lost the way a bit.'

'Never mind about losing the way, you've just lost us an hour.'

'I said I was sorry.'

'Okay then, sonny,' Maxwell said, 'just damn well stick close to me this time.' He started his engine.

'Hold it,' Webb pleaded. 'This thing's boiling.'

'Too bad about that. We'll stop in another five miles.'

For Webb the drive was mechanical agony. Maxwell led at a faster pace than on the previous night. He did not make his first stop for seven miles. All that time the catching truck boiled throatily, spewing back dirty water at the screen whenever they hit a bump. Webb hooted in vain for the Mercedes to stop. At last, when no more drops of rusty water appeared on the windscreen, Webb became desperate, for he judged that his radiator had boiled so low that the level was well below the header tank. As far as he could judge the going here was fairly flat and so it should be possible to see Maxwell for some distance ahead. Furthermore there was now sufficient light to give him a reasonable chance of picking up Maxwell's tracks. So he stopped and filled the radiator of his own accord. Even so he was unhappy about it for he dared not wait long for the water to cool in case Maxwell disappeared altogether. He poured the water in drop by drop and heard it hiss as it hit the hot metal. When he caught up with Maxwell and they finally stopped, Maxwell had not even noticed that he had dropped out.

At this halt Webb did not wait for Maxwell to dismount. Instead he sprang out of his own cab and ran forward to the Mercedes. Maxwell, still at the wheel, was lighting one of his hand-rolled cigarettes. In its glow Webb saw Nancy Maxwell sitting upright in that curiously stiff and artificial manner that her paralysis forced upon her. Webb shouted 'Do you want to wreck that bloody truck completely? The engine's damn near white hot.'

Maxwell looked at him without rancour and without particular interest. 'Keep her moving,' he said, 'we're going straight through to Makole.'

It was two in the morning when Maxwell stopped for the fourth time. Webb saw that this was no normal halt, for Maxwell flashed his lights, hooted, and almost immediately turned left nearly at right angles. Webb watched the nose of the big lorry lift as it went over some obstruction and then dip the other side. They had reached the track.

Webb felt only slight relief at this. He had never doubted that Maxwell would find the track. His only satisfaction in arriving was that they had demolished a quarter of the journey. The idea of driving on the track gave him no special pleasure. African dirt roads were liable to be worse than the bush when it came to handing out punishment to suspension and steering. Moreover, for the last thirty miles he had been listening to a faint but slowly increasing mechanical rumble. He was certain that overheating during the early part of the night had started the rot in at least one of the big-end bearings.

'Ten minutes' break,' Maxwell announced. 'Then we bash on. There's a river bed about a hundred and twenty miles ahead. We should make it by ten in the morning. We'll breakfast there. Give the animals a freshen up.'

Without waiting for Maxwell to finish this announcement, Jen said conversationally to Webb 'Of course, we'll be allowed to wash, too, when the hippos have finished with the water.'

They bashed on. There was a glorious half-hour when the sun punched its way through the green paper hoop of the dawn. Francolin, who had come to the road for an early dusting, rose with a whirr of wings at their wheels. A ground hornbill, black and grotesque as the extinct dodo which it somewhat resembled, trotted off through the bush with the absurd pomp of an American drum majorette. Oribi rose from the grass and jinked away to stand looking curiously at them, their heads poised like bambis, the spots inside their slender ears showing like the stitching on a child's toy. But then the sun tore the whole sky open and the body blows of unremitting heat began.

Maxwell left Webb to make his own stops now since there was no possibility of him losing the way. It was eleven in the morning when Webb topped a rise and saw that the Mercedes below him had pulled off the track alongside a narrow sandy gash in the landscape. Webb took his foot off the throttle and let the truck coast down the slope. On the over-run, the rumble was unmistakable and menacing. One big-end was at least half gone.

He drove up to the fire the boys had made with dried boughs. Maxwell stopped drinking tea long enough to say 'Bloody stream's nearly dried up.'

'So?'

'So there's no sense in stopping long. Just enough water to give the hippos a bit of a sloshing. They won't stand a long time in this sun without a breath of air.'

'F . . . the hippos,' said Webb with feeling. 'I want some breakfast.'

'Sure. Help yourself. How's Jen?'

The girl had climbed down and wandered off a way into the bush.

'Oh, no,' said Webb, 'don't tell me you're starting to worry about *people*.'

'Have some tea,' Maxwell told him.

When they had all eaten, Maxwell held an informal orders group. 'We've got about two hundred and ten miles to do. For the Merc, that's between fourteen and sixteen hours' driving. With luck I'll get there between two and four in the morning, but I'll have to keep going.'

Webb interrupted 'Well, I won't be with you. At that pace the big-ends will knock out inside twenty miles.'

'Sure. You're on your own.'

'Thanks.'

'Directly I've off-loaded the hippo in Makole I'll come back for you.'

'Nice of you to worry.'

Maxwell allowed himself a slight tightening of the lines at the corner of his mouth which might have been a smile. 'I'm worrying about baby. I'll come back and take the *toto* off you.'

'Charming,' said the girl.

'Now listen, Ron. If you have trouble, if you pack up, get that bloody animal in the shade, and keep it alive. And another thing: if you have to stop, stay by the track where I can spot you.'

Nancy Maxwell said 'Nguru, make sure the *bwana* and memsahib have water, food, a fly-sheet.'

'Every home comfort,' said Webb.

'You okay, Jen?' Nancy asked.

The girl put her arm through Webb's and looked at Maxwell. 'Why not?' she said.

Webb was happier now that he could make his own pace. The Mercedes gradually outstripped them until he could no longer even see its dust cloud. The intense heat of the early afternoon bounced up off the road surface so that the floorboards of the truck felt like an empty saucepan on a low gas. Webb began to drop off. He fought this by shaking his head sharply and by sticking it out beyond the screen. But the drowsiness was impossible to fight indefinitely. He awoke to feel the pain in his chest where he had slumped forward on the steering-wheel. The truck had slewed off the road and had come to rest in some soft sand. The girl seemed unruffled.

'I'll drive for a spell,' she said.

Webb nodded. He was both too grateful and too tired to argue. He climbed out and took the passenger's seat. Soon he was uneasily asleep. He woke once about an hour later to say 'Take it easy, watch those bearings.' The girl didn't answer, or if she did, he was asleep again before he had registered her reply.

At six he awoke fully and tried to remember where he was. He had made so many long journeys in the driving-seat of jolting trucks that for the moment he had difficulty in placing what was happening to him. Then he caught sight of the girl's profile against the passing sky.

'Hullo,' said Jen, 'had a good kip?'

He looked at his watch. 'Good God, you've been driving for four hours.'

'So that's a disaster?'

'Apparently not. Did you fill her up and all that?'

'Just about every half-hour, that's all. You weren't interested.'

'How is she?'

'Listen while I put my foot down.' She buzzed the accelerator briefly and, when the engine slowed, a hollow metallic clanking echoed from under the bonnet.

'Christ. You've done pretty well to coax her along. Is she getting worse?'

'No. Seems about the same. Think she'll hold up?'

'Might do. No telling really. Might just suddenly decide to knock the rest of the metal out and then that's that.'

'Oh well,' she said.

'Oh well,' he agreed.

'What about the hippo?'

'Sod the hippo.'

'No, don't. He's money in the bank if we get him there.'

Now that he was a little refreshed, Webb was beginning to feel interest in the truck again. He was darned if he wanted the patient to die on him after all the care he had expended on its recovery. He listened critically to the rumbling of the engine.

'You've nursed her along fine,' he told the girl with real admiration. 'How far have we done?'

'Ninety since the Merc left us. About another one fifty to Makole.'

'We'll carry on until seven and then pull up and have a meal and a few hours' sleep. We'll move off about midnight again. Shall I take over?'

'No, go back to beddybyes. You've got another half-hour, so make the most of it.'

When they finally pulled up, the baby hippo looked more than usually depressed. The girl asked 'What about him?'

'I dunno,' said Webb, 'and to tell you the truth I don't care all that much, except that he might mean the difference between getting paid something, and working for nothing. We can't afford to waste much water on him, that's certain. I don't know the country between here and Makole. It's probably bone dry. Give him a bucketful to drink and some grub and hope for the best.'

Webb lit a fire with dead wood. They opened some tins and made the invariable tea. Then Webb got his two blankets out from under the driving-seat and handed one to the girl. 'Me for a lie down,' he said.

He chose a patch of soft sand not far from the truck. After some minutes the girl spread her blanket a few feet away from him. Webb remained lying on his back, watching the sky darken with sudden twilight. He was conscious of the girl but not to any disturbing degree. As far as his unpoetic soul was capable, it was registering pleasure at the blissful falling of darkness. The emotion expressed itself in his mind as satisfaction that it had all stopped and for the moment he didn't have to hold on to the steering-wheel or listen to the knocking of the bearings.

'You scared of me?' the girl asked suddenly.

He sat up. Webb was young enough to resent the suggestion that he was scared of anything, let alone the girl.

'Scared?' he said. 'Hell no. I just don't understand you.'

'That's not surprising.'

'Sometimes you seem to want me to . . .'

'And do you?'

'Don't be bloody silly.'

'Oh God,' said the girl, 'everybody's so damn soft and gentle. Can't you be gentle, Ron?'

'Huh?' It was almost the first time she had used his Christian name. 'I tried being gentle once, remember. You made me feel a damn fool.'

'When?'

'Last night in the truck.'

'Was that being gentle?'

'I don't know about that,' he told her, 'but there's a term for what you were doing last night.'

'I know,' she said. 'The second word is teaser.'

'Well, you said it.'

'Here,' she said, 'come here.' She moved towards him on the blanket.

Still afraid that she would make a fool of him again, he said 'I don't understand you. You don't even like me.'

The girl pulled back from him a little at this and looked at him squarely as if weighing up the truth of this remark. He couldn't read from her expressionless face what her long deep look at him told her.

There was certainly no detectable softening. Just the same she moved in quickly towards him and put her mouth up to his.

Some minutes later she asked him urgently 'Have you got something?'

'Hell,' he said, 'this is a time and place to ask.'

'Well, have you?'

'Well, yes, as a matter of fact, in my wallet in the truck.'

'Don't be long,' she said.

But the excitement they had both experienced up to that moment was not prolonged, and, for the girl, did not reach a climax in their love-making. Afterwards, Jen rolled away from him and soon Webb knew that she was crying. He did not know what to say, so he said 'I'm sorry. It wasn't any good for you, was it?'

'It wasn't any *different*,' she said. 'I thought it might take away the feel of the other but there's no gentleness in this damned land.'

'The other,' Webb said, baffled. 'What other?'

Jen didn't answer, so, after a time, he got up and laid his blanket over her.

Webb couldn't sleep any more. At eleven he made her a hot drink. She took it from him without speaking to him or even looking at him. At twelve they started off again.

It was seven the next morning, when they were still forty miles from Makole, that the big-end bearing finally went, Webb pulled off the track with the naked end of the con-rod slapping the crank-shaft.

Twelve hours later Maxwell appeared in the Mercedes.

Webb and the girl had hardly spoken a word since they had stopped that morning. Maxwell found the girl camped about fifty yards away from Webb and the derelict truck, under a tree.

Webb had done his best for the hippo. He had given it every drop of water he could spare including what was left in the radiator of the truck.

Despite this, the young animal was dead.

They left the dead hippo for the vultures and towed the mortally wounded catching truck behind the Mercedes forty miles to Makole. Webb sat behind the lifeless steering-wheel possessed by an utter sense of failure: failure with the truck and failure with Jen. The girl at his side apparently neither saw nor heard anything that happened around them. Outside Makole, and close by the seven kilometre post, Nguru had made a camp by a shallow stream bed and already a *boma* was erected, its lower end running down into the shallows of the river.

As they drove in, Nancy Maxwell propelled herself out across the flat ground in her wheel-chair to meet them. Without speaking to Webb, Jen climbed stiffly down from the truck and ran towards the crippled woman who put her arms up to her and round her like a mother receiving a troubled child. The two women stayed like this for perhaps half a minute and then Jen broke away and, taking the handles of the wheel-chair, began to push Nancy Maxwell back towards the fly-sheet shelter.

Webb remained sitting behind his steering-wheel like a captain disinclined to abandon his dismasted and drifting ship. It was as if his whole reason for existing and his only reference point with living had been extinguished. For the moment he did not know how to take up with things once more and was too tired to care.

Maxwell leaned into his cab. 'Where do you want her?' he asked.

'Eh?' The idea that he could want any more of this tortured vehicle, or it of him, had not occurred to Webb.

'What did you say?' he asked slowly and stupidly.

'I said where did you want me to drop off the tow-rope,' Maxwell said patiently.

'What's the odds?'

'Sonny Jim, the odds are yours to work out. Sooner or later, you've got to get stuck into her, so have you any preferences? For instance, would you find it easier to strip the engine down if I dropped her in the river bed?'

'It's all one to me. She's had it anyway.'

Maxwell said 'Mechanics. I had one once that couldn't fix a kid's tricycle.'

Webb felt a faint surge of irritation and pride but not enough to stir him fully out of his lethargy. 'Oh, stick it over there under that tree if you like. As if it makes any difference. Even if I had a chance of lashing it up again, we'd never get any spares in this damned awful hole.'

Maxwell walked forward to the Mercedes and soon Webb heard the motor start. He felt the tow take up smoothly. Automatically he guided the catching truck for the last fifty yards of its journey towards the shade of the tree. Still devoid of any initiative, he sat there waiting for Maxwell to show up again and half hoping that he would order him to begin work on the damned engine at once. Instead Maxwell walked over to the women in the mess tent.

At last, feeling hurt and neglected, Webb decided to join them. 'Any *chai*?' he asked aggressively.

Maxwell handed him a cup.

'Well, what now?' Webb challenged.

Maxwell tilted his canvas-backed chair and impassively sipped his scalding tea. Webb looked quickly for support to the girl who sat with her back half turned towards the two men. When he got no response from her either, he felt that he had to go on. 'Well,' he said, 'can't anyone tell me what we do now? I say let's flog the five hippo we've still got and call the whole thing quits. What about you, Jen?'

The girl did not look round. What she now said was delivered in an emotionless tone that somehow made its impact on the group round the table all the more severe.

'I personally,' said Jen, 'no longer care what you do or don't do about the hippo, or the money. Nancy, I want you to know that I don't include you in this. He's your husband, so God help you, you're stuck with him. But Ted, I'm talking to you, Ted, and to you too, Webb. You both live in a great big make-believe boy's world. With Webb it's his bloody trucks. It's bad enough to have sump oil in your veins and to have a brain that can't think better than a carburettor. That must be limiting enough, but I give you this, Webb, dumb as you are, you do actually *know* that there are other human beings on this earth. You've come out from your damn grease pit occasionally just long enough to catch a glimpse of one or two, not that you're really interested. But you, Ted'—and now Jen turned and faced Maxwell, her voice rising in pitch—'you don't even know people exist. Or that they have feelings. Particularly you don't know that women have feelings. You're with the animals, Ted. You know more about animals and care more about animals than you do about people. As for love or tenderness—well, you belong up in the trees, or beneath them, like those bloody rhinos you think so much of. I've heard you go into raptures about a couple of rhinos on the job as if it was the most wonderful thing that God created. Well, mate, that's about your level. You're with them, only you're not so good at it. They do at least rub noses before they begin. You, man, are just a bloody animal without refinements. I've lived with this sort of travelling circus ever since I can remember. Well, I'm over it now. This trip with all its charm has cured me once and for all. When that truck leaves to take the hippos to the coast, I'm going with it. So good luck and farewell to the bloody lot of you.' She paused for breath. Maxwell had made no move to suggest that he had even heard her. Furious now, she shrieked at him 'And the first thing I'm going to do when I get among human beings again is turn myself back into a woman, not that any of you would understand the need for *that.*'

Then suddenly she began to cry, not noisily but with brimming tears that filled her eyes and streamed down her face, crumpled now like a child's. Nancy Maxwell started to push her chair towards her, but as she did so the girl turned and ran off into the bush, sobbing loudly and hysterically.

Maxwell put down his tea cup.

'I'm taking the Merc into Makole,' was all he said.

PART TWO

Maxwell was not at all disturbed by
Jen's outburst. He had heard it all, or something very like it, before.
The only problem that filled his mind now was how to find transport
to carry on with the operation to which he had pledged himself. So
he drove into Makole to see the director general of the Parcs
Nationaux, who was, of all surprising things in this particular colonial
administration, a Scotsman.

Maxwell disliked Makole as he disliked all towns. Yet, to most
people for two hundred miles around, it was a desirable metropolis.
Makole was the administrative centre of an area about the size of
Wales. It was the focal point to which isolated men came for justice,
for commerce, for supplies, and for what in these circumstances and
this land passed for luxury and high living. It was said that the intensity of any man's longings for the attractions of Makole was in
direct proportion to the distance by which he was separated from it,
multiplied by the interval since he had last visited the place.

As he drove the Mercedes in along the dusty red dirt road, Maxwell took in the town's features automatically and without enthusiasm. In shape the town was like a python that had swallowed a
goat and half digested it. Makole was thin at either extremity but
thickened up considerably towards the middle. It was the tail, or perhaps head of the town, through which Maxwell was now driving.

At first he passed the shanties of the African population. One or
two of these were of the traditional thatched, tribal pattern. A very
few were the new portable aluminium kind which threw back the

sun's rays as defiantly as a heliograph, and, in so doing, were said to keep their inmates pleasantly cool. But the majority were shoddy affairs of corrugated iron and mud bricks. Many of these bore signs advertising Pepsi and Coca Cola, or beer. No wall appeared to be too humble to carry the salesman's message. The irony lay in the contrast between the product advertised and the media chosen to proclaim its virtues. Outside several of the huts lay derelict car bodies, wheel-less and devoid of all removable fittings. In this way they resembled the skeleton of a large animal picked clean by vultures and indeed they had received much the same treatment. These hulks had no easily discernible purpose except possibly to offer shelter to the scrawny chickens which scratched in their shade. The litter and confusion of this outlying part of the town was only made bearable to the eye by the profusion of vegetation which grew up round it, for Makole, like most settlements in this part of the world, had been built in one of the few fertile oases in the surrounding bush. Many of the tin shanties were mercifully hidden by the slit, emerald green leaves of the banana trees. The miniature though sweet fruits which these palms produced were a major source of food and alcohol for the African population.

Maxwell registered the fact that this shanty town looked unusually deserted, but, as he drove into Makole, he began to meet more and more of the inhabitants, at first in ones and twos and then in groups, and all gravitating inwards. Only the women were still around the shanty settlements. They carried outlandish loads upon their heads with the insouciance, but without the showmanship, of highly skilled jugglers. Whatever was drawing the men towards town, the women, as usual, were not participating. Maxwell slowed the Mercedes to allow a group of big fat mammies in their cotton dresses looking like miniature flowered marquees, to cross the road. On the head of each was gyroscopically balanced a rectangular four-gallon petrol can filled with water. The weight was enough to impact the spinal column of any European woman and yet the mammies progressed with the dignity of swans while still managing to chatter and smile to each other as they walked.

A cluster of bright aluminium mushrooms ahead told Maxwell that he was reaching the police post. This post was strategically placed at the point at which the native huts gave way to the first of the white administrative bungalows of Makole proper. Blocking the way ahead now, between the lorry and the police huts, was a thick concourse of African men of all ages. One or two carried badly scrawled placards on which were the usual words about freedom, self-government and independence—*Uhuru*. He had seen similar slogans in almost all of the emergent African states. '*Uhuru*,' Maxwell muttered scornfully to himself. He had grave doubts about the wisdom or efficacy of self-government in any African community, at least within the next two hundred years. Some at least, he supposed, had a good chance—but this lot! Whatever else British administration had done or not done in the parts of East and Central Africa for which it had been responsible, it had at least given the resident population an inkling of how to run their own show. But this lot! Maxwell had no illusion, however, about the force of the will that drove the native populations, and through them the ordinary people, to believe that independence was a miracle that would change everything.

He had lived for a long time in a land like a political mine-field and so he approached the demonstration with caution. It looked peaceful enough but somehow it was too quiet. There was a watchfulness about it, a lack of overt excitement that restrained his hand from ramming down the horn button and his foot from pressing hard on the accelerator. This was different from a usual local gathering to listen to a visiting African politician. The crowd parted slightly for him. He drove into the chasm that had opened, expecting to remain enclosed and prevented from going further. But instead, when he had progressed a little, another avenue opened silently for him. Then he saw why he had been given a passage without having to hoot and curse, threaten and nudge the nearest in the crowd with his mudguards. Ahead, in strength, armed with batons and wearing tin hats, but equally silent and watchful, was the main body of Makole's police force, about thirty strong. An African police officer waved him through and in a minute he was on the open road to Makole again.

Once through the police cordon he was out of the African area of Makole. Now the bungalows began, small, white rectangles of administration garnished with neat beds of flaming shrubs. Notice boards announced what activity took place inside: tsetse fly control, veterinary service, medical officer of health. Of the activity itself there was no outward sign. Not even a breeze shivered the shades in the windows. Here, too, there were police, posted front and back of the official buildings. They lounged, leaning against telegraph poles and veranda posts, as listless as the flag outside the Game Department office. Maxwell's lorry enveloped them with the dust of its passing. They did not even bother to close their eyes but simply let it billow around them and settle on their khaki shirts and white riot helmets.

Maxwell registered all this and said aloud to himself 'Some bloody thing is up.'

He reached the centre of the town where administrative bungalows gave way to commerce. This was the thickened stomach of Makole: the place where the goat had stuck when the snake swallowed it. There were more police here than Maxwell had ever seen in Makole or any town like it. A stomach-griping smell of burnt rubber gave him the first clue to their presence. The stench seaped from the blackened frame of a burned-out Renault. One of the rear tyres was still smoking. Just beyond it, a frightened group of Indian store-keepers stood staring at a puddle of smashed plate-glass. Through the socket of a blinded window Maxwell glimpsed more police. European ones this time, with holstered pistols, standing inside the front office of the bank. On the streets there were few Africans. Many of the *dukas* were closed. Anything that can close down an Indian store-keeper during his most fruitful hours of business, reflected Maxwell, must be an event of moderately catastrophic proportions.

Just then an armoured car pulled up and nervously swung its turret to cover the main thoroughfare. Three lorries of European troops with automatic weapons followed.

Because he felt that this was not his fight Maxwell was only mildly intrigued. The riot could have been about so many things. Anti-European; anti-Indian; anti-African. These days you never could be quite certain. He turned the Merc left beyond the last *duka* and drove towards the residential area. Almost immediately he met a column of three armoured cars. A fourth was deployed away to the left upon a small grass mound. At least two platoons of white infantrymen were dispersed between the European houses and the rest of Makole. Two light machine-gun posts, manned and more or less alert, commanded the roadway. The whole thing looked like a field-day rather than a serious preventative operation. He had, however, seen such scenes turn with brutal and bewildering suddenness into real little shooting wars. One thing was now quite clear: it was the European element in Makole that felt itself in need of protection.

Beyond the platoon commander's wireless truck and in the direction of the well-laid-out European residences, all seemed entirely normal. The cool, commodious houses bathed themselves in pools of vivid greenery touched off with firework displays of poinsettia and bougainvillea. White children played in a garden. An African gardener jabbed his hoe at a flower-bed.

Each house had a box for mail at the foot of its driveway. Beside this, the resident's name was lettered neatly on a signboard. Maxwell drove on past these without looking at them. The house he was visiting was at the extreme end of the European residential colony where a green tongue of fertility licked out into the bush. Here, half in the town, half out of it, lived Alexander Richie. Richie's was something more than a mere residence. It was also a fair-sized *shamba* with rubber and vanilla plants, coffee, pawpaws and pineapples, maize and spices. Richie was one of the only Europeans actually to own land in Makole district. His father had bought the plot in some long-forgotten colonial attempt to introduce settlers. He had made a fair go of the holding and now Richie, besides his other work, kept the *shamba* ticking over and little more.

There was the sign by the letter-box now. Maxwell slowed up when he saw that a fresh slash of black paint underlined the name A. Richie. He had always been amused by the juxtaposition of the Scottish name and the legend inscribed beneath it: A. Richie, *Chef du Parcs Nationaux.* He was not amused now to find that *Chef du Parcs Nationaux* had been struck out by the daub of paint. He put it down to a piece of hooligan anti-white demonstration.

Maxwell tried to dismiss the implication. It was unlikely they would displace Richie. He had been an unmethodical but successful head of the Park. Maxwell had often wondered why Alex Richie with his obvious talents for getting people of different ambitions and colours to work together had not chosen to serve in a British Park or game reserve. Perhaps it was because his father had settled here or because he himself had married a Continental woman, now five years dead.

The lorry ground up the driveway under rubber trees, long past their best years, and came to a halt in front of the house.

Richie's home was something quite different from the domestic colonial architecture which was usual in Makole. It was an immense, solid, red brick affair that wouldn't have been out of place on the outskirts of Dumfries. Richie, who hadn't been back to Scotland since his schooldays, felt, as had his father who built the place, that it was a link with the homeland. If Richie senior had settled in British territory, he would, no doubt, have settled for the local style of building. But here, in distinctly foreign parts, he had thought it right to make the gesture. Alex Richie agreed with this. It was about the only thing in which he had agreed with his father either during his lifetime or after.

Maxwell jumped down from the lorry and stepped over the aged African who lay on the veranda porch on a dirty blanket, an antique spear propped by his side. The African did not stir. He was asleep.

Maxwell blinked in the cool darkness inside the house. He was always surprised to discover that this unlikely looking red brick pile actually did not glow incandescent in the sun. His eyes, growing accustomed to the murk, picked out the heavy Victorian banisters of the staircase, the grandfather-clock, the grand piano with its collection of silver-mounted photographs and, round the wall, the heads of kudu, impala, kob, buffalo, and eland. Even these, which were at least native to the place, seemed to have been robbed of their African quality. They were what the rest of their surroundings plainly said they were—the mounted trophies of some wandering Scottish Nimrod returned to his native land.

The houseboy in a long pink robe was snoozing in one of the red plush armchairs which Richie senior had imported from Maples via the Red Sea. Maxwell prodded him. The boy leapt to his feet with a frightened squeal.

'*Wapi bwana?*' Maxwell asked.

For one awful moment he thought that the riot he had seen in town had already swept over Richie's *shamba* with fatal consequences to the owner and that the servants were now in charge. But the scared look in the surprised houseboy's eyes reassured him that everything was just as normal. Richie was either hundreds of miles away in the Park or else out making the rounds of the *shamba*.

Just then Maxwell heard his name called, and, turning, saw Alex Richie bounding up the stone steps of the veranda.

Richie was about five foot six, slender, neat and mild-looking. He had on a large-brimmed straw hat—local make—which gave him the appearance of a genial planter from a rum advertisement. He wore an impeccably laundered and pressed bush suit of his own design, a variation on the romper theme. The tunic and trousers were in one piece. He apparently got into them through a hole in the back. Despite this minor touch of individuality, he might still have been taken for a submissive, middle-grade civil servant. It was only when you looked closely into the blue eyes behind the thin-rimmed, schoolmasterish glasses that you sensed that here was a genuine, one hundred per cent eccentric.

He stepped carefully over his sleeping veranda guard and held out his hand to Maxwell. 'Mustn't wake the devoted sentinels up,' he said cheerfully. He spoke with a soft, pure Highland Scottish accent.

Maxwell grunted. 'For a minute I thought the wogs had taken over.'

Richie skimmed his hat across the room to the now alert houseboy who, from long practice, caught it. 'They damn near have. Have a shandy.'

'Thanks, Alex. Nice to see you in one piece. You're fairly well out on your own here. When I saw all those armoured cars . . .'

Richie took the pint mug of shandy which the houseboy brought. 'Not nearly as bad as that—yet. No, I was just making the weekly tour of the *shamba* to see what they *hadn't* knocked off. Do you know, I've been growing a few pineapples here ever since I can remember, but I've never actually seen a ripe one on a stalk. Of course, they sell them back to me for my own use. The locals are pretty fair really. I get fresh fruit—my own naturally—at not much more than it would cost me to pay the labour to pick it.'

'You don't sound too worried about it all.'

Richie laughed. 'Worried? I'd go bonkers if I worried. No, just so long as I can keep slightly ahead of these lads. You can't really hope to do better than that. The old man knew something when he put in those rubber trees. Of course, they're getting a bit old now. I'll have to think about planting some more—if the coming régime will let me, naturally. But rubber. Rubber's good because it's the one crop they haven't yet found a way to pinch and sell. But they will,' he added confidently, 'they will.'

Richie said all this with genuine amusement and certainly without resentment.

'Well, I couldn't stand being done like that,' grunted Maxwell.

'But my dear Ted, you're done all the time.'

'Sure. But if I'm done enough, I just kick 'em out of camp and leave 'em to walk home. I don't have the fatherly attitude you have, and that's for sure. You surely don't expect any loyalty from them.

Look at that character on the veranda. I imagine he's supposed to be guarding your grand piano or something, but the bastard's sound asleep.'

Richie agreed, but added wryly 'Yes, but he was on night duty.'

'I'll bet he was asleep then.'

'I expect you're right, but having a sentry at all shows the locals that I've got my eye on them if they're thinking of carrying on their pilfering *inside* the house.'

'Well, if he was with me he'd be walking home right now.'

'Not much good, in my case. He lives on the *shamba*.'

Maxwell was now irritated at the way this irrelevant conversation was becoming protracted. He knew that he would never pin Alex Richie down to the thing he had come to talk to him about until the shandy and chit-chat had been allowed to run on a bit, but he wanted to wind it up.

'Anyway,' he said gruffly, 'I don't see that old twot with a spear stopping a rush of *pombe*-hopped up Magunga if they ever come to cut the *bwana's* throat.'

'I agree with you,' Richie said calmly, 'particularly since he's a Magunga himself. Now if he was an Ashota . . .'

'If he was an Ashota,' Maxwell couldn't resist replying, 'he'd get his own throat cut first.'

'Absolutely. You can't win with these lads.' Richie said this almost with affection, as if he was talking about a recalcitrant troop of performing chimps. 'Anyway, you haven't come to talk about my troubles.'

'Well, not yours, maybe, Alex. Ours. The Park's rhinos.'

'Oh, yes, the rhinos.' Richie sipped deeply at his shandy and looked over the top of his glasses.

'I've run up against a bit of trouble.'

'You have, have you? Well, that's too bad, Ted. Too bad. But the sad thing is I'm not so sure that it's all that important now. To the park, that is,' Richie added.

'Look, Alex, stop beating about the bloody bush. What's happening here? What's the meaning of the paint all over your signboard? Have you been chucked out of the parks set-up?'

'Well now, laddie, no. Not officially, anyway. But what's this about the signboard?'

'Someone's struck your title off. According to that, you're no longer head man in your own National Park.'

'They've done that, have they? Well, of course, that's just the local lads' idea of a joke. They've probably done it to every official with his name on a notice board from here to the border.'

'They probably have.'

Richie said gravely 'I don't imagine they've got my removal from office from a highly placed government spokesman, but, as it happens, the lads with a paint pot may not be all that much ahead of the game.'

'Oh Christ, Alex, I wish to God you'd sound a bit stirred up about it.'

'Now, Ted, what the devil's the use?'

'I suppose it surprises you to know that there's apparently been a riot in Makole. There's a car burnt out and the window of the bank smashed, and there's half a young army stationed on your doorstep.'

'Well, now, I haven't been in to town for a couple of days though I did hear they'd had a bit of trouble. . . . Did you catch those six young hippos we agreed to give you?'

'Five. One died.'

'Bad luck, Ted. Still five is something.' Alex Richie paused. 'As long as I'm head of the parks I suppose I oughtn't to suggest this, but maybe I could anticipate my own imminent demotion just a little. In which case, I'd just give you a wee word of advice—flog your hippos, Ted. Flog 'em and get the hell out of it back to British territory just as soon as you can.'

'What the hell are you talking about? The whole damn white rhino transfer was your idea. You said let's save what's left of the bloody animals. You said the poachers would get the lot if we didn't act fast. You had this high and mighty plan to shift a breeding nucleus into your bloody park before it was too late. And now you sit there looking like some bloody Scottish minister telling me to forget the whole thing. And you give me five hippos for damn-all into the bargain—or have I misunderstood you slightly?'

Alex Richie called out sharply 'Besuha.'

The sheepish houseboy popped out from behind a curtain.

'More shandy, quick.'

'Balls to the shandy,' said Maxwell. 'Drink more of that mosquito pee and what's left of your blood will turn into shandy—if it hasn't already. And then God knows what you'll suggest.'

Besuha brought two pint tankards to be on the safe side. Maxwell took his and hurled the contents out of the window. The house-boy blinked out after the vanished liquid.

'Must keep up the fluid intake,' Richie chided.

'What I want to know is: why have you suddenly become a bloody old woman? Why have you changed your mind about the rhinos?'

Richie said 'You obviously haven't heard.'

'Now, I suppose, we're getting to it.'

'This country,' said Richie, 'has been selected for a singular hon-our. The authorities are giving it almost immediate *Uhuru*.'

'But Christ, it wasn't due for independence for eighteen months and that would be five hundred years too soon.'

'Maybe, maybe, but you cannot stand in the way of progress,' said Richie sententiously.

'Progress! What kind of progress is that?'

'Well, it's kind of a backward progress.'

'Too true. But why? Why the hell?'

'Like everything else in this land it's politics.' This was a favourite explanation of Alex Richie's. To his way of thinking, it covered al-most every event, predictable and unpredictable, and as a matter of fact he was right.

Maxwell said 'But why suddenly put *Uhuru* all that much ahead?'

'Well, it's some damn great political fiddle and you know what politics back in Europe are like. I gather they know that there's a sort-out coming between the tribes in preparation for *Uhuru*. The Ashota, as you know, claim that the colonial authorities took away four of their tribal counties and gave them to the Magunga for services rendered. These services were almost certainly a bit of treachery on the part of the Magunga. They saw which side their bread was buttered, and fought with the colonials against the Ashota when the colonials grabbed the place. Mind you, all this was eighty years ago but that's a mere blink of a tribal African's eyelash when it comes to a grievance. They're rather like the Irish in that respect. Never forget Oliver Cromwell and Good Queen Bess, too, for that matter. Now there are a hell of a lot of Ashota and allied tribes and the first thing those lads are going to go for when good old *Uhuru* comes are the lost tribal domains. I don't have to tell you that here national boundaries as drawn up by us don't mean a thing. It's the tribal territory that counts.'

'That's what bloody visiting European politicians never realize,' agreed Maxwell.

'Quite. Now the old Ashota aren't likely to wait for *Uhuru* if it runs its full course of eighteen months. They're going to work right now, before Independence comes, so that they've already got their lost lands all lined up when the bell goes. This is pretty well inevitable. So, if *Uhuru* waits for eighteen months, it means a year and a half of trouble and strife before the locals can be allowed to start killing each other legally and in their own time.'

Maxwell knew most of this but knew, too, that Richie had to tell it all his way.

'Eighteen months of trouble,' repeated Richie. 'So long as there are colonial authorities and nationals here, then the dear old colonial power is bound to keep order and protect its lives and property and this means a hell of a lot more troops than they've got here at present. It's also going to mean spending a hell of a lot more money than they're spending on the place at present.'

'They've just about got the whole army in Makole now, I imagine,' said Maxwell.

'Yes? Well they'll need a lot more than that if they stay on, so what happens in Parliament back home? The so-called moderate opposition have been belly-aching for years about freeing the oppressed Africans. The Government is damned unpopular for overspending, anyway. They've raised the taxes as high as they dare and there's an election coming up. The moral is obvious: give the colony independence ahead of time. This will please the liberals and get the Government out of a spot—they won't have to ask for more money just before an election. So that's it. *Uhuru* is now exactly one month away from us instead of eighteen. What do you think of that?'

'I think,' said Maxwell, after a moment's consideration, 'that it's a bloody disaster. When did all this suddenly come up?'

'Well, the decision to give immediate independence popped up last week but it's been brewing for months past. It started to hot up about the time you went away chasing hippos.'

'And the park?' asked Maxwell. 'What about the park?'

'Anyone's guess. There's a fair risk they'll either let it run down, or else they'll wade in and clobber the lot—rhinos for horn, elephants for ivory, antelope and zebra for an immediate free meal.'

'But that's a bloody tragedy.'

109

'I agree,' said Richie, 'but there are worse things. For example, a few settlers are going to lose everything they've worked for. Some are probably going to get killed. Apart from the whites, quite a few of the local lads will get carved up. All of it's a tragedy.'

'Bugger the locals, and the settlers for that matter, too. But you must care about the park,' Maxwell persisted. 'You've put half your life into building the thing up.'

'I do care about it,' Richie agreed, 'but I don't care about it as a thing apart, on its own. I care about it along with this *shamba*, and the house my old man built, and the people I've known and worked with, white and black. That's the damned shame of it.'

Maxwell asked 'What are *you* going to do, Alex?'

'A lot of people,' said Richie, 'are getting out at once. The authorities are putting on a special air-lift and all that sort of thing. But I reckon I'll just stay on for a bit.'

'And get your throat cut?'

'Well, I don't think that's such a serious risk.' Richie waved towards the balcony where the night watchman was in process of rolling over and covering his head, against the flies, with the filthy grey blanket. 'I'm well guarded.'

'From what I see of it, there doesn't look as though there's a great future for you here, Alex.'

'No? Well, you could be right, Ted. Of course, at the start it's going to be sheer bloody murder—and that's just the word for it —but if we can survive this period it's bound to shake down in the end. Whoever runs the place, they'll need food and I grow quite a bit here.'

'Sure, they'll pinch the *shamba* straight away.'

'Some of the African politicians are pretty bright, you know. Give 'em time and they'll sort their own country out. One or two of them realize that chaps like me get more out of a bit of land than the local lads can ever do. It's the same with the park, too. Most of the nationalists can't see any sense in animals. To them they're just a dangerous nuisance and worth a bob or two if you can knock them over before they knock you. But there are small areas of enlightenment. For instance, the Magunga lad who may get to be prime minister is well conditioned to the thought that parks can in the long run bring tourists and that tourists bring foreign currency and that the bawbees are the one thing that this great new nation is going to find itself short of. He's all for building up parks. So we've got a faint chance of ending up with at least a pair of elephants if the Magunga come out on top. Their boy was trained at the London School of Economics.'

'And if the Ashota win?'

'Well, then, it's not quite so good. Their boy was trained by the witch doctor in a mud hut. If their party wins, there'll almost certainly be an immediate glut of powdered rhino horn on the aphrodisiac market and, of course, a consequent shortage of rhinos, both white and black, in this part of Africa.'

'Either way the immediate future for you and the parks looks pretty bloody.'

'The whole show will be absolute anarchy for a bit. But we'll just have to see—about the *shamba* and about the park. If we can weather this period and get through with some animals left, then we may be all right.'

Alex Richie got up and poured himself a large whisky from an old-fashioned mahogany tantalus. 'Now we've got the water table to the required level, I don't think a little of the hard stuff would hurt. You'll join me, Ted?'

'No thanks, I rarely drink Scotch.'

'Well then, we'll have a little late breakfast. I'll see if I can persuade the faithful steward to slice up one of those pineapples of mine —sorry—ours.'

When breakfast arrived Richie busied himself opening his mail. He was a sporadic and unsystematic correspondent and now he dealt with a pile of invoices, receipts, demands from merchants, pleas from debtors and threats from creditors, which had, apparently, been piling up for some days, if not weeks.

When Maxwell could stand it no longer he said 'I came here to ask for a bit of help. I also told you that I'd had a spot of bother.'

Richie put down the coffee-pot in the act of pouring himself a third cup.

Maxwell said 'How you can swill that stuff down on top of shandy and Scotch beats me.'

'Ah, the shandy is a replacement of liquid lost through perspiration. Very necessary. The Scotch is a mild stimulant to reinforce lost sense of purpose. The coffee is just to make negative any trace of disturbance which the previous mixture might have caused. But this trouble of yours, Ted. I do apologize.'

111

'My transport's wrecked.'

'Good God. Well, of course it can happen in this sort of country, particularly the way you lads drive the things. But I see you've got a lorry left and that's all you'll want.'

'All I'll want,' Maxwell repeated incredulously.

'Sure. To get the five young hippos to the coast. It's a pity you couldn't have made it six, but even five should show you a bit of profit on the trip.'

'You don't seem to understand. It's the catching truck that's gone for a Burton, walloped by a bloody great hippo in a hurry.'

Richie blinked at Maxwell, took off his glasses and began to clean them as if this action would help him to understand better what Maxwell was trying to tell him. 'Catching truck? What do you need a catching truck for now?'

'To catch your six white rhinos and put them in your park for you. That's the deal we made. Six hippo calves for me to sell to zoos. Six white rhinos shifted for you.'

'You must be mad. Come back in five years' time, or ten years, and then see if we've got any park left to put them in.'

'You may have a park but you won't have any white rhinos, that's for certain.'

'I concede that, but we won't have any rhinos left even if you shift them into the park now. They'll get speared for their horn wherever they are. The African politicos are going to have too much on their hands in the next few months to worry about stopping a spot of rhino poaching. That's why I'm telling you. Take your hippos and get out with them before the Magunga or the Ashota decide to cut those up too. They're very partial to hippo steaks.'

'Look here, Alex, you said yourself that the parks might have a chance. Some of those African wardens you've been training aren't too bad at their job. How can you be certain they won't keep the parks going whatever happens here?'

'I can't. But there's just one thing I do know. These same African wardens we so lovingly trained were tribal hunters before we took 'em on. What we stuck on will soon wash off. They'll revert to true form pretty quickly, I can tell you, particularly when the administration here grinds to a halt and they don't get their monthly pay packets.'

'That's what they said about the Congo,' Maxwell grunted. 'But the Parc Albert kept going from all accounts—*and* the wardens chased out the boys who came across from the Uganda side looking for meat and ivory.'

Richie agreed, but said 'The Belgians have been in the parks business longer than we have.'

'So what. Here you are lecturing me about staying on in Makole yourself and hoping things will shake down. In the next breath you're telling me to take the Parks' money—for that's what the five hippos amount to—and then not to bother to deliver.'

Richie said 'I'm staying on in Makole because running this *shamba* is all I really know how to do.'

'Sure. And catching animals with the faint hope that we'll end up with a few of the brutes left in Africa is all I know how to do.'

'But I have only myself to think of.'

'So,' said Maxwell slowly, 'have I.'

'Don't tell me you do it all single-handed. What about your wife and that girl and whoever else you have around your camp?'

'My wife does what I do. The rest can please themselves. You worry about people, Alex. I'll just worry about catching animals.'

'Very noble, Ted.'

'Not noble. Just plain sense. I like what I do. I happen to think that it's important. Profits. People. They can go and screw themselves.'

'Well, if you do this job,' said Richie, looking at him over the top of the glasses which he had replaced specially for the gesture, 'you may be lucky if you don't end up as powdered rhino horn yourself.'

'Oh, grow up. What's so different about this country? We lived through Mau Mau in my part of Africa. I'm asking you officially, as head of the parks, which you apparently still are, for transport, or at least spares, so that I can go and finish the job.'

Richie got up and straddled across the seat of an empty chair so that his face was close to Maxwell's. 'Ted, you're right. You *are* a big boy. You can look after yourself. I don't doubt that. You very probably wouldn't come up against any real trouble anyway—at least you might not. On the other hand we may shortly have a full-blown civil war to cope with. As head of the parks, I'd agree with you. The rhinos would have some sort of a chance inside the park, or at least a better one than they do at the moment, four hundred miles away, in the open bush, unprotected by anything except a few game guards who will knock them over themselves at the first opportunity.

I grant you all that, but, when you ask for transport, I'm absolutely helpless. There's such a damn flap blowing since the news about *Uhuru* got out that the authorities have taken every single truck they can commandeer (a) for the military and (b) to start evacuating outlying settlers who want to go home. They're going to bring them in to the airfields. They've taken everything off the Parks except a handful of Land-Rovers. You want to try catching three tons of white rhino in a clapped-out diesel Land-Rover? There isn't a single truck that would do your job for you in the entire province and your chances of getting spares are even smaller.'

Maxwell got up. 'I better get busy and look around then. Someone here must have a heavy, medium-sized truck with a bit of urge in it.'

'No one I know, Ted. Hereabouts it's all Land-Rovers and three-tonners.'

'Some settler, then?'

'If there is, then I don't know him.'

'Then I'll have to try and find one. There must be some transport about if everyone's packing up and going back home.'

'Same story. Land-Rovers and big wagons. That terrible catching truck of yours is a pretty rare bird in these parts. It is totally *kaput*?'

'New bearings. New crankshaft. New front axle. New steering linkage. Apart from that, it's as good as new.'

'The best I can do is to offer you a diesel Land-Rover.'

'Could I catch from it?'

'You couldn't overtake my devoted sentry at a hand gallop.'

'Then what's the use?'

'Well, it might help you to look around.'

'According to you, I don't have much time.'

'Very little, I'd say. The rains are not far away into the bargain.'

Maxwell turned his back on Richie. 'Well, thanks. Thanks for all the help you haven't bloody given me.'

'I don't want you to get yourself and that crippled wife of yours murdered for nothing.'

'Thanks again, but I'm not bothered.'

'Have you asked her?'

'I don't have to and anyway why don't you mind your own business.'

'And your ward?'

'She's pulling out.'

114

'Sensible kid. What about the rest of your crew?'

'Most of them are kukes. They're a long way from home. They'll come.'

'No other Europeans?'

'My mechanic, Webb. He can please himself. Now look, for the last time, Alex, do you know of any transport that would do me?'

Alex Richie hesitated, took his glasses off and polished them. Then he put them back. 'There's just one chap,' he said. 'Monkey catcher. Name of Ryan. Michael Ryan. Got a five-tonner and a fifteen hundredweight. He came in from the West Coast a month ago. Caught a wagon-load of monkeys—vervets and baboons chiefly, for zoos and pet shops. He calls himself a big-game trapper. He came to see me a couple of days ago. I believe he's pulling out shortly. Ever heard of him?'

'No. Where's he camped?'

'Along the Bembo road, about five miles out of town.'

'Well, why the hell couldn't you say so?'

'He may not be quite as crazy as you.'

Maxwell drove out through the groves of rubber trees that stretched away from Richie's house. Between the *shamba* and Makole nothing had altered. The armoured cars and infantrymen remained fixed in the same attitudes of soporific watchfulness. In Makole itself some life was flowing back into the veins of the town. Maxwell swung the three-tonner left at the main junction and onto the Bembo road. He found Ryan's camp just beyond the five kilometre sign. He saw immediately that there were two big lorries. He couldn't, however, spot what he wanted most to see: a fifteen hundredweight. Scattered about the camp were a number of small wooden crates which had, presumably, held the monkeys. They were empty. Maxwell pulled up, stopped his engine and looked round.

A man, naked except for gym shoes and a pair of very short pale blue trunks, came out from the trees and stood looking at the Mercedes. His body was sun-stained the colour of a cigar box. 'Good-looking bastard,' Maxwell registered. 'Looks as if he should be tossing a beach ball about in one of those you-too-can-have-a-body-like-mine ads.'

When he saw that it was another white man at the wheel of the Mercedes, the man in the trunks advanced.

'Hi,' he said.

'Hi. Are you Ryan?'

The man smote his well-developed chest. It was a gesture at once self-conscious, cocky and slightly comic. 'Me Ryan,' he said. 'You,' he pointed at the name stencilled on the door of the Mercedes, 'Maxwell.'

'That's me,' Maxwell agreed. He looked at Ryan closely. What he saw did not entirely please him. He summed him up quickly as a bit of a joker, a bit of a chancer, tough all right, but too much of a show-off. Maxwell did not approve of show-offs.

Ryan now abandoned his imitation Tarzan act. 'I've heard of you,' he said. 'I catch animals, too.'

'Where are you from?'

'South Africa in the first place. I've just worked my way over from the West Coast.'

'Monkeys,' Maxwell asked. 'Been catching monkeys?'

Ryan laughed. 'Well,' he said, 'there's a demand for them.'

'Catch anything else?'

'Anything,' Ryan assured him. 'Why?'

'Ever caught a rhino?'

'Lion, giraffe, eland, the lot.'

'But a rhino?'

'Before breakfast,' Ryan told him. 'Any day of the week. Black or white.'

'You've never caught a white rhino?'

'We've got bags of them down in the Union.'

'I wasn't disputing it,' said Maxwell. 'I simply asked if you had ever caught one.'

'They're pretty docile, I hear.'

Maxwell said 'Maybe. When they're just standing around perhaps they are. They're not so liable to charge you as a black bastard but what about when you start chasing one in a truck?'

'It doesn't like it.'

'No,' said Maxwell, 'I don't suppose it does, but if you've caught one you'll be able to give me the answer. How much doesn't it like it?'

Ryan laughed. His laugh came easily. He had film-star teeth and when he laughed his wiry brown hair bobbed around in a way that a woman would almost certainly find attractive. Maxwell, who wasn't over-endowed with feminine characteristics, did not find it pleasing.

There was, he thought, something fang-like about Ryan's good-looking laugh.

'Well, to tell you the truth,' Ryan admitted, 'I've only chased the black variety with a truck and they can be pretty nasty.'

'We've given up chasing black rhinos,' Maxwell told him. 'We just show them the catching truck and let them chase us. It saves time and petrol. Anyway, I knew you had never caught a white rhino. Up till now only a few have been captured and they were half-grown. The big 'uns weigh three and a half tons.'

Ryan did not seem to like being caught out. He half turned on his heels. 'Nice of you to drop in, anyway,' he said. 'I enjoyed our little chat. Or was there something you wanted to talk about?'

'I heard you had a fifteen hundredweight but I don't see it around?'

'I have. It's in Makole getting stores.'

'Is it any good?'

'It does me okay. Look, if you've got some proposition or something, come across and talk about it.'

'I have. I want to buy your truck—if it's any good.'

By the time they had reached the fly-sheet rigged beneath a tree, a shelter which served as Ryan's office, living quarters and store-room, the fifteen hundredweight came roaring across the grass with an African driver at the wheel. Maxwell noted that the engine sounded healthy although the sides were a little too high for his liking and the centre of gravity probably not really low enough. However it was considerably more use as a catching truck than a diesel Land-Rover.

Ryan poured out two glasses of beer from a bottle which lay in the shade beneath a canvas water-bag of the type which keeps its contents deliciously cool by slow evaporation. Maxwell sipped and, nodding towards the truck, asked 'That it?'

'That's it.'

'What do you use it for?'

'Well, right now, getting the beer from town. Apart from that we use it for catching.'

'With those sides?' Maxwell asked.

'We get by with it.'

'Want to sell it?'

'That depends. It's a valuable bit of my equipment.'

'You don't need it to catch monkeys, surely?'

Ryan gave his crocodile grin. 'As I explained, I occasionally catch other things. Anyway, monkeys or not, I'm fond of that truck.'

Maxwell said 'By all accounts you're pulling out shortly. This country's going to be a mighty troubled place. I've got to stay. You could easily buy another fifteen hundredweight in Kenya or wherever you're going.'

'It would cost me four hundred quid.'

'Well, allow a bit for exaggeration and say two fifty.'

'You say what *you* like,' Ryan agreed good-humouredly. 'I'd say four hundred.'

'I'd give you three for it.'

'Do you have it on you?'

'I don't normally tear around the bush stacked up with notes.'

'No. I suppose not. Anyway, even if you did have it on you, I really don't think I'd want to sell.'

'Look,' said Maxwell. 'I have a job to do. I need a catching truck. I have five hippo calves. They're worth £500 apiece, delivered. I'll trade one for the truck.'

Ryan poured himself some more beer. 'I heard about this job you're on from Alex Richie. Fine piece of conservation and so on. Of course, it's pretty doubtful whether it's worth doing, the way things are going up here.'

'We've been into all that, Richie and I,' Maxwell said impatiently. 'We think that it's worth doing.'

'Good for you. I daresay you're right. Of course, the white rhinos, even a pair of them would be much safer inside a nice zoo.'

'What are you getting at?'

'Do you know the price a European zoo will pay for a pair of white rhinos? Not less than £10,000. Send away four of those babies and you don't have to worry about the *duka* bill for quite a long time, not that I worry all that much anyway. It would be nice though. I could worry less about some other bill.'

Maxwell said slowly 'My deal is to lift six rhinos from a game area where they're daily threatened by poachers and to shift them to the comparative safety of the Parcs Nationaux.'

'I'm glad you said comparative. What makes you think the game guards in the park won't spear them for their horns once the administration packs up here. Far better to forget the parks and simply shift them straight to the peace and quiet of a nice zoo somewhere.'

Maxwell got up. 'My deal was with the parks. I've got my payment in the form of hippos. Those are what I'm flogging. The rhinos are the other half of the bargain, so I deliver them the way I said I would.'

Ryan smiled. 'I quite see your point, old boy, but I think you may have a bit of a job catching them from that Mercedes. My boys tell me that's all you have left.'

'I'll have to find a truck somewhere else then, that's all.'

'I suppose there's always a chance.'

'Look. Bring all your transport along with me on this job and I'll split the sale of the hippos with you.'

'You'd make precious little out of it.'

'That's my business.'

'What about the rest of your crew?'

'I'd see they got paid off.'

'And make nothing yourself?'

'I've lost on jobs before and, as I said: that's my business.'

'You're an odd one!'

'Thanks for the information,' Maxwell said. 'But the only information I want from you is whether you're on.'

Ryan said 'You're in a spot if you really mean to go through with this. Personally, if it were my show, I'd pull out now and sell my hippos. Maybe I'd come back later when the dust has settled here, and maybe I wouldn't. Now the way I see it, you're not only relying on me for a catching truck but you could use my big transport too, first to shift your hippos to the coast and secondly to get those rhinos into the park as soon as possible. With just your Merc it might take a very long time trundling back and forth four hundred miles each way between the catching ground and the park. Alex Richie told me a bit about the set-up. On top of everything else, the rains are coming as sure as *Uhuru* and both of them might make extended travelling with a busload of rhinos pretty sticky. So you really do want all the transport you can get.'

Maxwell nodded. 'I won't argue about any of that.'

'Now if I come in with you,' Ryan went on, 'I'm taking a bit of a risk. I don't have to deliver rhinos. It isn't my party. Come to that, I don't feel the same as you seem to about the need to deliver them. I catch animals for money, not for glory, for the joy of mankind, or the future of the world's wildlife. I like it, sure. It's a living and it suits me, but that's where it ends.'

'You're a big lad,' said Maxwell. He felt uneasy at being represented in the slightest degree as a selfless man; the image that he carried of himself was that of a man who regarded everything except the job in hand as expendable. Any suggestion of altruism was foreign to him and embarrassing. He repeated 'You're a big lad. You can please yourself how you feel.'

'I do. And the way I feel about this is that I want more out of it than half your hippos, which might add up to, say, £800 by the time we've deducted expenses. If I come along and help you, then I want a pair of white rhinos.'

'Don't be damned stupid.'

'I've heard about you. You've got a great reputation when it comes to animals. All right, you'd like to see Africa stocked with rhinos rather than people. That's your affair.'

Maxwell remained unruffled. 'Who told you that?'

'Oh, I can see that. You're a flaming sentimentalist.'

'Yes? I can think of some people who'd be amused to hear it said.'

'I daresay. I suppose you mean women. Well, I wasn't thinking of them—although,' he added, 'that makes a change. You're a sentimentalist because you want to keep things just the way they are, or rather were. Do you know that in the entire traceable history of the goddam world at least one million species of animals have gone their way to extinction? Don't ask me where I got the facts. Probably off the back of a cigarette card or maybe even from a book. Sometimes I read books. Now that's a hell of a lot of animals, even if my figure's not quite accurate. Why did they disappear? As I understand it, they went because they just weren't good enough to last. They couldn't adapt themselves. Something else came along and pushed them out.'

'About that truck,' Maxwell interrupted. His tone was still patient.

'The truck can wait for a second. I want to tell you something and if you keep interrupting me we'll never get to the point.'

'Does all this serve some purpose then?'

'Yes. I want to convince you why I'm offering you a bargain. So, you're a sentimentalist. That's your right, I grant you. If you'd had your way, none of those million kinds of animals would ever have disappeared. Right now we'd have a national park for dinosaurs. We'd be coughing up for a "Save the Sabre-Toothed Tiger Fund". So now you want to save what's left of Africa. You want to keep it the way you think it's always been, at least the way it was after the dinosaurs went out of business. Of course, you overlook one thing and that is that the present collection of animals deserve to go just as much as the dinosaurs did, because now something better than them has come along—*us*.'

'Oh, do me a favour, Ryan.' Maxwell pointed at Ryan's driver who was lying asleep under the lorry he had just driven into camp. His filthy khaki shirt was in ribbons, his toes stuck out through the soles of a ruined pair of gym shoes, his limbs sprawled in a slovenly and ungainly heap and his mouth lolled open. 'Is he the superior being you're so stuck on? Or are you, for that matter?'

Ryan grinned. 'In the long run, yes. Anyway, he's a start.'

'Sorry. I didn't see you as a strong African nationalist.'

'Don't worry, I'm not. Don't forget I come from the Union. Back there we have a system. It's called *apartheid* and it works.'

'For the moment.'

'I'm only concerned with moments, mate.'

Maxwell got to his feet. 'So am I. They're running out, too. Too bad you couldn't help.'

'But I can.'

'Not at your price, you can't.'

'Now you're being sentimental again.'

'Oh, drop dead. I'm just interested in sticking to a deal I made.'

'Yes? You're interested in more than that. You really care about preserving the bloody rhinos.'

'Is there something wrong with that?'

'No. It's just that your whole approach to the thing—in the present circumstances at least—is sentimental.'

Maxwell said wearily: 'Oh not that again.' He began to walk towards the lorry. Ryan followed him.

'No, listen. By sentimental I mean just not realistic. Save the rhinos if that's what your heart is set on, but at least be practical about it. What happens if you don't go after them and shift them?'

'They get speared for horn.'

'So, no rhinos.'

'That's about it.'

'Can you save them without my help?'

'I'll try damn hard.'

'Come off it. I'm ready-made. I've got more transport than you dreamed of. I know the trade. All I want is two rhinos for myself that would have been poached anyway. Who am I robbing? You? The park? No, I'm robbing the bleeding poachers who won't even eat the meat. They'll simply cut off the horns, sell them at 120 shilling per pound to some greasy Indian merchant who'll ship them out under cover to China where they'll be ground up into some loathsome powder and given to failing old men in the mistaken belief that next time they try to screw their girl friends they can take a quick swig of the stuff and get the horn themselves. Isn't that the size of it?'

'Yes,' Maxwell agreed reluctantly.

'Now supposing I do take two rhinos and sell them for £10,000, who'll buy them off me? No, don't tell me, I'll tell you. A zoo will buy them. So, instead of going to waste there will be two more white rhinos saved for posterity. What's more they'll be damn sight safer in a zoo than they will be on the hoof in this park. You'd be a bloody hero.'

'My bargain with Richie,' said Maxwell stolidly, 'is to give the parks six.'

'Well don't go on about it,' said Ryan. 'Still give him six but catch two more for me. That's my offer. I suppose there *are* eight left up there?'

'They reckon that the area holds between twenty and thirty.'

'Well, then. And don't say there won't be time. With my extra transport we'll catch eight easily. Of course, I wouldn't mention any of this to Richie.'

'Who said I was even thinking of agreeing with you?'

'No one, but then why have you sat down again?'

Ryan moved his camp to join Maxwell that afternoon. Nancy Maxwell watched the trucks as they came bumping across the bush towards the hippo *boma*. To her husband she said 'The transport looks sound enough even if the idea is crazy.'

'Are you worried?'

'What's the use?' she said. 'You'll do what you want anyway.'

'What about Webb?'

'I haven't seen him since you came bounding back this morning to break the news. He's been sleeping his trip off. If he wants to he can go back to the coast with the girl, can't he?'

'Has she still got that idea?'

'I haven't asked her,' Nancy Maxwell said. 'But you heard what she said.'

'Sure. I've heard her say that she's packing it in before.'

'If she did I wouldn't blame her. I wouldn't have blamed her before we heard what's happening here. Now I think she'd be mad not to get out of it.'

'She won't,' said Maxwell with more certainty than he felt. 'Look at Webb,' he went on, 'just look at him now. The sound of those lorries has woken him out of his beauty sleep. Anybody would think it was a troop of dancing girls coming in instead of a couple of three-tonners and a fifteen hundredweight.'

Webb had crawled out under the flap of his tent and, shading his eyes, was staring unbelievingly at the approaching lorries.

Nancy Maxwell said waspishly 'Well, where's wonder boy Ryan? Let's have a look at him, then we'll know what we're in for.'

'We've got his trucks, haven't we?'

'Sure, but what else have we got along with them?'

Mike Ryan had dismounted and was walking towards them across the burnt, flayed grass. He still had on his pale blue shorts but above these he now wore a well-laundered, well-pressed bush shirt. This was unbuttoned from top to bottom so that a strip of mahogany chest and hard, drawn-in stomach showed through. Above all this he wore his white-toothed grin.

'Christ,' said Nancy Maxwell piously, 'he looks like a fallen angel.'

'More like a Durban beach boy to me,' Maxwell grunted. He walked out to meet him.

Ryan, who had eight locally recruited boys, all Ashota, with him, made a separate camp one hundred yards beyond the pen holding the hippos. When he had settled in, he came across, at Maxwell's invitation, to hold a discussion. Maxwell introduced him to his wife. 'This is Mike Ryan,' he said. 'I told you about him.'

Nancy Maxwell adjusted the set of her wheel-chair so that she squarely faced Ryan. 'Ted told me what you propose,' she said without preamble. 'The first thing to do is to get those five hippo *totos* to the coast.'

The suddenness with which she had plunged to the heart of the business caught Ryan with his hand extended towards her but with the anticipated handshake denied to it. She left him with the hand extended. Ryan, however, managed to convert his gesture into a sort of general wave of greeting. He was not going to be thrown so easily or so early in the encounter. 'You agree with my proposition then, Mrs Maxwell?'

'My husband agrees,' she said. 'He makes the decisions. I help him carry them out.'

Ryan sat down and shook his head as if slightly bewildered at her bluntness but managing to convey a hint of admiration as well. 'I see,' he said. 'Let me know where I come into your husband's plans, then.'

'I will, Mr Ryan.'

'Just call me Mike.'

'No doubt we'll come to that stage naturally,' she said.

Maxwell continued to sit in his chair, chin lowered on chest, as if all this was taking place in the next room.

'Okay, *Mrs* Maxwell,' Ryan said with a grin. 'Doesn't *Mr* Maxwell come in on this staff conference?'

'Ted is the boss, the absolute boss of this outfit. You must understand that. Once we start operations, whatever he says everyone else does, including you, Mr Ryan. I want that clear from the start. I just do the planning.'

'I see,' said Ryan. 'If I may say so you do seem to be laying down the law a bit in view of the fact that it's me who's pulling your outfit out of the muck.'

'You've made your bargain. It's a fairly hard one as I see it. Just the same, once we've agreed to it, we will deliver our side of it. I imagine you want us to deliver. You'd be a damn fool if you didn't.'

'Sure. I want two rhinos crated and delivered.'

'Then you can't really object to us saying how things are to be done. First, you only get your two when we've put our six into the park.'

'If that's what you insist on.'

'We do and we want to make one thing quite clear: we only catch an additional two for you once the original six are safely in the bag. If we only catch six, or if there are only six to catch, then those six go to the park and you get nothing.'

'The way I hear it there are twenty or thirty still left up there.'

'So do we. But nothing is certain in this game. That's your gamble.'

'I take it that having caught your six you'll try just as hard to catch my two?'

'You have our word for that.'

'I'm inclined to believe you.'

'Good. Then I have drawn up a short agreement between us. There are two copies. I'd be glad if you would sign both and give one back to me.'

Nancy Maxwell handed Ryan two sheets torn from a ruled exercise book.

'Well,' he said admiringly, 'aren't you the girl!' He began to read what she had written. 'Seems fairly straightforward,' he said, 'though I don't suppose it would be exactly binding in a court of law.'

'I don't think that particularly matters. For one thing this is a thoroughly illegal arrangement and for another there isn't liable to be much law and order around for a bit. Now this is what my husband proposes.'

Without shifting his slumped position in the chair Maxwell took his cue. 'The very first thing,' he said, 'is to get those five hippos to the coast. We will crate and load 'em tonight. We'll use the Merc and one of Ryan's lorries to take 'em there. Ryan, I'd like you to drive your lorry and take your boys as a loading party.'

'What will you be doing all this time?'

'Tomorrow morning I break camp and leave with the catching truck and the other three-tonner and head north to the catching area. I'll take the rest of the boys. I'll make the recce. Those rhinos are going to take some finding. Four days from now you should be back from the coast and on the way to join us. By then we'll have built the *boma* and we'll be ready to start catching.'

'How do I know where to off-load the hippos and who to hand them over to?' asked Ryan.

'I forgot. Nancy will go with you in the Merc. Nguru will drive her. We've got a base camp to dump them in. It will simply be a question of off-loading. The agents will see to the rest. You can turn round and come straight back.'

His wife said 'Haven't you left someone out?'

'Webb? He can please himself. If he wants to quit, he can ride to the coast in the back of the Merc.'

Next morning the camp was awakened at four thirty. Maxwell sluiced his face in a bucket of lukewarm water and regarded the day with joy. Things were moving again. In an hour Ryan and the hippos would be out of his hair. In two hours he would be pressing on up the road, spewing out the miles behind in a cloud of choking dust and heading for new country. Just for the moment, at this early hour, the day was deceptively innocent. It smelt as cool as an iced melon.

The scrub around him and the forest beyond was liquid with the melting song of bush shrikes. This and hours like this one were the best times of his life. With satisfaction he saw that Nguru had the boys securing the final lashings on the hippo crates. He saw Nguru checking the supplies of food and water the animals needed for the journey. Beyond the *boma* he saw Ryan shaving himself with a battery-powered electric razor. He wrinkled his nose slightly at this. His gaze travelled back from Ryan's camp towards his own lines. There, he knew, was the flaw whose presence he had deliberately hidden from himself. Jen had kept away from all the preparations of the previous afternoon and evening. This did not mean that she did not know precisely what was going on. She would know from her boys or from Webb that the lorries were leaving for the coast at any time now. With a pain he did not suspect himself capable of feeling, he now saw that she was moving in her tent. Webb came sauntering across the clearing.

'Guess I'll come rhino-catching,' he said without preamble.

'All right, then,' Maxwell agreed. 'You may not get paid though.'

'Then I'll sign on with Ryan. I hear he earns big money.'

'Catching monkeys?'

'Or rhinos.'

'If you're coming,' Maxwell told him, 'I can do without the humorous remarks.'

'All right, so long as I don't have to try to make that old bastard of a catching truck go again. What'll we do with it?'

'We could just leave it here,' Maxwell suggested.

'Leave it, hell,' Webb told him. 'There are still a good few spares on her.'

'That's my boy,' Maxwell told him. 'Tell you what we'll do then. We'll tow it up to Alex Richie's *shamba* and dump it on him. He can keep his chickens in it. We can pick up the Land-Rover he promised me at the same time.'

'What kind is it? Long-wheel base?'

'Short-arsed and diesel.'

'Well,' said Webb, 'I suppose it might come in useful for something though it's hard to think what—catching dung beetles maybe. When are we leaving?'

'Just as soon as we've got the hippo convoy off towards the coast. So get your tent struck and gear loaded.'

As Webb strolled away Maxwell felt an overpowering urge to ask him whether Jen was leaving with the hippos. But he was afraid he knew the answer, for she had just come out of her tent. She was wearing something he did not even suspect she carried in her safari gear. She had on a flowered summer dress.

Jen did not appear at the brief breakfast the hippo party took in the mess tent. Ryan was there, well-shaven and talkative. So was Nancy Maxwell who ticked off a list of stores while drinking her coffee. At five thirty Nguru had the lorries started and the few boys who were going climbed aboard to stow themselves around the crated animals.

When the Africans were aboard Nguru walked across to the tent, grinned at Maxwell and then stood expectantly in front of Nancy Maxwell. She nodded and Nguru took the handles of the wheel-chair and pushed it across the grass towards the Mercedes. Then he picked her up and settled her in the passenger's seat.

Ryan watched her go and then said to Maxwell 'All right, then. Four days from now.'

Maxwell nodded.

Ryan walked across and climbed into the driving-seat of his three-tonner.

Maxwell was conscious now of a quite unaccustomed dryness in his throat. He tried not to look towards Jen's tent. The lorries were rolling forward, cutting off his view. The Mercedes was making quite a dust cloud so that it became harder for him to see what was happening. Then the Mercedes pulled off the grass onto the road and he saw that Ryan's three-tonner was slowing down. When it stopped he saw Jen standing just ahead of it, holding up her hand. She ran forward and began to speak to Ryan in the cab. Maxwell was just able to register the fact that this must have been quite a shock to Ryan who had not, as far as he knew, had any inkling until that moment that there was a girl in the camp. He imagined Ryan's grin. He could imagine him tossing his curls and puffing out his over-developed chest. For a moment Maxwell thought of running across the clearing and forcibly detaining Jen. Then he saw the door on the passenger's side of the cab swing open in invitation. The girl stood for several seconds looking back towards the camp. She stared first in the direction of Webb's tent which even at that moment was being pulled down, and then turned and looked longer and more deliberately at Maxwell. The Ashota driver leaped down and lobbed her two suitcases lightly into the back of the lorry before climbing up after them.

Then Ryan's arm appeared and helped Jen into the passenger's seat. The lorry engine raced. Ryan waved his hand out of the driver's window and the three-tonner ground its way towards the road where it joined its newly forming dust cloud to the tail end of the vanishing trail left by the Mercedes. The engines died away and the dust hung like smoke among the trees.

In the twenty-four hours since Maxwell had visited Makole the situation had changed, though it was hard to say in which direction. The main street was fully populated again and the Indian stores were open and doing a little business. There were, however, many more troops about and armoured cars stood at every major crossing. There was even a tank guarding the turning off towards the residential area and Richie's *shamba*. The infantry no longer lounged about in a loose cordon round the European section. Instead there were manned machine-gun posts, jeeps, a command car with wireless aerial raised. The situation seemed to have been stabilized. Just the same, anyone who had seen these things before could have detected the unmistakable smell of a slow-burning fuse. Outside the first European residence were two large lorries into which African servants were loading baggage and furniture. Maxwell at the wheel of Ryan's second three-tonner noted all this without particular alarm. Soon he would be out of it all, away in the unchanging bush. Makole would miraculously cease to exist. Behind him Webb registered little of what was passing. Seated at the wheel of the derelict catching truck he jolted at the end of a tow-rope. In Maxwell's wake, he saw nothing beyond an occasional glimpse of the lorry's tailboard. He was totally enshrouded in a cocoon of red dust. They pulled up at last outside Richie's mansion.

Alex Richie came down the steps to meet them. He looked first at Maxwell and then at the name neatly stencilled on the door of the three-tonner: Mike Ryan, *Big-Game Trapper*. 'Ah,' he said, 'so you succeeded.'

Maxwell said 'Yes, he agreed to team up.'

'Excellent. I'm delighted. Is he coming along just for the fun of it?'

'Is that likely?'

'On the whole, I should say not.' Richie let the remark hang, as if he half hoped that Maxwell would tell him without any prompting what Ryan's price for co-operation was. Instead Maxwell said 'Alex, I want to dump this wreck on you until we come back.'

'Of course, anywhere you like. Better stick it under the trees over there.'

Webb leant out of his cab. 'Good idea. We don't want to blister the paintwork.'

'Name of Webb. Ron Webb,' Maxwell explained to Richie. 'He tries to keep the transport going. Tell him where this Land-Rover of yours is.'

'Certainly. It's down outside the Park's office in Makole. I've had it checked for you. Do you still want it?'

'Better have it. We don't know what sort of a fix we'll be in up there.'

'Well, drop that wreck over by the trees and come in for a shandy.'

'I'd much rather get moving. We've got a long way to go. Besides this Makole place stifles me.' Maxwell roared his engine as a signal to Webb and then moved off, pulling the derelict towards its place in the shade.

By the time they had unhitched the tow-rope, Richie was back on the veranda with three pints of shandy in his hands. Maxwell did not intend to get out of the truck but Webb was already mounting the steps. 'By the time we've stopped to collect that Land-Rover . . .' Maxwell began.

Richie said mildly 'Oh come on, Ted. You must keep up the water table.' Maxwell, still with the fear that Richie might press him about his bargain with Ryan, reluctantly got down from the lorry.

When they had all taken their pint mugs Richie said 'Ted, there's one thing I must ask you.' Maxwell thought 'Here it comes. I'll have to persuade him Ryan settled for half the hippo money, but he's a canny old devil.'

But Richie said 'Are you quite sure you want to go on with this?'

'Would I be going otherwise?'

'You do know that it's quite unpredictable, what may happen here in the next few weeks? No one will be able to help you up there. The Game Warden who was going to take you on your recce has just received his notice. The Game Department is closing down. The chap is coming in to Makole within the next two days.'

'He's not bringing the rhinos with him, is he?'

'No, but he's bringing his wife. They're flying home.'

'That's their privilege if they've got the wind up.'

'I don't think it's that at all. They just feel that there's no future for them here.'

'Too bad. I'm sorry. I'm really sorry for anyone who loses a job they like doing. That's why I'm catching the rhinos. All I want to know about is your park. Will there be someone left there to take over the things when we deliver them?'

Richie said 'As far as I'm concerned the parks are carrying on. We're building tracks now so that you can bring the rhinos into the release area. We're sticking up a ramp, too, to make unloading easier. You bring them in from the north by the Itangi track. We've dammed and bridged a couple of little streams for you. The dams will hold until the rains really break. Look, I've got the maps for you.'

'What would I want with maps? I know the place.'

Richie said patiently 'You know the park all right, but what about the catching ground? That's five hundred square miles of sweet damn-all.'

'Okay. If you insist.'

'Your wife—' began Richie.

'Gone to the coast with the hippos.'

'Good. I wouldn't want any women about on this safari if I could help it.'

'She'll be back in four days' time,' Maxwell told him.

'You're crazy. Well, watch her and watch yourself. And you, young man. Any damn thing could happen.'

'You're the one that's got to watch it, Alex. I bet they aren't guarding the rhinos with armoured cars like your *shamba* here. You take care of yourself.' Maxwell waved his hand and started down the steps.

'The maps,' Richie called.

'I'll take 'em,' said Webb. 'I doubt if he can read anyway.'

Richie watched them drive away, then went into the house to bawl out Besuha while he still had the chance.

By the time they got to the Parks' office in Makole the other two lorries, the Mercedes and Ryan's fifteen hundredweight, were drawn up by the side of the road waiting for them. So was the diesel Land-Rover. Maxwell signed for this and gave the receipt to the grave-faced African clerk in the office.

'Who's in charge down in the park now?' Maxwell asked.

'Mr Enriko.'

Mr Enriko was an African who had been trained as assistant warden.

'What's happened to *bwana* Bertrand?'

'He is on leave in Europe.'

'Does Mr Enriko expect us to start bringing him white rhinos soon?'

'Oh, yes. He knows all about it.'

'Is Enriko disturbed by what's going on up here?' Maxwell gestured in the direction of the distant sound of hubbub that was building up in the street.

The clerk said simply '*Bwana* Richie has told everyone that the parks will continue whatever happens.'

'And do you believe this? Does Enriko think this?'

'If he has been told so,' the clerk said with dignity.

'Good. What tribe is Enriko?'

'Ashota, *bwana*. All the game guards are Ashota. They make very good game guards because they understand the animals. The Ashota are a hunting people, not like the Magunga. The Magunga are banana and maize growers.'

'You, I take it, are an Ashota.'

The clerk stood up straight for the first time during the interview. 'Most certainly, sir,' he said. He touched the slanting tribal scars upon his cheek.

Maxwell nodded, acknowledging the man's pride of blood, but said 'The only trouble about converted hunters is that they convert back just as easily.'

'I beg your pardon?'

'Never mind,' Maxwell told him. 'When was the last pay parade down in the park?'

'Last week, *bwana*.'

'And the next one?'

'In one month's time.'

'And is there money for that?'

The clerk looked flustered. 'Without *bwana* Richie's permission . . .' he began.

'All right,' Maxwell told him, 'I'm not going to blow up the safe. *Bwana* Richie wouldn't have given me the Land-Rover if he didn't trust me, would he? I just want to know how long I can expect the game guards to stay game guards rather than game hunters.'

'*Bwana* Richie has told us all that the parks . . .' the clerk began again.

'Sure. Well, I hope he's right. Telling is one thing but paying wages and keeping everyone happy is another.'

The clerk was stung by Maxwell's tone. 'You need not worry, *bwana*,' he burst out. 'There is money for . . .'

Maxwell held up his hand. 'Good. That's all I wanted to know. Don't let anyone, Magunga or Ashota, or anyone else for that matter, pinch it.'

At that moment, Ron Webb opened the office door and poked his head round. As he did so the noise in the street rose in intensity. The increase in volume was not entirely geared to the opening of the door.

'Ted,' said Webb, 'looks like we're parked in the middle of a riot. We'd better be moving out.'

'Thanks. You take the Merc. I'll drive the fifteen hundredweight. I might as well see what it's got inside it. Ryan's spare driver can wreck his own three-tonner. That leaves the Land-Rover. Have we got a driver for that?'

'Better risk Mgulu.'

'That clot?'

'He can just about make things go.'

'All right, stick him in front of you. You bring up the rear. I'll lead.'

'Right.'

But by the time they had sorted out the drivers, the uproar was steadily drifting down the road towards them, though nothing could yet be seen of the demonstrators. As Maxwell started his engine, a mob of Africans carrying banners appeared round the slight bend in the road one hundred yards ahead. Before them four African policemen, waving truncheons, fell back like cork floats swept on the front of a breaker. Suddenly one of these slipped and fell in the path of the crowd. Fearing the mob would simply trample him to death, the policeman swiped out in panic with his truncheon and brought down a white-robed man carrying a banner. In the next second the remaining three policemen were lashing out with their truncheons, too.

Maxwell heard transport approaching behind him, fast. In his driving mirror he saw a lorry loaded with armed African police reinforcements coming up flat out, and behind it the turret of an armoured car of the colonial forces. The two vehicles roared past him and stopped. When the dust had settled he saw that the three policemen had escaped from the crowd, dragging their fallen comrade with them. Armed reinforcements from the lorry had now formed themselves in a line across the road and stood with their rifles at the ready. The armoured car with two helmeted European soldiers in the open turret had pulled right across the road, well to the rear of the opposing African groups. The soldiers smoked and watched, the turret and the muzzles of their machine-guns swung more or less towards the disturbance. Otherwise they made no attempt to look businesslike or ready for instant action. Perhaps they judged that the presence of the armoured car was enough.

'That's that,' thought Maxwell. 'In a minute these silly bastards will get fed up and go home. Then we'll be able to get on our way.'

The situation, however, remained at stalemate for some minutes. Then several members of the mob made short, feinting rushes towards the police cordon, shouted slogans and abuse. The police merely raised the muzzles of their rifles slightly and the demonstrators fell back. Next the sergeant in charge of the police stepped out in front of his men and began to address the crowd. Immediately there was a volley of counter-shouts. The sergeant stopped speaking until the noise fell away and then tried again.

It was all entirely predictable and slightly comic. And then something very different happened. A youngish man ran out from the body of the mob with an iron bar in his hand. He stood poised for a second, five yards from the sergeant, and drew back his hand. He remained like this for fully another three seconds and then he hurled the bar. This in itself was a ridiculous and inept action. The bar was never in danger of hitting the sergeant or anyone else. It flew lopsidedly through the air, turning end over end to pass four feet wide of its target and crash in the roadway.

The gesture of violence triggered off a deep sigh from the mob and a tiny wave of motion ran through it, but still it did not charge. The moment of danger which the young man's action had brought very close had broken and passed. The crowd had missed its chance. The young man turned to run back into the crowd. As he did so Maxwell saw the tribal slashes of the Ashota upon his face. He had not completed his turning movement when a burst of Sten-gun fire from the right-hand man of the police cordon cut him down. The sergeant, his simple, flattened Magunga face open with terror and surprise, turned to see which of his men had fired and, in this second, the crowd turned tail and ran, leaving the young man face downwards in the dust, lying in the pool of blood that seeped from beneath his chest.

In the turret of the armoured car the two helmeted soldiers still looked on. One had put down his cigarette and lowered himself slightly towards his weapons. The other remained unmoved. Two African policemen carried the young man's body back towards their lorry, its head bumping in the dust.

Maxwell started his engine for the second time and waved to the truck behind him that he was moving off. As he drew up alongside the armoured car he slowed and shouted to the man in the turret 'Couldn't you brave soldiers have stopped that?'

'Not our orders,' said the cigarette smoker.

'Christ almighty, I should have thought your orders were to stop people killing each other for nothing.'

'That's their affair,' the soldier told him. 'The cops are Magunga. That was an Ashota demonstration. What else do you expect?'

'I'd have expected you to break that lot up before anyone got killed.'

'What's an Ashota or two the less? Our orders are simply to protect European life and property.'

'Christ,' Maxwell told him, 'no wonder you bastards are getting chucked out.'

'Watch what you're saying,' said the soldier, 'my sergeant's down in the turret. We could easily stop you from going wherever you think you're going.'

'Yes, but I don't reckon you will. You boys have got enough trouble on your hands.'

As Maxwell drove past the spot where the young man had died the flies were thick on the newly-shed blood. Overhead, a single white-backed vulture was circling optimistically.

Once out of town they made good going. Maxwell led at the fastest pace the dirt surface allowed, for he wanted to get Makole and the killing of the demonstrator as far behind him as he could. His main conscious object in clipping along at this speed was that he sought to drive a sense of urgency and purpose back into the expedition. Moreover, he did not know how much the Africans behind him in the other trucks had seen. They would certainly have heard the burst of Sten fire and they had probably spotted the corpse as they passed the police lorry. On the morale of his own boys the experience could hardly have been beneficial. Ryan's retainers, he reminded himself, were Ashota.

After an hour he stopped and found himself, as he had expected, alone. Five minutes later the dust of the next lorry appeared over the tree-tops. He stepped out in the road and waved the convoy down. When all three vehicles were in, he walked down the line telling the Ashota driver in Ryan's lorry and his own wide-eyed boy, Mgulu, at the wheel of the Land-Rover, to check their loads. Webb was already seeing that his crew did this.

As Maxwell came up Webb asked 'What the hell was that all about?'

Maxwell said quietly 'An African got the chop.'

'That burst of machine-gun fire. The armoured car?'

'No. His fellow-Africans. One of the police cut loose with a Sten. The fellow wasn't dangerous. He'd thrown an iron bar, that's all. It missed. Trouble was he belonged to the wrong tribe, so the opposition took a chance to pay off an old debt.'

'They're lovely boys,' said Webb. 'Simple children of nature.'

'You think the Europeans did so hot?'

'Well at least they didn't open fire.'

'Exactly. A couple of bursts over the heads of that crowd and they would all have gone home to mammy. The trouble is the bloody colonials have abdicated. They don't want to know. They're not taking any responsibility any more. They're going home to let the original owners sort it all—and each other—out.'

'This worries you?' Webb asked unbelievingly. 'Since when have you been worried about the poor African?'

'Sonny,' said Maxwell, 'there's only one thing that worries me and that's my way of living. When the animals go from Africa, I go. When the colonials pull out there's a better than even chance that the animals in that part of the world will get their notice shortly after. And that's all I care about.'

Webb looked at Maxwell closely and seemed satisfied with what he saw in his face. 'Good old Ted,' he said, 'I knew I could rely on you to stay in character. I'd be disappointed if you'd turned out to be a bloody human being. Or are you really a hard old cookie with a soft centre?'

'Don't talk crap.'

'That's better. How's that fifteen hundredweight going?'

'There are a few things you could do for it, but it'll get by. Now let's be moving. Next stop in two hours. Can you keep up?'

'You're straining it a bit, particularly with that dopey bastard Mgulu. He's done a little cross-country work with the Land-Rover twice.'

'Off the road?'

'Yes. He probably falls asleep.'

'Well, he can't afford to. Tell him that if the crash doesn't kill him, I will. We've about two hundred miles to do. I'll shake him up a bit as I go up the line.'

A few seconds later Webb heard the familiar rich pattern of Swahili and Anglo-Saxon twined together in a whiplash of admonition and abuse. He smiled. This was the Maxwell he knew and just occasionally almost loved.

They drove first through partly wooded country, surprisingly green in the breathless heat, the leaves motionless as if preserved and held fast for ever in the burning amber resin of the sun. Apart from a rare vervet monkey and the sudden electric fire-flash of a grey-headed kingfisher, there was no wildlife to be seen and not much human life either. What there was of the second had obliterated the first. To the locals, anything that moved in this area, which was neither game reserve nor park, was simply meat on the hoof, here today and in the pot tomorrow. Maxwell found this country acutely depressing.

When eighty miles had ticked up on the clock they came out of the forest onto open savannah. Here there were at least birds and even occasional antelope which had evaded the hunter's net and spear. Through the hatchway above his head Maxwell could see a soaring Bateleur eagle, its stubby body more like that of a moth than a bird. Bateleurs always gave him a pleasant prehistoric thrill. They looked as if they lived out of their time and were some long-forgotten, outlandish cross between giant insect and bird. Maxwell acknowledged to himself that as eagles went they weren't up to much. They lacked the cruel, tearing talons and steel leg sinews of the tawny or the martial eagle and they'd eat anything that moved on the ground, even crickets. He did not particularly care about their lack of aquiline fibre. But they were part of a scene, an aerial signpost that this was limitless, rolling, open Africa, the Africa he knew best. The Bateleur soared out of his square of vision through the hatch.

Later on the road ran through swampy ground. An old buffalo bull who had somehow escaped with its hide, probably by sheer guile and the terror it managed to inspire in local hunters, glared at him from the reeds surrounding a small water-hole. He remembered the description he had heard some smart-aleck white hunter give his client. 'Buffalo,' this man had said, 'always managed to look as though they have just stolen your wallet or are about to seduce your wife.'

The swampy ground continued until they ran down an escarpment onto a river bank, and there by the bridge was an aluminium-roofed police hut and a barrier thrown across the road.

The askari who guarded the barrier carried a carbine. He saluted.

'What's all this about?' Maxwell asked.

'Inside please, *bwana.*'

'Oh, come on. Pull the bloody barrier down, we're in a hurry.'

'I'm afraid you must see my sergeant, *bwana.*'

This was the second time that morning that Maxwell had been threatened with a sergeant. He began to wonder if there was something in his appearance that didn't accord him the attention of an officer. He climbed down sadly. Inside the stifling hut—perhaps the aluminium wasn't all that good as a reflector after all—an African sergeant sat at a desk behind an impressive row of untouched pens, unsullied notebooks and blotless blotting paper. Maxwell wondered how long he had been waiting for a customer. His heart filled with dread at the thought that he might be the first, for the sergeant would then make a banquet of the proceedings.

'What's up?' Maxwell asked politely. He knew better than to try to push his way with African officialdom.

'You are going into a troubled area,' said the sergeant.

'I reckon I've just come out of one.'

'Very possibly so, but then in Makole the situation is well in hand.'

'Is that so?' said Maxwell. 'Is that so?' He was just going to add that he had only that morning seen a man shot down, but sensed correctly that this would only extend and prolong things.

'What is your reason for wanting to travel on?'

'I am working for the Parcs Nationaux. I'm going to catch some animals for them.'

'I see. Can I examine your papers?'

'Papers. . . .' He was about to say that he didn't have any papers, but checked himself quickly.

'You have authorization papers of course?'

Maxwell thought fast. He didn't have even a letter from Richie.

137

In fact, Richie had never written him one. It had all been by word of mouth. Then he remembered the maps. 'I have papers,' he said.

'May I see them, please?'

As Maxwell stepped out of the hut into the roadway, the sun hit him so that even he felt its impact. Perhaps the aluminium construction was more effective than he had imagined. He found the maps under the dashboard of the truck. He ripped open the envelope. Inside were two maps, one a small scale with the roads from catching ground to park marked in red: the other a far larger scale sheet of the catching area itself. There was also a pencil sketch of the route across the park to the release ramp. Clipped to the latter was a sheet of Parks notepaper—the first he ever remembered seeing. On this was typed a note from Richie's clerk which said 'Please find attached the maps M Richie says you will need for catching and delivering the rhinos.' It was signed 'Alex Richie, Chef du Parcs Nationaux.' The writing was the clerk's.

The sergeant held the maps upside down and examined them at length and with considerable enthusiasm. Next he held up the letter as if checking for a forgery. Then he began to fill in an interminable series of forms, demanding information which began with Maxwell's father's age and nationality. Maxwell, biting back the urge to give the sergeant a dressing-down, sat and sweated while his stomach made enough acid to burn a hole in the table. A full forty-five minutes had passed before everything was at last signed, countersigned, stamped and stamped again.

'Will this lot get me through now?' he asked wearily.

'You are free to travel at your own risk.'

'What's going on up ahead?'

'We do not know. We can only warn you that you are now travelling in a disturbed area.'

'Fine. Well, if I get shot at I'll simply stick these forms next to my heart. Nothing will penetrate this lot.'

The sergeant saluted gravely as Maxwell left the hut. One valuable hour after they had stopped at the barrier, the convoy ground its way on across the bridge.

At first, as they pushed on through the blistering afternoon, there was little sign of trouble. In one or two of the larger villages they met police patrols. Once they were stopped and asked for papers. Maxwell waved his stamped and countersigned document at the grinning askari who then signalled them through. Maxwell recognized in his high cheek-bones and protruding teeth the typical Ashota face. In one small town, a political meeting was in progress. Under banners demanding return of lost lands, an African speaker shouted hysterically. A police patrol stood by, but there was nothing unusual in any of this. On the surface, the area appeared far less troubled than Makole had been, but Maxwell reflected that if anything was cooking it was being brewed in a forest clearing or inside a chief's hut and not in the main streets. Only once did they run into real evidence of trouble. In this particular village the motionless air was filled with the stench of burning. By the side of the road sat a party of dispirited women and children. Beyond them were the remains of five charred huts. The women had the typical rounded, rather stupid face of the Magunga. A police lorry stood witness to the facts of violence. Burning a man's house was a common African way of showing disapproval. Probably there had been fighting, perhaps even casualties. Now only the women sat there, resigned. Maxwell had seen all this many times in other places.

Towards late afternoon the landscape began to change. Low knobbly hills sprang up out of the plain. At a distance the hills seemed to be speckled with small bushes, but when you got close you saw that these were large trees. In the open spaces between the trees, outcrops of rock shouldered their way through the thin jacket of the soil. As the road wound between these foothills, Maxwell watched it gloomily through the insect-plastered windscreen. This was heartbreak country as far as he was concerned. Richie, who knew something of animal catching, had described the white rhino territory as fairly good going. But here even the flats between the hills were impenetrable, the rocks sticking up all over the scrub like blackened canine teeth. The truck he drove was not so close to the ground as his own wrecked fifteen hundredweight had been, but those teeth would rip the bottom out of the sump within seconds of turning off the roadway into the bush. However, he consoled himself with the thought that there was at least fifty miles to go and the landscape could change several times in that distance.

To his relief, in the last twenty miles, the road began to drop away onto lower ground again. It was still not quite the grass country which Maxwell hoped for, but it would do at a pinch. In July the elephant grass here would stand eight or nine feet tall but now it was burnt brown and scythed flat by the sun. This was scrub country, with small thorn trees everywhere and a light sprinkling of rocks over which the truck would have to take its chance. But the ground was fairly level and packed hard by the sun and by bush fires. There were the marks of fire on almost every tree.

Just after five, Maxwell stopped at the fork which led to the catching area. The road on which they had travelled was little more than a rutted track. The fork leading away from it was simply a crease on the tired face of the landscape. He looked at the faded name on the signboard. IMGI. Imgi was where the white rhino were supposed to be. According to Richie, the game warden in charge of this area had had a permanent safari base there. By all the rules Maxwell ought to have called there on his way, but, in the circumstances, it hardly seemed worth it. He decided to push on and make camp.

After twelve miles of bumpy going he found a site close to a stream into which the track dipped and momentarily drowned its dust. When the track emerged on the far side of the stream, it ran through country lightly wooded with young trees, ideal timber, he noted, for building a *boma*. One tall tree, the survivor of countless bush fires, stood out well above the rest. It promised shade throughout the day. Maxwell stopped beneath it just as the light was dropping out of the sky like colour from the cheeks of a man suddenly dead. In the next instant it was night.

Maxwell wakened the camp at five next morning. Normally he reckoned that he needed four full days, in any new situation, before he was ready to start catching. One day had already gone. In three days from now the remainder of the transport should be back from the coast and he wanted to put the first rhino in the bag on the day following their return. But for the moment he forgot the rhinos altogether. The routine work had to be done first. So he split his force into two working parties. Webb he put in charge of Ryan's Ashota boys and a handful of his own Kikuyu who were experienced at *boma* building. Not knowing how used the Ashota were to this kind of work, he rightly assumed that at least they would know how to fell timber with a *panga*. Webb would see that the Kikuyu built the *bomas*. *Bomas*: he wanted two for a start. There was no sense in catching rhinos if he didn't have somewhere to hold them until they could be crated. Maxwell himself took four of the handiest of his own boys and set them to unload the pile of rough but new timber which Webb had collected while they were in Makole. Then he marked out, by scratching with a pickaxe in the iron-hard soil, the ground plan of the two crates he had in mind. Crate-making was the inevitable prelude to all catching operations. Rarely did one type or size of crate do for two jobs. What fitted a giraffe was not the right shape for a zebra. The trouble was that one never knew what animal the next catching assignment might involve. Some of the crates which had taken the hippos to the coast would do for any young rhinos he caught, but Maxwell was planning for the really big stuff, the three-and-a-half-tonners which he knew might come his way if all went well.

The two parties worked throughout the day with frequent breaks for tea and, in the case of the Africans, swills of stream water drunk from an old petrol can. Maxwell never ceased to marvel at what Africans could pour into their stomachs without dying of disease. By late afternoon Webb's party had cut all the timber necessary for the two holding pens and the ribs of the first large crate rose from the ground like the skeleton of a wrecked wooden ship. Maxwell judged that he could now leave things to Webb, so he took the Land-Rover and drove back down the track to look for the Game Department's safari camp.

He soon found Land-Rover tracks leading into the bush and, after following them for half a mile, spotted thatched huts on top of a low hill. As there was no transport outside these he judged that if anyone was there it would be the African game guards responsible for patrolling the area and conducting the rare hunting parties that started their safaris from this point. At the camp, he found a single African washing his khaki shirt in a cut-down five-gallon petrol can. When the African saw him he left his washing and ran inside the hut. A few seconds later he emerged, more or less properly dressed in a bush shirt and a khaki beret in which was the impala badge of the Game Department. This was faintly encouraging. At least the system still worked to some extent. The game guard saluted.

Maxwell asked him in Swahili if *bwana* Bertrand was in the area.

The guard replied that the *bwana* had left two days before and that he himself was now in charge of the area. Yes, he knew about the rhinos. There were still a few rhinos left but, alas, their numbers grew fewer every day. It was impossible for three men, and this was the full strength of the post, to patrol and punish poachers in a territory this size. Maxwell privately agreed but commented to himself that the whole operation was probably made much more difficult if the game guards themselves were assisting in the poaching.

He asked the African if there was another white *bwana* taking over the area. The man said that he had not heard so and repeated that he was in charge. *Bwana* Bertrand had instructed him that he was to act as guide to the catchers. He was not optimistic, however, of being able to find many rhinos. He began to explain again about the poachers. Maxwell cut him short with instructions to report to the catching camp the following afternoon. When he drove away the man was stripped again and washing his shirt. Maxwell wondered how much rhino horn he would have found buried under the floors of the safari huts had he decided to search.

They started work early again next day. Once the skeleton of the second crate was well in hand Maxwell gave half his time to helping Webb with the *boma*. After the Africans had dug pits in soil which had the consistency of badly set concrete, the thicker tree-trunks that served as uprights were tamped home. Then began the business of binding the cross members to these uprights with thick wire, each lashing being twisted into place with a heavy tommy bar. Maxwell and Webb critically examined each tree-trunk as it went into place. They had known black rhino tear flimsily fixed wire apart with a single blow from their horns.

Just after three the game guard reported for duty. When they were ready to leave, Webb and the guard climbed up in the back of the fifteen hundredweight and they set off along the track, leaving the stream and the camp behind them.

Before long the African indicated to Webb that they should bear off right-handed into the bush. Webb passed the information down to Maxwell by sticking his hand through the roof hatch and extending his fingers to the right in front of his face. They cruised in a more or less straight line for ten minutes without sighting anything except a few oribi. Suddenly the guard held up his hand. Webb banged on the roof and Maxwell stopped. The guard pointed away to the left. Webb looked and saw a pile of whitened, vulture-scattered bones. When Maxwell got down and examined the bones he found the typically long skull of the white rhino and noted the small round crater in which the front horn had once sat, marvelling as he did so that such an offensive weapon was not an integral part of the head itself but was merely stuck to it by sinew and hide. The horn, of course, was missing. It was for its horn that the animal had been killed.

'Speared,' the guard explained. 'Speared only a week ago.' He added that there were many other skeletons.

There were. The guard seemed bent on taking them on a conducted tour of dead white rhinos. He showed them seven skeletons, the last of which was still sufficiently close to death to attract an attendance of squabbling vultures and a single marabou stork which, when the vultures flew away at their approach, advanced alone towards its meal with the furtive tread of a grave-robber.

They drove for another hour, grinding over the bush in third, swerving constantly to miss rocks and wallows. They saw other animals, a leopard up a thorn tree with the carcass of a baboon, a small herd of elephants with young, a few impala and several parties of buffalo. But there were no rhinos, black or white. So far they had only explored the country to the east of the track. Maxwell now turned back towards the track itself, but, when he reached it, aiming to reconnoitre the bush on the far side, the guard said to Webb 'No rhino. Rhinos all where we come from.'

'Dead 'uns, you mean,' Webb told him.

'No. All the rhinos this side.'

Maxwell had stopped the truck just beyond the track to allow it to cool down. 'What's he say?' he asked Webb.

'Says all the bloody rhinos are where we've just come from.'

'Yes. I saw them but I'm not interested in catching dead ones.' He turned to the guard. 'Where are the rhinos?' he demanded in Swahili. The guard pointed back the way they had come.

'You're a bloody liar,' Maxwell told him conversationally in English. The guard seemed to understand this for he shook his head.

Maxwell pointed towards the country ahead of them. 'What about this way?'

The guard shook his head again. 'No rhinos,' he repeated.

'Okay,' Maxwell said, 'we'll go see. I bet the bastards have knocked off the lot where we've just been. This is probably their private poaching preserve up ahead.'

'Very bad ground. Truck not go there,' the guard said sulkily to Webb.

'Too bad,' Maxwell said. 'Tell him we're insured. Hang on, son.'

They started off again. The guard had been right about one thing. The going was certainly rougher. There were many more fire-stunted trees as well as large patches of elephant grass which, though dry and crisp, had been missed by bush fire. In ten minutes Webb spotted the first rhino, a monster cow with a calf. He banged on the roof and stuck his hand down for some left rudder. Maxwell shouted with joy and began to circle the pair, keeping at a distance so as to avoid giving them the idea that a truck was something alarming. Even from a hundred yards the size of the cow was impressive. Maxwell put her at well in the three-ton class. He had a strong attachment to black rhinos with their close-coupled look of packed power, their short bruisers' heads growing straight out of their shoulders and their neat, tucked-in, aggressive snouts. The white rhino struck him as slightly comic, despite her bulk and the size of her front horn which was longer—far longer—than all but a few freak horns he had seen on the black variety. She was a heavyweight all right, but the weight seemed to hang from her enormous backside as though she had dropsy of the buttocks. Her head was long and her mouth satchel-shaped and she was cropping the grass peacefully. He eased up to her and stopped his engine fifty yards away. Webb, who only had experience of black rhino, looked at her in amazement.

'Think she'll charge?' he asked Maxwell.

'Doesn't look like it. Looks as though you could walk over and stroke her.'

'If she'd been a black she'd have nailed us by now. Think she knows we're here?'

'Sure. Look at her swivel those ears. See the way they're fixed to her bonce? Kind of like tubes at the bottom where they join the skull. Now a black rhino's ears are open all the way down like a dog's.'

'Thanks for the nature notes,' said Webb.

The animal put up her head and stamped a forefoot.

'Wind's changed,' Webb told Maxwell. 'She's got our wind. Better start the engine.'

'She won't charge.'

Almost as if she had heard him, the big cow put down her head and started to graze again.

Maxwell told Webb 'They're grazers. That's what the wide mouth is for. As a matter of fact that's how they got their name. *Weide Monde*. It's Afrikaans for wide-mouthed. *Weide* . . . the word's been changed to white, although they're just the same colour as black rhinos. They eat grass and stuff. Now the old black 'un's a browser. Eats off trees and bushes. That's why his mouth's a different shape,

144

probably why he's so damn bad-tempered, too. All those thorns he eats must pepper him up a bit.'

The wind was now blowing more strongly from the truck towards the rhinos. The female moved round so that she was between her baby and the vehicle. She began to toss her head about.

Maxwell said 'I don't think she'll charge but I don't want to stir her up too much. Let's move on.'

Webb, secretly relieved, said 'She seems pretty tame.'

'Maybe. But there's no telling what she'll be like once we get chasing her. We'll be giving away a lot of weight.'

In the next half-hour they saw two rhino skeletons and five more live animals. When Maxwell at last stopped to give the truck a breather, he walked round, climbed up on the back of the lorry and took the game guard by his shirt.

He spoke quietly in Swahili, shaking the guard all the while. 'You,' he said, 'are a liar and a thief. I believe you and your friends have been killing rhino. You told us there were none here. Listen to me carefully. If we find one more dead rhino in the bush we will come and take you to prison. If we catch you or anyone else poaching you will not even get a chance of going to prison. We shall shoot poachers in self-defence.'

He stopped shaking the guard but the man went on shaking of his own accord. Maxwell said 'Come in front, Ron. Leave the bastard up top.'

When they were both in the cab, Webb said 'He looked as if he believed you.'

'Good thing if he did. I aimed to make an impression on him. Now Bertrand's gone I suppose these boys see the chance of a quick clean-up.'

Some minutes later Webb pointed towards a small group of grey rocks amid which another larger rock suddenly moved. 'Bull,' he said. 'It's a young bull.'

'Right,' Maxwell told him, 'let's see what sort of speed they've got.'

Webb felt his stomach muscles tighten as the engine began to rise to a howl in third. He jammed his feet hard against the metal plates under the dashboard and his back against the upright part of the seat. Between these two points he let the truck hit him if it could. The front of the truck was by far the most uncomfortable place at catching speed. He often wondered how Maxwell managed to stay behind the wheel. Up behind in the catcher's position it was rough, but your leg muscles took a good deal of the pounding and there was a bar behind you to stop you being flung out backwards—not on this vehicle of Ryan's, though, for Webb had not yet modified it. But that was the game guard's worry. Webb concentrated on the chase.

The white rhino bull was certainly showing a fair turn of speed. Despite his bulk he was making a good twenty-five miles per hour which meant that Maxwell had to do thirty-five to get up with him. He could turn check and turn, too, with surprising agility. Twice he jinked more in the manner of a hare than a rhino. Maxwell braked and put the wheel hard over so that the truck bounced sideways on two wheels before dropping onto all fours again. Just before Maxwell got up with the bull and ran neck and neck with him he touched a large rock with his near-side front wheel. Webb felt himself hit the roof hard. When he came down in his seat and could focus on the situation again, the rhino had half-turned on the slowing truck and had walloped his horn straight through the front mudguard. Maxwell let him back off and when he came in for a second charge swung the truck out of harm's way. When they stopped a good hundred yards away, the rhino had turned and galloped off.

'Not bad,' Maxwell said admiringly. 'They've got a bit of go in them, and he was only a little feller, about half grown.'

The engine was boiling again. When Webb got out to fetch the water can from the back he saw that the game guard was no longer with them. He told Maxwell this. Maxwell said 'I thought he might not be. Well, you know my motto. When they muck you around, let them walk home.'

Three days had gone and there was still plenty to do. On the fourth, Maxwell switched his attention to completing the second *boma*. For the moment, the crates could wait. They could be finished off even while the first rhinos were being caught. If the trucks came up the road from the coast by nightfall he wanted to be ready to start catching in earnest next day. Meantime, Webb modified Ryan's fifteen hundredweight. As Maxwell had predicted, the sides were too high for easy manipulation of catching poles and lassos. The disappearance of the African game guard had made something else quite plain: before they could use the truck for catching, a crossbar must be erected behind the cab to prevent the lassoers from being pitched out backwards.

Webb, therefore, began his modifications by cutting away with an oxy-acetylene torch the metal sides of the lorry towards the front. Then he built a kind of goal-post across the back behind the cab, at shoulder-blade height, to be for the two catchers rather like the ropes in a boxing ring—except that the bar was not quite so soft and yielding when you bounced back against it. Next he cut up an old inner tube and stretched several bands of rubber between the cab and the uprights of the goal-post, to seal off the ends of the catcher's platform. This was more by way of moral than physical support.

One vital piece of equipment remained to be fixed to the sides of the truck before it could start catching. Webb took four six-foot tree-trunks, slightly thicker than pit props, and, having drilled them, bolted them with three stout bolts apiece to the remaining metal freeboard of the lorry. When he had finished, the trunks stuck up, two on each side, one pair just behind the catching position and the other well towards the tailboard. These were bollards round which to take the rope once a rhino had been hooked.

Webb was intensely happy in his work. He felt an unaccustomed warmness and companionship for Maxwell which he did not bother to analyse. It was just something that had been more or less with him since the convoy had left for the coast. Dimly he felt that the camp was happier without the women. Perhaps he was even relieved that Jen was gone for good.

Webb finished his modifications at about four in the afternoon, just as Maxwell was backing one of the lorries experimentally down the sloping pits dug in front of the gate of the *boma*. When the lorry stopped, the base of its tailboard was about six feet from the opening and level with the ground. This would be fine when it came to unloading the rhinos. Webb wrapped his beloved tools in their satchel, cleaning each one, checking it for burrs and blemishes, even feeling the edge of the hacksaw's blade. Then he put the satchel in front of the Mercedes for safe-keeping.

At six they stopped for a meal. Afterwards Maxwell sent for Mbagi, the Acholi tracker who was deputizing as head boy in Nguru's absence. He told him to take Mgulu and the Land-Rover and drive back the way they had travelled until they reached the fork of the main road. They were to camp there until the lorries came up from the coast. Then they would guide them in.

In the cool of the evening Maxwell sat outside the tent, rigging the heavy sisal ropes on the lasso poles. He felt fairly satisfied.

PART THREE

The trucks didn't come that evening,
but in the early hours of the following morning Maxwell stirred and
woke. He propped himself up on one elbow on his safari bed and
strained his ears. At first he could hear only the dawn chorus in the
bush. Then he caught the sound that had broken his sleep: the low
growl of transport far away. He swung out of bed and went to the
mouth of the tent. The noise of engines was now unmistakable. He
judged that the convoy must be about a mile away. A great relief
filled him, for he had not withheld from himself that many kinds of
trouble might have delayed the return of his transport for days or, if
real fighting had broken out in the colony, even for long enough to
cripple the operation: cripple it, not stop it, for if the worst had happened he would have gone on with the men and trucks he had available. Not once, in these calculations, had he consciously given
thought to the possible plight of Ryan, the Africans in the trucks, or
even of his wife.

He pulled on his slacks and strolled across the camp to the point
at which he knew the lorries must turn off the track. As he did so he
kicked the flap of Webb's tent. 'Hey, Ron, they're coming. Get those
bloody cooks out and get some breakfast cracking.'

When he reached the track he could see the dust raised by the
lorries' approach. Then he caught sight of the Land-Rover leading
them in and, behind, the bulk of one of the bigger lorries. He made
out the outline of the Mercedes. Ryan must be bringing up the rear.
As the truck came nearer he could see the empty hippo crates jump-

ing about in the back. He didn't know what else he expected, but he was relieved at this evidence that the hippos had been disposed of.

The Land-Rover came lurching and bouncing up the track, finishing on a spirited and undiesel-like burst. Mgulu, wide-eyed and crazy looking, swung the wheel and careered past him into camp. Next, after a two-hundred-yard interval, came the Mercedes. Nguru drove, grinning with pleasure at his return to the fold. By his side, Nancy Maxwell sat upright, strapped in, and as if on parade. She looked grey and tired and covered with dust. She raised a hand in salute and shouted something to him at the moment Nguru changed down to make the turn, so that her words were lost in the grinding of gears. Ryan was still barely in sight. Trust him, Maxwell thought, to be out on his own. He decided not to wait and turned back into camp. By the time he had walked the seventy yards or so Nguru had already unstrapped Nancy Maxwell from her seat and carried her into the tent. Maxwell was anxious to hear how things had gone and was curious to know what she had called out to him. But, before he could reach her, Ryan's lorry came in and stopped with its back towards the tents.

In the next few seconds Maxwell knew what his wife had tried to tell him. He saw Ryan, in an even brighter pair of blue shorts than when last seen, jump lightly down and run round the bonnet of his lorry to open the near-side door. Then he put up his hand to help someone out. Jen stepped down and stood holding Ryan's hand. She looked fresh and almost gay and she wore a dress which, although it had suffered from its journey, was still feminine and becoming. She waved to Maxwell and called out 'Didn't expect to see me back, did you?'

Maxwell said 'You'd better get out of that thing now you're here. We're going to start catching after breakfast.'

Jen slipped her arm through Ryan's. She looked up at him appealingly. 'Shall I, Mike?' she asked, 'or would you like me to stay like this? Do you like me like this?'

Ryan put his arm round her shoulders. 'Bush baby,' he said, 'I like you anyway. Anyway at all.'

'Oh Christ,' said Maxwell. 'Sweet lovely Christ. So that's why you came back?'

Jen said lightly 'Well, you didn't think it was to catch rhinos or join the he-men again, did you? Mike persuaded me.'

'Yes,' said Maxwell slowly, 'I can imagine. Get some breakfast then get some sleep. We've all got work to do. Ryan,' he went on, 'your tent's over there. We'll put one up for *bush baby*,' he pointed in the opposite direction, 'over there.'

Ryan smiled disarmingly. 'Yes,' he said, 'that will be nice. Very nice.'

Nancy Maxwell was lying back on her safari bed when Maxwell walked in. She still looked exhausted though she had sponged some of the dust off her face.

'Well?' Maxwell asked.

'You've seen her?' she said.

'Yeah.'

'Ryan,' his wife explained. 'She went for him straight away.'

Maxwell fell back on the remark with which he invariably disowned responsibility for any other human being's actions. 'She's a big girl now,' he said.

'I agree. I thought you might not see it that way, though.'

'Ryan? How was he?'

'Charming,' she said, 'that's what did it. Right from the start he treated her like a woman, a pretty woman.'

'Yes,' said Maxwell scathingly. 'I heard. *Bush baby*. Did Ryan act up at all?'

'No. He drove all right. He kept going.'

'Did he do what he was told?'

'Up to a point. He wanted to stay an extra day in town with her when we'd unloaded the hippos.'

'They all right?'

'Yes. They all made it. The agent's arranging to ship them. We'll probably get about £2,000 out of it.'

'Well,' Maxwell said, 'it won't leave much profit but at least it'll pay the wages. What about this day in town? You didn't let him stay.'

'He's back, isn't he?'

'Let's hope he's some use now he's here. If not, Webb and I will do the catching.'

'He'll behave. Or at least until the moment we've caught his rhinos. I suppose there *are* some rhinos?'

'Yes,' he said, 'there are rhinos all right. But Jen . . .' Maxwell spoke the name as if it had to be pulled, like a stubborn tooth, out of his mouth. 'Jen, what did she want to come back for?'

'Well,' she said, 'you saw the dress.'

'Ryan,' Maxwell began, 'do you reckon they . . . ?'

'Oh, be your age, Ted. And anyway, why should you care? Why shouldn't the kid have a bit of fun? What have you ever done for her and, tell me, why should you suddenly act so bloody prudish, or should I say bloody jealous?'

'Jealous,' Maxwell said. 'Jealous! Jen is damn nearly my daughter.'

The crippled woman heaved herself over on her side so that her face lay towards the wall of the tent. 'In that case,' she said, 'I've heard damn nearly everything about the upbringing of children.'

Maxwell stood there looking down at her back. 'You could have told me what kind of trip you had.'

'I didn't exactly hear you ask.'

'Okay. Well, now I'm asking. What was it like?'

'It wasn't a rest cure.'

'I can imagine.'

'We damn nearly didn't get here at all.'

'Trouble in Makole?'

'No. It was pretty quiet there except for the numbers of settlers coming in. They've put up a transit camp by the airfield for them. Plenty of troops about but no sign of real trouble. That'll come when the administration finally pulls out. They say the colonials are backing the Magunga. We heard they're leaving them guns, armoured cars and so on.'

'Hm. Three weeks to go.'

'Less than three weeks now. More like two. No, we hit it fifty miles south of here. The Magunga had run loose and burnt an entire Ashota village. The African police refused to let us go any further but just then an armoured car patrol came along and wanted to know who we were. Ryan told them we were going north to bring in some stranded settlers. So because it meant their people, they made the police let us through.'

'Pretty quick-witted of Ryan.'

'Oh, he's that all right, don't fear. Now, do you mind if I get some sleep.'

'You'd better all get some sleep. We'll make our first catch this afternoon. I'll tell Ryan.'

Maxwell took the catching truck and one of the boys, Mbagi, the tracker, and made a recce on his own. After sweeping round on the west side of the track for an hour, he found three white rhinos. The first, a big bull, was up on some high, rocky ground. The others were a pair, mother and son, the son about two years old. They were grazing quietly on good flat country. He decided that he would make his first try for these two and it wasn't the terrain that made him pick them. He had no idea how white rhinos might behave once they were penned inside a *boma*. For all he knew they might pine their hearts away and refuse to eat or drink. Some animals were like that. He felt instinctively that he had a better chance of settling down this first pair if the mother was still feeding her young. The calf would be happy because his mother was around, and would take her mind off the bitter reality of unaccustomed captivity. He left his boy under a tree, telling him to watch the rhinos and keep in touch with them if they moved off. The African sat down quite happily to wait. He had no water or food and he felt no need for them. Then Maxwell drove back to camp to make final preparations for the chase.

They ate their midday meal together. Ryan and Jen sat at the far end of the table. She had changed from her dress into new cream linen slacks. She no longer wore her usual bush shirt. Instead she had on a blue candy-striped blouse that set off skin on which tan glowed like a bloom. Webb, seated close to Maxwell and his wife, could hardly take his eyes off her. He had never seen her so alive. He had never been so aware of her breasts before. He had always thought of them as small, firm and well-shaped but now the nipples seemed to punch their way into the fabric of her blouse. Every ounce of latent, explosive femininity in her had suddenly detonated and Ryan was the cause of it.

Ryan and the girl sat close to each other, their thighs nearly meeting. Whenever opportunity offered, he touched her lightly—her bare arm, her hand, her hair. He passed her food, poured her water, and these actions themselves were to her the essence of courtship. Before this she had never known her companions to treat her as anything but an equal. Previously, if she had wanted a drink she would have had to get up and fetch it for herself. If she had lacked a knife and there was no boy handy to bring her one, then she would have had to reach across the table for it. Now Ryan attended her as if she sat at his side in a smart restaurant.

Maxwell ate in silence. He noticed all these things and he felt the screw of anger turn in his stomach, but he had other problems on his mind. He was wondering how the big cow rhino would fight.

Ryan was the first to get to his feet. 'Well,' he said, 'let's go and catch us a rhino or two.' He shadow-boxed nimbly away from the table. Jen looked up and laughed with infatuated pleasure.

Maxwell spoke to the girl. 'If you're coming, you can follow us in the Mercedes.'

The girl said stolidly 'I go with Mike.'

'That's right,' Maxwell told her, 'in the Mercedes.'

Ryan stopped skipping about and leaned over the table. 'Who says I go in the lorry?'

'I do,' Maxwell told him.

Ryan turned to the girl. 'I'm catching this first one, eh, bush baby?'

The girl looked squarely at Maxwell and said 'Well, any objections? It's Mike's transport. You wouldn't be catching at all but for Mike.'

Maxwell said evenly 'He'll get plenty of chance to show you his muscles later.'

Nancy Maxwell brought down her voice like a cleaver across the argument. 'Now let's get this straight. I told you all before we started that what Ted says everyone else does.'

Maxwell put his hand on her shoulder. 'No. Changed my mind. Let Ryan drive. We might as well find out whether he's got the stuff. Ron and I will catch up top. Nguru can bring up the Merc.'

Jen put her arm round Ryan's shoulders. 'There, Mike. I told you. I'll come in front.' Together they walked off arm-in-arm towards the catching truck where the boys were just preparing to load the lassos.

When the whole crew was mounted, Maxwell strolled up to Ryan in the driver's seat. 'There's a cow and calf,' he said. 'Go about a mile up the track and turn off by a big outcrop. I'll direct you through the hatch until we find our tracker. You're on your own after that. Get us up close and don't bump 'em.'

Ryan smiled. 'Nothing to it.'

'They're not flipping monkeys, you know,' Maxwell told him.

'Oh, for Christ's sake.'

Maxwell ran his eye over the entire outfit. He saw Webb standing above him in the left-hand catching position. Behind Webb crouched six Africans. Balanced on top of the cab were the two eight-foot-long bamboo catching poles. The poles and the heavy nooses which hung from them shook rhythmically with the vibration of the engine as if they, like everyone else, were keyed up to be off.

Maxwell climbed up behind the cab and banged on the roof. As the truck started forward, the Africans began to sing their usual song about brave hunters off to catch a rhino.

Above the din of the engine and the whistle of the wind Webb shouted to Maxwell 'Why the hell did you let glamour-pants drive?'

'Give the lad a chance,' Maxwell said. 'He's never caught a rhino before, so he might as well show us how to do it.'

The tracker had gone from his post. This meant that the rhinos had moved, too. Nguru inspected the base of the tree and read the signs the tracker had left. The rhinos had moved off east about two hours ago.

They drove on slowly and soon picked up the spoor. Half a mile further on they met the tracker standing happily in the minute pool of shade shed by an acacia thorn. Nguru and he held a short excited conversation. The mother and her calf were, it seemed, grazing on the edge of some unburnt elephant grass not four hundred yards away. Nguru pointed down the gradual slope that fell away at this point. At first even Maxwell could see nothing that looked like a rhino, but when he had climbed on top of the cab he made out something which for a long time he took to be a rock. Between the rock and this object the landscape jumped and fluttered in an ecstasy of heat haze. If you looked long enough, every inanimate object had life in it. The big rock shimmered with the rest, but then, all of a sudden, it did something different; it became two rocks, or rather a rock and a half, for the young bull had moved into view round the flank of his mother. Maxwell leapt down and banged twice on the roof.

Ryan shouted from the cab 'Well, what's up? What's happening? Where do we go from here?'

Webb felt almost sorry for Ryan. 'Ted,' he said, 'he can't be expected to know our drill.'

Maxwell grunted. 'Tell him to get weaving straight ahead. You yell directions to him through the hatch.'

By now Jen had translated the double knock signal and the truck had started off uncertainly. As Webb slipped goggles down over his eyes to protect them from flying thorns he saw Jen's face snarling up at him through the hatch. Her voice, shrill with fury, could not compete with the rising whine of the truck in second gear but he guessed that she was telling him not to bitch Ryan about. He smiled sweetly at her. They moved down the hill at what was, by Maxwell's standards, a funeral pace. If he'd been driving he would have tried to get up with his quarry as quickly as possible. For the moment he did not spur Ryan on, for the rhinos had vanished from view as the truck slid into a hollow. When the truck topped the far side of the dip, there were the rhinos one hundred and fifty yards ahead, just breaking into a trot. Maxwell banged three times for full speed. Ryan went about five miles per hour faster. Webb leant down through the hatch and yelled 'Step on it.' He had a glimpse of Ryan at the wheel, tense but still grinning, and he knew from the look of him that this was the first time he had driven on a rhino catch. Maxwell was banging again for more speed and shouting like a maniac. Ryan heard some of this and put his foot down suddenly. As he did so, they hit a patch of elephant grass which swallowed the truck completely. The effect from the driver's point of view was like hitting a water splash at speed. Vision was instantly cut off. Ryan took his foot off and they stopped. Maxwell leant over the cab and shouted down through the window 'If you can't drive the bloody thing, for Christ's sake why not say so.' Turning round, Webb saw two of the boys grinning. He swore at them in Swahili and the grins became wider. Before he could deal with this situation the truck was out of the grass and moving in the clear again.

The ground here was fairly level and Ryan at last put his foot well down. Two hundred yards ahead the rhinos were still trotting. Ryan could now see their dust for himself and gave chase. They began to gallop. He soon discovered that it was impossible to watch anything but their dust cloud. The rhinos were now making about twenty-five miles an hour. To get anywhere near them he would have to average at least thirty-five with occasional spurts at forty. Concentrating on the target ahead left him no chance to spot obstacles in his path. The first of these was a tree which he took full in the centre of the radiator at just under forty miles per hour. He ducked instinctively but the tree mysteriously folded up and disappeared beneath his wheels. He slowed a little and instantly touched a rock with his off-side wheel. The truck reared up on two wheels and fell with a thud. Ryan felt the sweat streaming down under his shirt. Maxwell bawled at Webb 'For God's sake give him hand signals.'

Webb saw the wallow ahead and knew that not even the most violent turn could keep them out of it. He stuck his hand down in front of Ryan's face with the fingers pointing to the floor. Ryan instinctively put his foot on the brakes. The truck slewed, bounced, straightened and nosed down into the wallow. They came to rest at the bottom with the front wheels buried in soft mud. Maxwell sorted himself out from the pile of boys who had slid forward on top of him and jumped down.

'All right,' he said to no one in particular. 'Now that we've got the comedy turn over we'll start catching.'

Ryan was grinning stiffly but with an obvious effort, determined to seem unabashed. 'How did I do?' he asked Maxwell.

Maxwell looked at him without expression. 'Much as expected, son,' he said. Maxwell walked round and opened Jen's door for her with a faint but unmistakable imitation of Ryan. 'Down you come,' Maxwell said agreeably.

'You bastards,' she said as she got down. 'You never gave him a chance.'

'Suit yourself about that.' Maxwell turned away from her. 'Ryan, you'll drive the three-tonner this time.'

Ryan seemed about to argue, but then smiled and shrugged.

'Jen, you'll get in the Mercedes with him. I'll want Nguru for roping.'

'Like hell, I will.'

Maxwell raised his hand slowly and brought it down with an almighty crack across the seat of her cream pants.

Ryan said 'Easy, dad.'

'Ryan. Just one more thing. If either of you don't do what you're told on a catch from this moment on you haven't a chance of getting your rhinos.'

Ryan grinned. 'As you say, dad.'

But he had his small moment of revenge. As he walked away with the girl towards the Mercedes he rubbed his hand soothingly across her smarting bottom.

They took off again immediately the truck had been winched out of the mud by the Mercedes. Maxwell made a long detour, well clear of the rhinos, so that he would come on them from the front and drive them back into the territory he had just crossed. Despite the rocks and trees he judged this as being the most promising catching ground he was likely to find.

This time the rhinos had the wind up. They broke into a gallop when the truck was still a hundred and fifty yards away. Maxwell put his foot flat down and kept it there. Up top, Webb leant forward, his stomach pressed against the hot metal roof of the cab, his backside jammed hard against one upright of the goal-post. He held on to his catching pole like a knight riding at full tilt into a joust. On the opposite side of the truck Nguru did the same, the slipstream forcing the lips back from his prominent teeth in an exaggerated grin. At forty-five Maxwell hit a large tree slap in the radiator. It disintegrated as if it had been struck by a shell. Unlike Ryan, Maxwell did not bother to duck or wince. He knew that the tree, like most of the trees in these parts, had been desiccated by fire. Externally it was green and living, inside, it was as brittle as pitch. Above him Webb cursed as the fragments whipped past his head. They were closing fast on the rhinos now. Taking a short cut, Maxwell drove straight at a clump of elephant grass. It crackled like crumpled cellophane as they hit it. Webb felt something strike the eyepiece of his goggles. A two-inch thorn stuck in his wrist like a dart, and the wind drew a line of blood from the wound right back to his elbow. But his attention was fixed on the rhinos. They were barely twenty yards ahead, running at full belt, the cow outside her calf. The going was rougher here so that Maxwell had to slow down. But the cow, sensing danger for her *toto*, slowed too and crossed behind the calf so that she ran between it and the catching truck. The cow would soon be perfectly placed for Webb to rope her but he guessed that Maxwell wanted the calf first.

Maxwell wanted the calf for a very good reason. The *toto* was a young one. If he went for the mother first the baby would be left alone and helpless for several hours. It would wander off into the bush and might even be jumped by a lion.

Maxwell eyed the thundering backside of the cow six feet ahead of his off-side front mudguard. He knew he had two alternatives: to cross over to the right of them both and let Nguru rope the calf from the left-hand catching position; or to make the cow ease away to the left and catch the calf where he now was. Maxwell had nothing against Nguru's roping ability—in fact, he had quite a respect for it—but he liked to catch on the right-hand side of the truck. In this position he felt himself totally in control. Most important of all, there was less chance of him ramming and damaging the catch.

The rhinos had picked up speed again. They were still galloping at a good twenty miles per hour. Maxwell swung the wheel right-handed, taking the truck suddenly across the cow's stern and behind the calf. The little animal gave a squeal and spurted away to the right so that there was momentarily a gap between mother and son. At the same instant the cow checked and looked towards her calf. Maxwell chose this moment to edge back to the left. Almost gently he tapped her on the flank with his left front mudguard. She swerved away and the gap was wide open. He moved into it at full throttle until he had the calf running and squeaking close in by his own door. The next instant he saw Webb's lasso pole dip and the rope drop neatly over the *toto*'s tiny horn. Maxwell slowed gradually so that the calf could run ahead and break the noose from the bindings attaching it to the pole. He kept going just slightly slower than the calf so that there would be no jerk on its neck once it reached the limit of free rope. Meanwhile he kept an eye open for mum and spotted her charging at full bore on the left flank. He saw her horn coming in with a wild uppercut and swung the truck at the last moment so that the blow hit empty air. Now he heard the boys up top shouting at the cow to keep her at bay. He forgot her and concentrated on the calf. Every time the calf stopped bucking and fighting he eased the truck up to it so that Webb could shorten the rope and twist it round the tree-trunk bollards on the side of the lorry. A few seconds later he saw that Webb and Nguru were down on the floor with the lassoed *toto*, darting round its rear end like rival scrum halves waiting for the ball. Maxwell now kept his eye on mum, half expecting her to charge again. She hung around, tossing her head angrily, but when Ryan drove up in the Mercedes she edged away. Maxwell judged that she had made her bid for the time being. Now everyone could jump down and get on with the tying.

The baby rhino fought with every pound of his quarter-ton weight but soon he was flat on his side and securely trussed. Then the whole crew heaved the little bull into the back of the catching truck.

'We don't need the Merc for him,' Maxwell told them all, 'but somehow I think mum will be different.'

They drove the little rhino back to camp and let him loose in the *boma*. As soon as Maxwell eased the last rope off his feet he leapt up and charged. Maxwell side-stepped like a bull-fighter and jumped for the walls. The *toto* wheeled and hit the timber six inches beneath Maxwell's plimsolled foot, making the tree-trunks jump in their wire lashings. Maxwell laughed out loud.

'Little bastard,' he shouted admiringly to Webb. 'Did you see that? He nearly got me.' Maxwell said this in the tone he might have used of a puppy who had tried to nip him when he took its rubber bone away. 'Little bastard,' he repeated.

Ryan stood by the door of the *boma* as Maxwell jumped down.
'One,' he said. 'That's number one. Now let's go and get number
two.'

'She'll come a bit harder,' Maxwell said. 'She's not going to love
us.'

'I know. This time I'll want to be with the roping crew.'

'Suit yourself,' Maxwell told him indifferently, 'but just remember
your monkeys didn't have a horn three foot long on the end of their
noses.'

Because of her size Maxwell ordered an extra pole and lasso to be
loaded. When they set out again, Ryan rode in the open part of the
truck behind Webb and Nguru. At the last minute, when Maxwell
was tucked away in the cab, Jen had climbed up too. Ryan stuck her
protectively in between Webb and Nguru.

Ryan told Webb 'I want to go over and rope this one.'

'You nuts?'

'No. I watched you. Doesn't seem to be much to it.'

'Get him!' Webb said.

Ryan insisted 'I'll come down and help you tie her up.'

'You won't help me,' Webb told him. 'This baby will need two
lasso ropes on her. I'll be playing yo-yo up here for a bit. Nguru's
going to tie this one. He'll get the first rope on.'

'Then I'll help him.'

Webb said 'You don't have to, you know.'

Ryan pointed towards the cab. 'Old stone-face made a monkey
out of me.'

'I reckon you asked for it.'

'Maybe I did, but I won't let him have that on me for the dura-
tion.'

The engine began its familiar crescendo.

'Here we go now,' Webb shouted.

'Any last minute suggestions?' Ryan asked.

'Yes. Let Nguru go over the side first and tie the back feet. You
get the second rope on. That's the one on the front legs. And if anything goes wrong for Christ's sake hang on to the rhino's tail. It's the
only hope you'll have.'

As Maxwell had forecast, the big cow was something different. He
caught up with her after a long, fast chase during which Webb had to

signal three times for immediate avoiding action. They successfully side-stepped a buffalo wallow and a large rock, but they clipped the side of an anthill with a jolt that made Webb feel for a second as though his lower teeth had bitten the underside of his brain. When he looked round to see if the boys were all still there he caught sight of Ryan balanced on the balls of his feet like a sailor riding a pitching deck and with not much more trouble. The only hold Ryan had was on the girl's shoulder in front of him, and it was she who was being steadied, not him.

From the driving-seat Maxwell was impressed with the speed of the cow. He was also impressed by the size of her horn with which, even while at full gallop, she tried to give the tormenting truck a poke in the vitals. Out of the corner of his eye he saw Webb's lasso pole begin to dip and he screamed 'Not yet—for Christ's sake not yet.' He could not tell whether Webb heard but he saw the pole hesitate and then withdraw skywards out of vision. In fact, Webb had not heard him. He was totally baffled by the problem of trying to drop the noose over a horn three feet in length while the nose of the rhino remained out in front of the bonnet. Maxwell saw fifty yards of reasonably smooth ground ahead and put his foot on the floor. The truck climbed laboriously to maximum revs in third gear and slowly the rhino fell back until her eye was disagreeably close to Maxwell's own. When he shot out his hand to tell Webb to rope, his fingers touched the animal's skull. He saw the pole dip as Webb took his signal. But the rope caught over the horn and wouldn't fall fully over the rhino's snout. Maxwell was now screaming loudly and continuously for Nguru to cross the truck and put the second lasso on, which he was already doing, but not because he had heard Maxwell. As Nguru began to move from his side of the goal-post, Jen instinctively ducked out and under to let him pass, while Webb, still fighting with his pole, leaned right out over the rhino's back to give him room. Nguru was luckier with his rope. The cow flung her head as he dropped the noose and the rope passed over the horn and down under her lower jaw. But in doing so it caught the end of Webb's catching pole.

Maxwell saw the second noose go home and began to brake. The rhino spurted ahead, tearing the pole out of Webb's grasp. Bound tightly to the rhino's head, the ten-foot pole stuck up ludicrously, like a long wireless antenna. For the rhino, the pole, not the truck, now became the enemy. Her first thought was to get away from the creature which made her head feel top-heavy and unmanageable. So, as Maxwell slowed down, the rhino accelerated. Webb watched the remains of Nguru's rope snake out over the side and saw the inch-thick fibres part like a piece of string where the end was secured to a tree-trunk. The cow was now attached to the lorry by Webb's rope alone and his had only a precarious hold. However, it didn't snap like the first one because the rhino had stopped dead and had begun to fight the pole. It did this by thrashing its head up and down until the pole tilted downwards. Then it smashed it against the ground. At the second attempt the pole broke its fixings to the rope and came flying end over end over the top of the lorry. The rhino paused for breath. It was still attached to Webb's rope but this remained caught only round the horn and the animal's upper jaw. At any second, another spasm of fury might fling it loose.

It was then that Ryan went over the side with a length of foot-rope in his hand. The rhino was still preoccupied with the lasso round its nose. Its tiny brain was fixed on this situation. It had killed one enemy and was now ready for the next. It was used to ox-peckers sitting on its snout and picking the ticks out of its hide, but their touch was insignificant. This thing now glued to its upper jaw was oppressive and objectionable in the extreme—moreover it jammed one nostril so that breathing was difficult. While the rhino paused, Ryan ran round behind it and took a turn round one hind leg. Webb watched him, mesmerized. Ryan had moved so quickly and unpre-dictably that, for the moment, he had no reactions available. All he knew was that this was no time for anyone to be down there on his flat feet beside that rhino.

The rhino had made up her mind. The thing on her nose had to be got rid of. She flung up her head and swung it sideways with a steam-hammer blow. The rope slipped off her jaw and remained coiled loosely, like a ring in a hoopla stall, round her enormous front horn. Webb did the only thing he could think of. He pulled the lasso tight.

Ryan, in the act of passing the rope round the other back foot, did not even know that the head rope had slipped. The rhino then dropped its head so that the noose slid up its horn and fell to the ground. For a second she did not realize that she was free.

Webb began to bang the sides of the lorry to scare her off. He saw Maxwell jump down from the cab and double round the front of the radiator, hoping to draw the rhino's attention and make her charge the truck. He saw Jen go past him in a clean flying leap. She hit the ground beneath him in full view of the rhino and stumbled. The rhino still hesitated. At that angle Jen was beneath the creature's line of sight.

'Stay down,' Webb yelled at her. 'Get back under the truck.'

The girl, however, was determined to make a diversion. She got to her feet and ran back towards the tailboard of the truck. The rhino saw her, put down its head and charged, tearing its foot-rope free just as Ryan was about to make the second lashing round its free leg.

Now, for the first time, Ryan realized that the creature was running loose. As it started forward he grabbed for its tail and held on. The rhino didn't even feel him. Ahead, through the dust kicked up by the charge, Ryan had a glimpse of Jen running for the tailboard and then Nguru cut across his vision—Nguru running with the third lasso pole. The rhino checked and swerved to hook this new attacker, but Nguru dropped the noose cleanly over its head and threw himself beneath the truck. The rhino hooked the truck just above the point at which Nguru had disappeared. Webb took up some of the slack on the new rope and let the rhino bash the truck. Now the big cow began to go to work on it in earnest.

By this time, Maxwell had regained the driving-seat from the far side. The girl climbed in beside him. Only Ryan remained on the ground. Maxwell slipped into gear and prepared to tire out his catch.

The girl tore his arm with her nails and screamed at him:

'He'll be killed.'

'His own bloody fault. He damn near killed all of us.'

'You bastard. Mike was the only one who had the guts to go over and start tying.'

Maxwell kept his eye on the cow who was backing off again against the rope to make another charge.

'Stupid bastard just didn't know what he was doing.'

'If that other head rope goes, he'll be killed.'

'Well, I'm not stopping now,' Maxwell said. 'We want this one.'

He began to take the truck round in a slow circle, letting the rhino back away and then come in and hit the truck so that Webb should shorten rope a little each time. The girl craned frantically out of her side of the truck, looking for Ryan. Ryan had picked himself up and was keeping about ten yards behind the rhino.

At last Maxwell stopped the truck but kept the engine running. He judged the big cow had had about enough now. This part of the operation was like playing a huge fish on a very slender line. He hoped to God she would pack up soon. Each one of those crunching blows at the truck hurt him badly. There was already a smear of blood on the side of her head. He bawled at Webb 'For Christ's sake get her in close.'

The rhino obliged at once. She came in and hooked a front tyre hard. Then she lifted her head and bounced it a couple of times on the top of the radiator so that the whole truck rocked. Next she gave the lorry a sideways buffet that hurled one of the Africans over the tailboard.

'Nguru,' Maxwell yelled. 'Rope her before she bashes herself to pieces.'

But by the time Nguru went over with a fresh length of rope, Ryan had moved in and had both back legs neatly tied. Shortly after that the whole crew piled on to her and the cow crashed over on her side.

When they had tied her up tight, Maxwell went away by himself and lit one of his untidy hand-made cigarettes. He did not want to talk to anyone, least of all to Ryan. He could see him alongside the trussed rhino, shaking his head and grinning and indicating by every gesture that he had thought his number was up. Maxwell watched the girl kiss Ryan full on the lips. Nguru sat apart. Maxwell noticed that Ryan did not thank him for what he had done.

Three hours later the big cow had joined her son in the *boma*.

Maxwell had watched over every phase of the operation with anxiety and, occasionally, even agony in his heart. First the boys had to dig away a pit in the baked surface of the bush close to where the trussed rhino lay. This had taken half an hour and had cost the rhino nothing. She had remained tied up but relaxed, snorting from time to time, trying to lift her great head every now and again but, since the head-rope was still in place and lashed to the lorry, failing to get far with the manœuvre. She lay there recovering the strength and energy she had expended in the chase and fight.

The big cow was lactating. Perhaps because of her struggle her twin udders were running with milk. While the rest worked, Zakari, the cook boy, had broken some dried boughs from a thorn tree and brewed up, only to discover they were short of milk. So Ryan had taken his tin mug of nearly black tea and, straddling the rhino's hind quarters, pulled a teat so that some thick milk squirted into his cup.

'Leave her alone,' Maxwell had ordered.

Ryan shrugged, then raised his cup in a mock toast to Maxwell.

When the pit had been dug, Webb backed the lorry down into it so that the dropped tailboard lay close to the cow's hind-quarters. The boys laid two sets of metal loading rollers between the rhino and the sloping floor of the lorry. Then they splashed the rhino, the rollers and the back of the lorry with water to ease her ascent. Webb meantime had run a long winch cable round a block fixed immediately behind the cab to the open floor of the Mercedes. He hooked one end of this to the rear of the catching truck. The hook on the other end Maxwell himself fitted to a rope loop tied to the rhino's back legs. When everything was ready he told Webb to get in the catching truck and to mind that he watched his hand signals.

Maxwell positioned the rest of his men, including Ryan, on hand-ropes fixed to the front and rear feet of the cow. He raised his hand slowly. When he dropped it, Webb inched the catching truck away at right angles to the Mercedes so that the winch wire became taut round the block and began to take the strain.

'Heave,' Maxwell shouted to the hand-ropers. The rhino moved backwards a trifle. '*Heave.*' Again she jerked a little further towards the rollers. As the third heave came, she lifted her head and crashed it down on the metal ramp. Maxwell ran round her and slipped a straw-filled sack under her head. The rhino rewarded him by trying to hook him in the leg. 'Steady girl,' he said. 'Right. *Heave!*'

This time her backside overlapped the first rollers.

Maxwell turned towards Webb to see that he was watching him closely, then he had raised his hand slowly. Webb let in the clutch. When Maxwell's hand fell, Webb began to creep forward and the wire became taut a second time. '*Heave,*' shouted Maxwell and the rhino's bottom overlapped the second roller. As Webb took the truck steadily forward, she began to jerk and jog up the slope. Half-way up she jammed momentarily. Maxwell roared obscenities for Webb to stop pulling, but Webb had seen the commotion, guessed its cause and stopped almost before the first syllables were out of Maxwell's mouth. No damage had come to the animal, but, in the pause that followed, Maxwell walked slowly across to the fifteen hundredweight and shouted at Webb 'For God's sake watch what you're doing, you clumsy sod. Do you want to pull the legs off her?'

Webb had looked calmly at Maxwell. He had seen him like this over the welfare of his catches before. He nodded mildly enough and said 'Keep your shirt on. I'm watching you.'

After that the rhino was winched onto the lorry without further incident. Aboard the Mercedes, they tied her up so that she looked like Gulliver on the shores of Lilliput. Like Lilliputians they were taking no chances with this monster.

Back at camp she made the reverse journey into the *boma* with only one bad moment for Maxwell. This came when she was half-way down the metal rollers. There was no room to use a winch cable so she had to be pulled out of the Mercedes by manpower. This time everyone pulled on a single headrope and relied on the creature's weight to slide her down the slope. There was, however, little room to work. In the excitement the whole party became momentarily jammed in the log gate of the *boma* so that tension went off the headrope. In that instant, finding the pressure relaxed, the rhino lifted her head and smashed it down on the rollers with a blow that Maxwell felt to the soles of his feet. This time he said nothing, but, when he had successfully untied the cow and she stood pawing the dust in the *boma*, he remained looking at her long after the rest had dispersed to their tents.

When they all met again at supper the atmosphere had relaxed. Far from feeling any shame or even embarrassment over his part in the two catches, Ryan was at his most talkative. He talked mainly to Jen who, again, sat close to him. Maxwell ate in silence, looking out through the velvet night towards the *boma* where the great bulk of the cow rhino could be seen moodily looming beyond the logs. His first inclination, after the catch was over, had been to have an immediate show-down with Ryan, telling him what risks he was prepared to see his crew exposed to in the normal run of things and making it quite clear that there were no risks he would see taken to save the hide of show-off bastards like Ryan. But then he had remembered that he himself had taken a certain risk on Ryan's behalf by jumping down to tempt the cow to charge. Had she charged there would have been at least a thirty per cent chance that he would not have made it out of harm's way, round the bonnet of the truck. He did not want Ryan to remind him of this. Maxwell was pleased with his double catch. Things would have gone better but for Ryan, but they had gone well. He had to admit Ryan's undoubted guts. When all was said and done he had stayed with the rhino and put the rope on even before Nguru could get there. And he did not want Ryan to remind him of that either. So Maxwell sat, said nothing, let the night sounds fill his ears with pleasure.

Ryan, however, needed an audience. He had that trick of talking about anyone who remained outside his conversation until they were eventually needled into replying. For a long time Maxwell took no notice, hearing himself referred to repeatedly as 'old Ted', as if they had been friends for life. He ignored such deliberate provocations as 'Of course, old Ted and his Wild West antics will soon be out of business. Down in the Union they're perfecting dope darts for rhinos. Soon you won't have to chase them any more. You'll just shoot 'em with a cross-bow and walk up to them and lead them into the *boma*.' But a direct question Maxwell could not leave unanswered without appearing to sulk. So, when Ryan followed up with, 'Well, what about dope darts, Ted? How will you feel about them when your life work disappears?' Maxwell replied quietly. 'The point may not strike you, Ryan, but doping will make it far easier on the rhinos.'

Ryan clapped his hands. 'Right on the button,' he said. 'The good old humanitarian as always.'

Nancy Maxwell said 'Funnily enough, Ryan, that's what he does worry about. The animals.'

'Just the animals, Nancy . . . sorry Mrs Maxwell . . . That's what I heard about him. Ted Maxwell, they said, doesn't give a damn for people.'

'Wrap it up, Ryan,' said Webb.

'No, seriously. I'm just interested. I like to know the people I'm working with. I've always thought of myself as the chap who didn't give a damn about people.'

'Or animals,' said Maxwell. 'Or nothing. You're running on your own.'

'Maybe,' said Ryan quite good-naturedly. 'But I'm just as anxious that you should be consistent, too. You see, I don't think this big tough reputation we've heard about is quite deserved. If it is, then what were you doing running around inviting a rhino to charge you this afternoon just to save my miserable skin?'

'Oh, wrap it up,' Webb said again. 'I suppose if I'd thought quicker, I'd have had a go, too. You do it automatically.'

'But *you* didn't?'

'Now, look,' Webb began.

'Oh, I'm not saying you were scared, so don't worry. You were just mentally tougher or more sensible. You thought: if that stupid clot wants to get down there and risk his neck, then that's not my affair. And I confess I'd have thought the same, too.' Ryan turned to the girl. 'As for bush baby here, she jumped down, bless her, because she likes me. But old Ted staged a diversion because he really likes the whole damn human race. That's why he goes to all this trouble saving rhinos. For him it's not the money like it is with me. I'll give him that. But here's the big surprise, it's not really the rhinos, either. It's because he thinks the whole damn animal creation is something put there for the glory of man.'

Maxwell got to his feet and looked down at Ryan. His lined face was without emotion as he said 'I don't know what the hell you're talking about and I don't all that much care. I'll just tell you this, though, Ryan: if you play to the gallery any more, no one will help you out. And if they do—and I don't care who it is—I'll drive the damn truck away and leave all of you to do the bullfighting on your own. Now I'm going to turn in.' He stopped in front of the girl's chair and said 'Don't forget *your* tent is over there.'

Next morning they went for the bull that Maxwell had spotted on the high rocky ground. He had moved down onto the level. They caught up with him after a short, fast chase, but, as Webb was about to put the lasso on, the animal stumbled and staggered to the left. Maxwell put the wheel over as hard as he could to avoid him but, even so, the truck hit the rhino a punishing blow on the flank. After this, roping and tying was easy. Winded, the rhino had lost the urge to fight back.

As they drove the catch back to camp, Ryan said to Maxwell 'Maybe you've got a new technique there.'

'What did you say?'

'Bumping 'em like that. Slows them up. Takes the fight out of them.'

'We'll be lucky if he lives.'

'He hasn't got a mark on him.'

'Same goes for some people who get run over by cars, but they pack up later, just the same.'

When they unloaded the bull and released him in the *boma* he seemed fully recovered. Ryan insisted on untying the last leg rope this time and Maxwell raised no objection. If Ryan was going to prove handy after all, he didn't see why he shouldn't do as much of the dirty work as possible. Watching Ryan work, Maxwell had to admit that his particular brand of bravado and coolness were well suited to roping. Ryan eased the last knot apart so that the rhino, still lying on its side in the *boma*, had no idea that it was free. Ryan stood there grinning and looking round to make sure that the girl, seated astride a top log of the *boma*, was watching him. Then he kicked the animal's rump with his rubber shoe and walked casually away. The bull was up on his feet and came at Ryan with a blundering charge. At the last second he turned to face it and side-stepped. '*Olè*,' he shouted. The bull backed off and swung to make another charge. Ryan stood his ground and stamped his foot. 'Hey, *toro*,' he shouted, striking an attitude. When the bull came this time he was a little too slow and the horn caught him a glancing blow on the outside of his thigh. When he had climbed out of the *boma*, Maxwell said 'From now on you can cut that out, too.'

Ryan had his arm round the girl who was rubbing his leg. 'Just a small bruise,' he said.

'I wasn't thinking about you. That rhino hit the *boma* wall hard. He's in enough trouble already.'

'Trouble?' said Ryan. 'He didn't seem to be suffering any ill effects to me.'

Maxwell repeated grimly 'We'll be lucky if we don't lose him.'

They didn't try to make another catch that day. For one thing both *bomas* were full. For another, Maxwell suspected that the steering had been damaged when he hit the rhino and he wanted Webb to check it. But he had another deeper reason. He was worried about all three rhinos and he wanted to watch them and see the way they were shaping. To begin with, the calf was listless and seemed reluctant to suckle. His mother had refused so far to eat or drink, and this, coupled with the discomfort of her over-full udders, had made her moody and savage. Mostly she stood around staring out between the logs of the *boma*. Every so often she relieved her feelings by hooking them hard. The skin at the base of her horn was knocked away and raw and the flies had found it. Maxwell had experienced this situation with black rhinos. In the wild, rhinos had no natural enemies. Being caught and subjected to undreamt-of indignities seemed to hurt their pride. There was often a crisis period lasting for two or three days during which they refused to eat or drink. If the fast went on longer than this, then there was a very good chance that the animals would die. But, if they came through, they settled down to captivity remarkably quickly.

Maxwell spent the afternoon with two boys and the Land-Rover driving about in the bush, gathering every different kind of grass and ground vegetation he could find. Then he sat on the *boma* wall offering bunches of it first to the cow and then to the calf. They showed no interest in any of it.

This was bad enough, but the mother and son were at least undamaged. The bull, however, worried him even more. He had a long scar on his left flank where the lorry had hit him and now he was leaning wearily against one wall of the *boma*. Maxwell ordered the boys to pour water from an empty oil drum into a puddle already excavated at one corner of his pen, but he didn't even sniff at it. Nor did he react to the buckets of water which Maxwell himself threw over him. Big animals like hippo, elephant and rhino appreciated a cold bath. They needed a mud wallow to keep their hides supple. Frequently when water was showered on them, they lay down in their drinking pool and plastered themselves with slime. But the bull just stood there. Maxwell shook his head doubtfully. He was about to send for more water when the sky, which had suddenly clouded up, provided a short torrential rainburst.

That evening when Maxwell was having a wash-down himself before supper, Nancy Maxwell said to him 'I suppose you've thought about the rains. They're coming up fast now. That shower this afternoon was no accident.'

'Sure.'

'Those storms are going to get more frequent from now on. Catching's going to get harder and harder. It's lucky we've got three rhinos already. We have got three, haven't we?'

'I'm not sure.'

'I know you're not. I saw you down at the *boma* all afternoon. Now look. All I'm saying is, we owe Ryan two rhino. We didn't say they had to be perfect rhino. So don't go wasting any.'

'Ryan? What's Ryan got to do with it? We're catching eight rhino. Good ones. I don't want any sick rhino.'

'What's the odds? Give him the ones that aren't so good.'

'You leave the rhino to me.'

'All right, but I'm telling you not to forget that the weather is not going to get any better and we've no idea what's going on outside this godforsaken place. We've got a long way to go once we leave here with 'em and that's another thing. What about petrol and diesel?'

'What about it? That's your department.'

'Certainly. When the pumps are working and there isn't a civil war going on, then I can supply it, but how do I know what's happening back in Makole or at the Park, or anywhere?'

'You don't. How much have we got here in camp?'

'Enough to finish catching with and a bit besides, but we'll need plenty more for the lift and we don't have that.'

'So what do you suggest?'

'I suggest we send out a recce just to discover whether we can still get fuel on the trip. Apart from that, I'd like to know what's going on in this part of the world in general.'

'Okay,' said Maxwell, 'I'm not quarrelling with that, but just leave the rhinos to me.'

'You'll not miss Ryan then, if I send him out in the Land-Rover tomorrow?'

'Miss him? Are you serious?'

At supper Nancy Maxwell told Ryan what was expected of him. He accepted the plan without a murmur, but, to Webb, he said 'Just keep on catching them at the same rate while I'm away, sonny boy. We all took an afternoon off today and we can't afford that.'

'We didn't. The catching truck did. It needed it.'

'Fine. Well, now it can get back to work and catch three more rhinos by the time I return.'

'Three,' said Maxwell, 'what makes you think we've got three?'

'Well, haven't we?' Ryan asked.

'We've got two doubtful starters and one dead loss,' Maxwell said glumly. 'Unless they all pull themselves together soon I may have to let the lot go.'

Ryan said 'You must be stark raving bloody mad. You mean you'd turn those rhino loose again?'

'If they didn't have a chance otherwise—yes.'

'Look,' said Ryan, 'let's not mess about. You may be bloody soft, but I'm not. You give those three rhinos to me. Crate them and load them and I'll pull out now and take my chance and you can return the rest of the transport later. Do what you like with the trucks but that's £15,000 quid's worth of rhino on the hoof down there.'

'Not if it all dies,' said Maxwell quietly.

'It won't die. Even if one dies, then there are still two. I'd take my chance with those two now.'

'Well, you're not going to have a chance. I'm not considering you.'

'You're not even considering the rhinos. Turn 'em loose and they'll be speared in the end. You've said so yourself.'

'Maybe. But I decide what chances the rhino have to take. One thing I do know: they're not going to die inside my *boma*.'

Nancy Maxwell cut in. 'So that's decided, Ryan. Understand? You take off in the morning with whatever boys you need to drive, and recce the petrol situation. Find out anything else you can, too.'

Ryan made one of his rapid recoveries. He put his arm round the girl. 'Boys?' he said, grinning, 'I don't need *boys*. I'll take Jen here along with me. We'll have a day out, won't we, bush child?'

Maxwell said 'Yes, a day. But be back tomorrow night.'

When he left the table to walk down to the *boma* he said to the girl, much as he had said the night before, '*Your* tent is over there.'

Ryan and the girl drove out of camp before breakfast next morning. Maxwell watched them go from his perch on the top of the bull rhino's *boma*. He had been up there, on and off, half the night. The rhino was now more or less exhausted. It had rallied during the early hours, but, when daylight came, it had used its new-found strength continually to bash the walls of the *boma* as if this enclosing creature was its present tormentor and its past assailant. It was quieter now but was more obviously than ever groggy at the knees. The skin at the base of its horn was raw and red. Maxwell got down at last and shouted for breakfast. Webb came strolling across to him. 'Aiming to go catching today?'

'Dunno,' said Maxwell.

'Truck won't be ready until after lunch. You shifted the axle when you hit that rhino.'

'Fix it then.'

'I am.'

'Well then, why ask me about it?'

'Ker-rist,' said Webb and walked away.

About mid-morning Maxwell bawled for Nguru.

'Get the *boma* open,' he ordered.

Nguru called for some of the boys who were filling in time by finishing off the crates. Together they heaved away the logs which sealed off the gate of the pen.

The bull faced the newly-made opening but did not move, so Maxwell climbed on top of the log wall and pushed his rump, hard, with one foot. The animal did nothing but stand there impassively for several more minutes. At last, Nguru took off his shirt and danced across the open door with it, flaunting it in the rhino's face. At the third attempt the rhino suddenly lurched into a charge, and, hooking the wall of the *boma* as he passed, galloped out into the open. The boys backed apprehensively behind the crates on which they were working. Maxwell sat watching. The bull halted, and once again he did not move.

He was still standing in the same position five minutes later when Nguru said to Maxwell 'He will die, *bwana*?'

'Dunno.'

'He will be easier for the poachers to spear.'

'One thing I do know. He'd have died if we'd kept him here.'

After a time, while the bull still stood there, the life of the camp returned to normal so that, when he eventually moved off into the trees, he was hardly seen to go except by Maxwell who still sat on top of the *boma* wall, watching.

At lunch time Webb pressed Maxwell again. 'When do we start catching, Ted? Truck's ready.'

'When those other two stupid bastards start to eat. That's when.'

Ryan didn't come back that night but then Maxwell had hardly kidded himself that he would. After supper, Maxwell took the fifteen hundredweight out on a test run. He drove along the stream for some way. He drove slowly, because he was still puzzled and depressed by the behaviour of the big cow. He was certain that if he could once get her eating, then the calf would have no problems at all. By a small drinking pool where he had stopped to watch some impala coming down to water, a cow rhino with her calf suddenly ambled out of some trees and came on calmly towards the stream. When she got there she didn't drink but began to munch a short, rush-like grass that grew by the water-side. Her calf, who was smaller than the one in the *boma*, copied her. Maxwell watched them with a feeling of great elation, certain that he had discovered something that would tempt his captives, but he didn't try to drive them away until they had finished feeding. When they moved off, he jumped down and tore up great armfuls of the grass, cutting his hands on the sharp edges of the blades. At last he had a pile of it in the back of the catching truck. He drove flat out back to camp and pulled up with a screech alongside the *boma*. Ten minutes after he had piled the fresh greenery onto the floor, the cow still stood and glared at him gloomily while her calf lay morose and abandoned in the corner. Maxwell slammed the door of the truck shut in fury, and, leaving the vehicle just where it was, walked to his tent and threw himself down on his bed.

His wife said 'You needn't fret yourself. They won't be back to-night.'

He looked at her without comprehending. Soon afterwards he fell asleep, but two hours later he woke, crawled out under the tent flap and went down to the *boma*. The cow was eating happily. Her calf, close by her side, was nuzzling her and obviously about to suckle. Maxwell gave a great cry. One of the boys poked his head out from his blankets. 'She's eating,' he shouted at the Kikuyu. He saw the boy's white teeth gleam as he grinned in the darkness. 'Stupid bastard,' thought Maxwell. 'He'd have grinned at anything, just to hear me shout, or because I wasn't shouting at him.' Maxwell felt he had to tell someone else. He walked over to Webb's tent. Webb was sound asleep with his mouth open. Maxwell picked up the end of the safari bed on his foot and dropped it heavily. Webb sat up with a strangled grunt. 'What the hell . . .' he began.

'The cow's feeding and the *toto*'s about to start.'

'Hooray, hooray,' said Webb. 'Now do you mind if I go back to sleep?'

'Sleep your damn head off,' Maxwell said happily. 'We start catching again tomorrow.'

Ryan drove in next morning, just after breakfast. He looked fresh and the girl radiant. They had plainly not driven far that morning. Maxwell made no comment when they sat down to coffee but Nancy Maxwell, anxious to forestall what she saw as an inevitable scene over their night's absence, said quickly 'Well, come on. Let's have the whole story.'

'Things are not too clever,' Ryan said. 'We went half-way to Makole and then swung round on the Adoge road towards the park. There's been quite a bit of local fighting between the tribes and one damn near pitched battle. Looks like the Ashota and their allies burnt a Magunga village in revenge and about twenty got killed. Then we ran into a convoy of European settlers pulling out. They told us, though they hadn't seen it themselves, that one white farm had been burnt down and the family chopped up with *pangas*. They also said that they'd heard the administration was arming the Ma-gunga before they pull out. They'd heard some tale about giving them an aeroplane or two, though I shouldn't think the Magunga would be too flush on pilots.'

The girl spoke for the first time. 'One of the wives said it wasn't the Magunga who were going to fly them but some hired hands the Magunga were paying.'

'Mercenaries?' asked Nancy Maxwell.

'That was her story.'

'Well, it's not impossible. The administration might even put up the money if they wanted the Magunga to win.'

Nancy Maxwell asked 'What about our petrol supplies?'

'We found two petrol points open. They're few and far between, as you know. But the chances of them staying open if any real fighting starts are pretty slim. We brought as many drums as we could carry in the Land-Rover.'

'It looks as though we should send a lorry in and load up while the going's good.'

'It's a fair way to the nearest petrol point. Why burn up some of our own supply on the off-chance of getting replacements? The situation may have changed by the time we get to the pumps. They may have closed down, then where are we? Short of a lot more petrol, that's all?'

'How much did you bring?'

'Twenty gallons, but I know where there's a lot more.'

'Where?'

'Where we spent the night.' Ryan looked directly at Maxwell as he said this but Maxwell didn't move a muscle.

'Where?' Nancy Maxwell insisted.

'At the Game Department's safari camp.'

Maxwell continued drinking his coffee.

Nancy Maxwell said 'But that's only five miles from here.'

Ryan smiled. 'That's right.' He was still looking at Maxwell but Maxwell seemed not to have heard him.

'How much petrol?' Nancy Maxwell persisted.

'More than enough for us. At least a hundred gallons in five-gallon drums. It's stacked in one of the huts. It must have been stored there for safari parties.'

Maxwell spoke at last. 'Get it then. Take a truck right after breakfast and load it before the wogs find a use for it. We can let the Game Department have it back later. They won't want it now, that's for certain.'

'Certainly,' said Ryan easily. 'Bush baby and I can go back.'

Maxwell looked at Ryan for the first time and said slowly 'I let the bull rhino go.'

The smile vanished from Ryan's face for a second.

'Well?' said Maxwell quietly.

Ryan smiled again, slipping his arm round the girl's shoulders. 'Well,' he said, 'we can't have everything on this safari, I suppose. Meeting bush baby *and* finding some sheer common bloody sense as well would be just too much to ask.'

'You get that petrol,' Maxwell told him.

As soon as Ryan returned with the petrol and had unloaded it, they went out after the cow and calf Maxwell had seen the night before. Almost as soon as they left camp, Webb spotted a thermal of vultures. He shouted down to Maxwell that there was a kill of some sort up ahead. Maxwell swung off to investigate. By the time they got near, the vultures were down out of the sky. They could see them sitting in rows in the tree-tops, and, when they finally drove into view of the kill, the birds flew up in a great brown, squawking cloud.

The carcass was still fresh. So far, hyenas and jackals in the night and vultures since daylight had only found one point of entry through the thick hide. This was around the long spear wounds in the flank. The head and back were already streaked with dirty white splashes of vulture lime. Despite all this the identity of the victim was beyond doubt. It was the young bull rhino Maxwell had released less than twenty-four hours previously. The motive for its murder was also quite evident. The horns had been hacked from its snout.

Maxwell got out and walked morosely round the body.

'Game guards,' he said. 'Those bloody game guards clobbered it.'

Ryan leaped down and faced Maxwell so that he stood directly in his path back to the truck. 'You damn stupid stone-faced old bastard. *You* wasted it. You flaming wasted it. If you hadn't been so damn soft and let it go the thing would still be in our *boma* and eating out of your hand. It would have recovered and that would have been one less rhino to chase.'

Maxwell looked at Ryan but said nothing.

'You flaming humanitarian. You're using my transport. You've no damn right to decide to let something go just because you think it's got a headache.' Ryan kicked the corpse on the ground. 'It's got damn sight more of a headache now. You make me flaming sick.'

'Then be sick,' Maxwell said. 'Right here. Sick your miserable stinking little heart up for all I care. When you spit it out you'll probably find it's a stone but you might be well rid of it. Now get up in that lorry or flaming walk back to camp.' Without looking at Ryan again Maxwell walked round him and got back into the truck.

They found the cow and her calf, a little female this time, close to where Maxwell had spotted them the previous night. They surprised the *toto* and caught her almost before the pair had got under way. The cow, which was slightly smaller than the first one they had caught, fought dearly for her freedom. The close country was to her disadvantage, however, so she was lassoed and roped comparatively quickly. But she had one surprise in store for them. While she was lying on the ground, apparently securely tied, she suddenly heaved herself half-way to her feet and made a great lunge upwards with her horn. She was lying close in to the catching truck at the time. The horn went in at the bottom of the petrol tank and came out of the top.

When the Mercedes had taken her back to camp and off-loaded her with her calf in the *boma* left empty by the dead bull, the big lorry had to return and tow the fifteen hundredweight in.

Perhaps because of the presence in the neighbouring *boma* of the first pair of rhinos, now steadily feeding and drinking, the second mother and calf settled down quickly. By late that evening, after the camp had turned in, Maxwell, standing in the shadows, watched the cow begin to munch the same riverside grasses he had seen her take in the bush. Soon afterwards, the small calf knelt to feed from its mother. He smiled in the darkness, amused as always at the considerate and practical way in which rhino calves knelt to save their mothers the discomfort of being prodded in the teats by a tiny but none the less sharp horn.

After the row over the released rhino, Ryan had kept away from Maxwell, but next morning he was about again, talkative and unabashed.

As Ryan came up, Maxwell was telling Webb the good news about the second pair. 'Well, well,' Ryan said. 'At last we're getting somewhere. Two more today and we're nearly there. Just two for your uncle Mike after that. When do we go out catching?'

'We don't,' Maxwell said flatly.

'Why the hell not?'

'Because the *bomas* are full.'

'For God's sake empty them. Can't you get the first load of rhinos on the way down to the park?'

'When we go,' Maxwell said, 'we go all together. I'm not wasting petrol and taking chances in these conditions. We all go together.'

'Look here,' Ryan shouted, 'I told you before that you're using my transport. Give me two of those animals, the two you owe me, and let me get out of here.'

'It would be a pleasure,' Maxwell said, 'but I told you: we all move together. Then, if there are two rhinos in good shape when we reach the park, you get those.'

'Christ, I should have known you'd pull some trick like that.'

'It's no trick, Ryan. I told you from the start we get six into the park first of all. You signed an agreement.'

Ryan's good-looking face was twisted like a frustrated child's.

'Look at those clouds,' he said, 'if you wait around much more we'll be swamped by the rains anyway.' As if to emphasize the truth of this, a single leaden drop splashed on Maxwell's face.

'Maybe,' Maxwell agreed. 'But that's the way we're going to do things. So we'll just have to get cracking and build two more *bomas*.'

'And how long do you think that's going to take?'

Maxwell permitted himself a slight crack of the features. It wasn't quite enough to call a smile. 'We've got a lot of cut timber, so, if you pull your finger out,' he said, 'we might be ready to start catching again by the day after tomorrow. But you'll have to put your sun-bronzed back into it.'

It took them all of two days to build the new *bomas*, though the job was made somewhat easier because they built them alongside the pens already standing and thus were able to use two of the existing walls. Maxwell put Ryan's boys onto making two more large crates. Nancy Maxwell took charge of this operation, sitting all day, hatless in the sun in her wheel-chair, bossing the Ashota around and occasionally whipping round the crate at high speed to criticize, direct or bawl out. Webb spent the first day taking the damaged tank from the catching truck and then brazing on patches top and bottom where the rhino's horn had penetrated. The girl worked, too, but only for Ryan. She hovered around him, cutting him lengths of binding wire, picking up a hammer he had dropped, handing him pliers when he needed them. Maxwell drove them all hard and had no

178

complaints about the way anyone, including Ryan, worked: he had no praise to spare either.

During the first day there were two short, stinging storms of relieving rain. When they sat down together to eat, they were too relaxed with sun and work and the feeling of driving activity that the camp had suddenly taken on to find time or energy to fall out. But the second day was different. Perhaps the cause was the weather. All day long the thunder-heads piled up like gigantic bronze cauliflowers in the blazing sky. Thunder growled but rain never broke. They ate in silence. Even Maxwell was now conscious that the weather was turning against them, though he never admitted as much. After supper he drove them all out again to finish the second *boma*. There was a short spat about this. Ryan complained: 'Hell, there's only the door to finish. We're not likely to fill both the *bomas* in one catch. Someone can finish the door tomorrow while we're out catching.'

Maxwell said 'You were the one who was all for bashing on. What's wrong? Getting tired or something?' Once again Ryan shrugged and walked away but he turned up at the *boma* with the rest.

They finished the whole job about eleven. By then they were running with sweat. The usual cool had not fallen with the darkness. The rain hadn't come and breathing the air was like gulping down lumps of medicated cotton wool.

Some time after they had all gone to their tents, Maxwell decided he would have a quick dip in the stream to wash the work out of his muscles. As he walked among the trees he heard the girl's laughter coming from Ryan's tent. Maxwell changed course immediately and flung open the flap. Through the shimmer of the mosquito net he could see the girl and Ryan lying together.

Maxwell said quietly 'I told you that your tent was over there.'

Ryan sat up. 'Oh, be your age,' he said.

The girl sat up, too. Maxwell saw that though she still had on her candy striped blouse it was undone and was the only thing she did have on.

'I don't allow womanizing in my camps,' Maxwell said gruffly.

'Oh no?' Ryan said. 'That's not the way I heard things.'

'I don't care what you heard. That's the way it is. As long as that girl is here I'll say what she does or doesn't do.'

'That's what I heard, too,' said Ryan. 'Only she doesn't do it, not any more, not with you.'

Maxwell felt a growing despair and helplessness. This was a situation, he knew, in which he was desperately vulnerable and could do nothing—and what's more was entitled to do nothing. Maxwell was not a violent man. For many people violence would have been the way out of an indefensible position. He could have torn down the mosquito net, hit Ryan on the jaw, anything, but instead he felt himself driven to say something futile, something which he knew would leave him even more exposed than before, and this, perhaps dimly, he felt he deserved. He said quietly 'I'm responsible for Jen. I'm damn nearly her father.'

The girl spat at him at once, as he had sensed she would. 'And since when have fathers slept with their daughters? I didn't learn much at school but I've heard of a word called incest.'

'You're not my daughter,' Maxwell said quietly. He spoke as if fending off a blow. 'You're my ward.'

Ryan said quickly 'Whether she's your daughter or your ward it doesn't seem you've much right to lay down the law to me. Now do you mind going?'

But the girl hadn't finished with Maxwell yet. 'He wouldn't care,' she screamed. 'It wouldn't make any difference if he had a birth certificate proving I was his daughter. Ken Maxwell is with the animals. Bull rhinos have it with their daughters. Cow rhinos are screwed by their sons. So, according to him, it's all right for everyone else.'

Ryan gently put his hand over the girl's mouth. 'Listen, Maxwell; rhino catching, *boma* building—in the end I'll take your orders because it suits me. But what I do in this tent is right outside our deal. Now get out.'

But Maxwell had already left. When he arrived at the stream he hurled himself into the water just like the girl had done at the hippo camp the morning after they had made love—if that was the word for what they had done. He lay there in his clothes. He was still lying in the shallows when the thunderstorm broke.

In the morning it was Maxwell who ate his breakfast on his own. Ryan and the girl appeared as usual in the mess tent. They showed no signs of the row of the night before, and Webb, if he had heard anything of the trouble, gave no indication either.

When Maxwell had returned from his bathe in the stream the previous night his wife had, apparently, been sound asleep and he had had no desire to awaken her and tell her what had taken place. It was impossible to tell from her face the following morning whether she had heard the disturbance or not. Everyone was playing it very cautiously. When Maxwell himself at last appeared, all he said was 'All right, then. This morning we start catching.'

The morning was a trying one. The thundery atmosphere had built up again. They chased two separate rhinos, a cow and a young bull, but each time they were foiled when the animals retreated onto rocky ground where catching was out of the question. When Maxwell organized a walking line of beaters to try and drive them onto more favourable terrain, the rhinos refused to budge. The bull did something that partly revised Maxwell's view of white rhinos as peaceful enemies. It broke into a trot, charged the boys, and actually succeeded in treeing one of them.

In the afternoon the storm broke and the face of the bush became a muddy paste which was unthinkable as a catching surface. By evening it had dried out a little and Maxwell invited Webb to join him in the Land-Rover on a reconnaissance. Rather to Maxwell's surprise, Webb jumped at the idea.

For a whole hour Maxwell drove, smoked and said little.

This did not disturb Webb. In fact he was enjoying himself as he had at the early days in the camp before the convoy had come back from the coast. As they wound through the scrub Webb was surprised to hear himself finally give form to his thoughts. 'You know,' he said, 'things were a hell of a lot better when we were up here on our own. I suppose it's Ryan. Have you noticed the way . . .'

Maxwell said 'There's a rhino up ahead. Let's go and look at him.'

But Webb was struck with his line of thought. 'It's the women,' he said, 'the flaming women.'

'Hang on,' Maxwell told him. 'We'll see what this orange box can do.'

Next day was better. The sun shone and they cut the bull out from his rocky stronghold before he could make it back to high ground. He was a fine young animal, about half-grown and just coming into prime breeding age. For his size he fought strongly. They put him into one of the new *bomas*. That made five.

At night Ryan and the girl openly went to bed together. Maxwell said nothing. At all times now he spoke to Ryan only when it was strictly necessary. The girl he ignored, although she made no attempt to avoid his eyes.

When Maxwell turned in after seeing the new capture was settled down peacefully, his wife said to him 'Glad to see you're letting them get on with it.'

Maxwell grunted.

'It's much better for her. Ryan's not my favourite man, but still . . .'

Maxwell said 'I suppose you're just saying that you're glad it's not me.'

'Since you say so. Not that I was jealous. What right have I got to be jealous? I just worried for her."

'She's a tart,' said Maxwell.

'That's hardly reasonable in the circumstances.'

'Well, what happens after this?'

'Since when have you been one to worry what happens after anything?'

Maxwell grunted again. 'Ryan'll just disappear. She'll never see him again.'

'Then that solves itself.'

'Hm. Maybe. Let's get some sleep, shall we?'

They spent most of the next morning stalking another half-grown rhino. At first they couldn't get close to him because of rough ground, but, when the chance finally came and they got up to him, Maxwell saw that he was a bull very much like the one they had caught the day before. Although they were nearly alongside and Webb was on the point of dropping the noose, Maxwell suddenly slowed and stopped. The bull thundered off on his own.

'Well, what was that all about?' yelled Webb.

Maxwell said 'Young bull.'

Ryan snapped 'So what?'

'Bulls don't breed with bulls.'

Ryan said with heavy sarcasm 'So now we're going to get a lecture on homosexuality in rhinos.'

Maxwell had climbed out and leaned against the open door of the cab. 'The idea, Ryan, is to give the park a breeding nucleus. So far we've got two big cows and two *totos*. I want a cow today to match the bull we caught yesterday.'

Ryan shouted 'That bull would have done for me, though.'

'You get what I give you. I want this catch as well balanced as possible.'

In the afternoon the luck changed. They found a cow who

matched the young bull in size and weight almost perfectly. She was an easy catch until they came to put her into the *boma*. They released her with the bull in the belief that he would be glad to have a female companion. Instead he immediately started knocking hell out of her.

It was nearly dark by the time they got her crated and the crate shifted against the door of the empty *boma* so that she could be turned out on her own.

Maxwell reckoned that they had now worked out the rhinos within easy range of the camp. Two more skeletons found during the last two days' catching confirmed that the poachers were still helping to cut down the local population. An empty morning of search, during which more valuable petrol vanished down the throat of the catching truck, prompted Maxwell to call another halt. So the following afternoon he left Webb in charge of the boys to finish off crates while he made a wide sweep to the west in the Land-Rover. At first he saw no rhinos, but, just as he was coming to the limit of possible catching ground where the bush toppled over the edge of a steep, rocky escarpment, he found two animals in quick succession. Such was their size and power that Maxwell stopped first the truck, then the engine, so that he could just sit and look at them. One was a cow; the other a bull. They were grazing within two hundred yards of each other. At first he thought they were the biggest rhinos he had ever seen, black or white. But then he decided that it was a matter of condition that made them look so splendid; that and the length of horn. Both front and back horns were beautifully developed but the main horn in each case was as long and perfectly proportioned as a cavalry sabre. If two animals were needed to found a new dynasty inside a national park, then these were the king and queen. Maxwell started the engine and made a wide, respectful circuit of the rhinos. Then he put his foot down and took the Land-Rover back to camp at the fastest pace he could coax from its labouring diesel heart.

He came into the compound much as Mgulu, the half-daft Kikuyu driver, had done on his return with the convoy, revving and sliding, kicking up the dust and finally slithering to a stop with a squeal of brakes. He pulled the plug to kill the engine and, leaving the poor, over-heated thing to splutter itself to extinction, leaped out, bawling for Nguru. When the head boy came running, Maxwell told him of his find.

Nguru said 'Good horn. Good horn for the poachers.'

'You've got it. That's why we're going to mount guard on them. Take any three boys you like. Better include the tracker. Load your gear in the catching truck. I'll lead you out there in the Land-Rover. Camp within sight of those two rhinos. Don't let anyone get near them. Keep the catching truck for the night. We'll save petrol that way. First thing in the morning we'll join you and catch the two finest rhinos you've ever seen.'

Nguru grinned and went off to pick his men.

When Maxwell took the Land-Rover over to the transport lines to top up its radiator, Webb emerged from beneath one of Ryan's three-tonners. He wiped the grease from his face. 'Just checking the springs and everything's okay for the road,' he said.

'Good,' Maxwell told him. 'You're going to need good springs. I've just found two of the biggest rhinos you've ever had to load on a lorry. We'll all be overloaded. We'll be moving any day now.'

By the time Maxwell got back from leading Nguru out to the rhinos, the news of his find was round the camp. A new feeling of expectancy and excitement had overtaken everyone. The boys were singing as they cooked their buffalo meat, cut from a beast Webb had shot four days before. At supper Ryan said 'Those two you've just found will do for me.'

'Whatever else you get, you don't have those two,' Maxwell told him.

Ryan laughed. 'As far as I can see I can't lose anyway.'

'No,' Maxwell agreed. 'Just so long as we unload six into the park.'

'I think even you'd admit that I'm entitled to know which rhinos I get.'

'As I said, we see what's left after we deliver.'

'Okay. But supposing we get them all there—and I can't see why we shouldn't—which ones do I get, always supposing that I agree?'

'You've *got* to agree.'

'All right, well, same question: which ones are you *kindly* going to give me?'

Maxwell said 'I don't want to give you a single damn rhino, but a deal's a deal. We catch those other two and we'll have two evenly matched breeding pairs for the park. Couldn't be better. That still leaves two cows with their *totos*. One *toto* is a female. She'll grow up and breed, so you don't get that pair, which leaves cow number one with the bull calf. As I said, you're in luck. Any zoo will pay good money for a mother and bull calf.'

Ryan kissed the girl's hair. 'There you are, bush baby. Ten thousand quid to set up house on. We certainly are in luck.'

'You announcing an engagement or something?' Maxwell asked sarcastically.

'Something like that.'

'I'd rather bet on my chances of getting all eight rhinos into the park than her chance of roping you at the altar.'

The girl said quietly 'Whatever Mike and I have got it's something you couldn't even begin to understand.'

'Why not?' Maxwell asked. 'As you told me the other night, the one thing I do understand is how animals go on.'

When they went for them next morning the king and queen were grazing side by side. Maxwell eased the catching truck towards them, revving the engine loudly. He made the boys shout and bang in the hope that one animal would break away and leave them a clear, isolated target. But it was as if this pair were living together as mates for life, for both stood their ground until the truck was within a hundred yards, and then broke into a concerted gallop, running side by side. After two hundred yards, the rhinos divided a little so that there was less than a truck's width between them. Maxwell drove straight at this gap, but still the rhinos refused to let him in.

Webb saw the wallow hidden by the elephant grass ahead of them just as Maxwell nuzzled the bonnet in between the rumps of the two animals. Webb shouted 'Oh Christ' and hung on tight, closing his eyes and nearly dropping his lasso pole. The next instant the nose of the truck dipped into the wallow. Webb prayed, expecting them to somersault on their backs and knowing that there had been no time to warn Maxwell with hand signals or anything else. Surprisingly the bottom of the wallow was not only dry but level. The truck careered down one side and up and out of the other. As if they had deliberately tried to lure the truck to destruction, the rhinos now peeled off, one to either side. But their course had taken them far apart and it was with the cow, running to the right, that Maxwell now closed. Webb got the rope home over her front horn without much difficulty and they slowed to fight it out. Five minutes later they were still shortening rope and the cow was not yet beaten. Finally it was Ryan who cut the engagement short by jumping over and, among the thrashing hooves and scimitar slashes of the horn, got a leg rope on.

Maxwell watched him from the cab. He had to admit to himself that Ryan did not lack physical courage. He even went further and did not bother to deny that Ryan was as quick and neat with a rope as anyone he had ever seen. But he stopped dead there. Any admiration he might have had for Ryan's performance was more than cancelled out by the man's lack of interest in the creatures he caught, the purpose of the operation or its value in the field of conservation. And even had Ryan appreciated or cared for any of these things, Maxwell would still have disliked him, for he found his brashness and boastfulness intolcrable.

When the cow was tied up securely, Ryan gave a virtuoso performance of arrogance and conceit. He was doing it for the girl's benefit and his target this time was Webb.

'What were you waiting for, sonny boy?' he asked.

'To get the rhino on a short rope, of course.'

'Hell,' said Ryan. 'Are you scared or something?'

'Oh drop dead,' Webb told him.

'I thought you were going to spew your heart out with fright when we hit that wallow.'

Webb said 'All right, so you tied up the rhino. We were tying up rhinos while you were still learning how to catch monkeys.'

'Oh, listen to him.' Ryan turned to the girl. 'Just listen to him. Pretty nice and safe and sound up there on his tin fortress. You want to try it down here at ground level, mate.'

Webb was young enough to allow himself to be goaded. He put his hand on the side of the truck as if ready to jump down and have it out with Ryan. 'Now listen, Ryan . . .' he began.

Maxwell got out of his cab and walked between them. 'You listen to me, both of you,' he said. 'Webb's job is lassoing. Not because it's safe or because it's dangerous, but because he's best at it.'

Ryan gave his toothy grin. 'Oh sure. I just thought someone else might like to have a go at the dirty work for a change. We monkey catchers have a union, too.'

When Maxwell had walked away to inspect the roped rhino, Webb said to Ryan 'All right, you clever sod. Next time you put the lasso on. I'll tie.'

Directly he saw them coming the big bull was full of hate for the truck. He did not run but stood his ground, head lowered. This time Ryan was in Webb's usual position, inside the goal-post and holding the catching pole. True to his word that he would tie this one, Webb crouched behind Ryan with a length of foot rope in his hand. Webb did not care for roping, though he had done it on many occasions. He had even tied black rhino. Each time before the moment came to jump he experienced the deepest dread. Once down there, darting and squirming for a handhold, he was too busy to worry any more. He wished now that the moment to jump would come quickly. He looked with considerable distaste at the bull squaring off at their approach.

At first, it seemed as though it was going to be too easy. The bull lowered its head and Ryan made a quick dab with the lasso. Webb, from behind his shoulder, guessed that he had missed. The next instant he felt the truck jolt as the rhino horned it hard somewhere up front. This time Ryan got the rope home. Webb could hear a hissing noise and guessed correctly that the bull had stuck its horn through one of the heavy duty front tyres.

Webb now did a stupid thing. He passed under the goal-post and jumped on top of the cab. He did this to get a better view of the rhino but also because he wanted to see what damage the bull had done to the truck. The animal was now running free at the full stretch of its rope. The split-second when Ryan might have recovered rope had gone. Webb was in no danger so long as the bull stayed well out to the right of the truck, but now it suddenly changed its mind and ran across the front of the lorry so that it could charge the left flank of its attacker. In doing so it took the taut head-rope across the top of the cab, just as the hawser of a ship momentarily out of control might sweep across a quayside. The rope caught Webb above the ankles and pitched him to the ground between the rhino and the lorry.

Like all rhinos this one had poor eyesight, but Webb's fall had crossed its line of vision. It knew that a fresh enemy had entered the battle and it attacked blindly and at once. It did not see Webb particularly well but it guessed where he was. It missed him with its horn but caught him with the full weight of its body just as he rose to his feet, smashing him against the side of the truck. By now both Ryan and Nguru were trying to draw the rhino off. Eventually, they managed to entice it round to the right side of the truck again and there at last it was fought to a standstill, roped and thrown.

Maxwell took no interest in the rest of this battle. He sat on the ground with Webb, cradling him in his arms.

Webb did not say anything, though he tried to speak several times. His ribs were crushed and both lungs punctured. About the time they got the rhino under control, blood rushed from his mouth, his eyes glazed over and his fair hair fell forward across his face. Maxwell was still holding him when he died.

Ryan began to explain how it had happened. While he did so, Maxwell stood looking at him without expression. He did not even appear to hear what Ryan was trying to tell him. Jen who had never, except for one brief, experimental five minutes, felt anything except hostility for Webb, sat sobbing in the cab of the three-ton lorry. She was as far from the body as she could get. She had seen many things but she had never before seen a man she had known crushed to death.

'What'll we do with the rhino?' Ryan kept asking.

Maxwell dimly heard this. 'Do?' he said slowly, in a puzzled voice. 'Do?'

'The rhino,' Ryan was almost shouting in order to get through to Maxwell. 'The rhino that killed him. What shall we do with it?'

Maxwell surfaced at last. 'Do?' he repeated flatly. 'Load him, of course. Load him and get him into the *boma*. I want that one more than all the others put together.'

Maxwell turned away. He walked slowly round the truck and took Webb's body from under the hasty shelter of cut thorn branches which the boys had laid over it. He placed it carefully in the back of the catching truck and wrapped it in the only covering he could find —a tarpaulin. Then he laid the cut boughs on top of it and drove alone back to camp.

There could be no delay about burial in that climate. They dug a deep grave on top of a little knoll overlooking the camp, and, as soon as the rhino had been released in the *boma*, they buried Webb in a shroud of fresh-cut river grasses. There was no time to make a coffin and, anyway, to Maxwell a coffin did not seem appropriate.

Webb had shown no noticeable attachment to any religious belief. From her wheel-chair, Nancy Maxwell repeated as much of the burial service as she could remember. Everyone else, the boys, Ryan, the girl, stood silently round the grave as Maxwell and Nguru lowered the reed-wrapped body. Already there was a faint smell of corruption on the air. When the grave had been filled in and everyone else had gone to their tents, Maxwell remained and saw that rocks were piled high above the place where Webb lay. Hyenas had their place in the scheme of things but he intended to see that their place was not here.

When he returned from this job, Nancy Maxwell tried to draw from him the whole story of how Webb had died. She seemed to want to force him to admit that he thought Ryan, however indirectly, was responsible, but all he would say, dully, was 'Webb was on top of the cab. He knew you could get knocked off. Ryan didn't put him there.'

'Oh God,' she said. 'If only we hadn't had to catch those two extra rhinos. Those were for Ryan.'

Maxwell looked at her. He was without anger at the edge of hysteria in her voice but equally without pity for its cause. He said slowly 'Those two, aren't for Ryan. They never were and they certainly aren't now. They're the best. Webb bought those. If they're for anyone, they're for Webb.'

As he walked out of the tent he called to her over his shoulder 'I'm moving out as soon as possible.'

'When?'

'Just as soon as we can get those rhinos crated.'

'And not wait for the last two to settle down?'

'I can give 'em until tomorrow night, then we load and move, all together.'

In the darkness outside, Ryan caught Maxwell's arm as he walked towards the *boma*.

'Webb,' Ryan began. 'He didn't have to rope. I tried to draw the rhino off him.'

'Yes,' said Maxwell flatly. 'I saw you.' He shook his arm gently free. 'We're moving. Tomorrow evening. Can't stick around here. Besides, do you know what happened today?'

Ryan's face fell open. He thought that Maxwell was going to accuse him of Webb's death. For once, no words came.

'Well, if you don't,' Maxwell went on, 'let me tell you. Today was the date set for this country to get *Uhuru*. Now do you mind getting the hell out of it?'

Maxwell walked on alone towards the *boma* where the big bull stood quietly alongside the younger male they had caught several days earlier. Maxwell felt his eyes drawn towards the spot where they had buried Webb. He could see the pile of rocks outlined against the starry night sky. He could see something else there, too. When he approached the grave he found that a rough cross had been built over it. He guessed correctly that this was the work of Nguru, who had been mission-educated. Appropriately enough, the cross was made of two broken spring leaves from the catching truck, lashed together with heavy gauge wire.

In the morning Maxwell gave his orders for loading the rhinos. He had lain awake a good deal of the night thinking about this problem. Even with Ryan's two three-tonners and the Mercedes they were still under-equipped for shifting eight animals at least four hundred miles across rough country. With Webb dead they had not only lost the man who could keep the trucks going but also their best long-haul driver. In these circumstances even the tired, borrowed Land-Rover became valuable.

What Maxwell eventually decided upon was this: the two finest rhinos, the bull who had killed Webb and his consort, would share the Mercedes. Maxwell himself would drive this. He did not intend to let the king and queen—he had come to think of the two animals in these terms—out of his sight or control.

By the same token, Ryan would drive one of his own three-tonners carrying the big cow and her bull calf, the first pair they had caught and which would eventually become Ryan's once successful delivery to the park was completed.

The other big cow, the cow with the female calf, would go on Ryan's second three-tonner and this would be in the charge of Nguru.

That left the young half-grown bull and the young cow of almost equal weight and size. This was the weak link in Maxwell's plan for there was nothing left to carry them except the fifteen hundred-weight catching truck, since each rhino weighed about a ton, this was obviously asking a great deal of it, especially after the hammering it had taken during the last two weeks of catching. There was no choice but to make Jen drive this. Maxwell had thought hard about this decision, too, and in the end had come down firmly in favour of it. Not only was the girl a sensitive driver quite capable of handling the situation, but the arrangement had the virtue of keeping her away from Ryan who would then have to concentrate on the work in hand. Maxwell admitted to himself that anything that could keep Ryan and Jen separated gave him positive personal relief, if not actual pleasure.

This left the Land-Rover. Unfortunately there was nothing for it but to surrender this to the mad Kikuyu driver, Mgulu, who had shown no sign of improvement since originally put at the wheel of this vehicle. He had, however, got the thing up from Makole and he could, presumably, get it to the park. It was essential that he did so, for the Land-Rover was going to have to carry a good deal of the safari gear, not to mention some Africans as well.

If any truck broke down, then they would have no choice but to leave it under guard, press on to the park and return for its rhinos once they had unloaded and released their own.

Maxwell's plans for the move were received in silence but without argument. It was as if everyone concerned now realized that this was the last lap of a very difficult race and that, even if he or she had a stone in his shoe, the time wasn't very far distant when the finishing line would be reached and the irritant could be shaken out and forgotten. The girl looked quickly at Ryan when Maxwell made it clear that they would be driving different trucks, but that was all. Everyone appeared to realize that Maxwell's plan was not only sound but almost certainly the only one.

Finally, Maxwell gave orders to start crating the two big cows with their calves and to get them aboard the three-tonners. Next, the small bull and cow were to be loaded on the fifteen hundredweight. The king and queen rhinos, however, were not to be touched until nightfall. This would give them the maximum opportunity to settle down.

Camp, except for safari beds and mosquito nets, would be broken after the evening meal. Everybody would then get as much sleep as possible until four a.m. They would move out in convoy at five the next morning.

As they worked throughout the day, no one was unconscious for long of Webb's grave on top of the little mound. Even in the sweat of sliding crates up to *boma* entrances, driving and tempting the rhinos into them, bolting home the crate doors and, finally, pushing crate and rhino up the rollers and onto the backs of the lorries, each one of them found himself stealing a glance towards Nguru's steel cross. Each one of them, African and European, wanted to be gone from the place, and quickly. The Africans, especially, felt the aura of death. They were unusually silent as they worked. Their superstitious natures took Webb's death as an omen. Maxwell knew this and drove them on far harder than usual. He swore and cursed at them a great deal. Once he raised his fist at some stupidity, though he did not strike the blow. More than anyone present he wanted them up and out of the place. This was no time for any cracks in morale. He knew that as soon as he could get the Kikuyu and Ashota on the road and moving, their mood was likely to turn instantly to one of disproportionate good spirits.

Once, during the afternoon, a griffon vulture swung circling above the camp and then swooped in to land with a great frowsy flapping of dirty brown wings. It sat on top of the rocks piled over Webb's grave.

Ryan wanted to fetch a rifle and shoot it, but Maxwell snapped, 'Leave it alone. It can't do him any harm and you can't do him any good.'

They moved out in convoy in the clear early light of the following morning. Maxwell led in the Mercedes. Behind him the girl drove the overloaded catching truck. Then came Ryan followed by the Land-Rover. Nguru, in the second of the three-tonners, brought up the rear.

Nancy Maxwell sat, as usual, strapped in beside her husband. Perched on top of the huge crates behind were the cook boys and their gear. The two big rhinos were still restive and Maxwell was not happy about them. The big cow had settled down to feed and drink but the bull was far from resigned to captivity. Being jolted and jarred in a crate wasn't going to help him.

In the fifteen hundredweight Jen was alone except for Mbagi, the tracker, who was, after Nguru, the most reliable of the boys.

Ryan drove alone. The other front seat of his lorry was stacked with camping gear. Up behind with the cow and bull calf, and somehow wedged between the crate, supplies of petrol and camping gear, were the majority of the Kikuyu. Mgulu's Land-Rover carried the balance of Maxwell's boys as well as a great load of gear. Aboard Nguru's three-tonner were Ryan's eight Ashota.

As they moved out onto the track, Maxwell took one long look back at the camp, the two deserted *bomas*, the litter of planking left over from crate-making, a pile of empty petrol drums, assorted human debris, and, overlooking it all, Webb's mound where the solitary vulture once again sat. Then he put it all behind him and began to ease the lorry along, feeling for its reactions to the six tons of rhino it carried. Directly behind his ear the bull gave a great hissing snort. Somewhere down the convoy he could hear the Kikuyu singing their usual song. So far, so good.

They made about twelve miles in each hour and kept going until ten o'clock, by which time, despite the snail's pace at which Maxwell led, the convoy had become well strung out. Two heavy, stinging storms had turned the surface to slippery paste and this hadn't helped their progress. Thunder-heads were mounting into the sky, threatening heavier rain to come. If this really was the start of the rains proper, then, Maxwell realized, they could be in considerable trouble, for there were several rivers between them and the park and the park was still four hundred miles distant. While he waited for the other trucks to come up, Maxwell consulted the maps which Richie had forced upon him. He saw that three of the streams were well bridged, but that the fourth, the river nearest to the park, frequently became impassable during the rains and was marked accordingly. If this bridge was down, then it would mean a detour of a further eighty miles to find a guaranteed crossing point. Maxwell passed the maps to his wife who said 'Why didn't you tell me you had these? You drive. I'll look after the route. Now just you concentrate on the animals and the convoy. That's your business.'

Maxwell frowned. 'What about petrol if we have to make that detour?'

'I'm doing the sums now. I think we might be in a spot.'

When the rest of the trucks had pulled in behind, Maxwell walked back to inspect the rhinos and to talk to the drivers. No one had any trouble to report. Except for Maxwell's big bull, the animals seemed quiet and relaxed.

They stopped for an hour and ate a meal of tea and canned beans.

Early in the afternoon, when they had covered nearly one hundred miles, they had an unexpected bit of luck. They reached a small town and found a garage. The garage was closed but, after a good deal of shouting and banging on doors, the proprietor, a turbanned sikh, came out. At first he insisted that he had no petrol. There had been no deliveries for his pumps for several weeks and, now that *Uhuru* had come, he did not expect any. Moreover, only the day before, a convoy of lorries loaded with Magunga militia had come through and commandeered his canned supplies. The sikh spread his hands despairingly. There had been no option. The town lay in Magunga tribal territory. The militia had been well armed with automatic rifles, the type previously used by troops of the colonial administration. Their camouflaged smocks, too, had been similar to those previously worn by the colonial forces. The sikh explained that, though he had had a great contempt for the militiamen themselves, he had a certain respect for their automatic rifles. When it had been made clear to him that the rifles were loaded he had parted with the petrol, even though he had received no payment, merely a receipt signed by the white officer in charge.

Maxwell had interrupted 'White officer?'

'Yes.'

'Wearing Colonial Administration badges?'

'No. Wearing a new kind of badge.'

'What kind of a badge?' Maxwell had pressed.

'Look,' said the sikh, rummaging in his pocket and producing a crumpled piece of paper.

Maxwell looked and saw that this was a docket for 500 gallons of petrol. Crudely printed at the head of the paper was a coat of arms which included a broad-bladed Magunga spear and the leopard-skin robe of their ceremonial tribal dress. Printed above this were the words: 'Magunga Independence Army'.

Maxwell said quickly 'They gave you no money. I can pay you.'

'But I have no petrol.'

'I will pay well for it.'

'I need the petrol for myself and my family so that we can get away should fighting break out here.'

'And has fighting broken out?'

'Between the Magunga and Ashota? We hear only rumours but a man who came through from Makole tells me that there is street fighting in the town and that in many places to the south of here there have been battles also.'

'How much petrol will you sell?'

'You will pay double the price?'

'How much will you sell?'

'Seventy gallons.'

'And diesel?'

'Twenty gallons.'

194

Maxwell said 'Double the price is far too much. I will pay you half as much again but that is all.'

The sikh grinned.

Half an hour later they had loaded the drums and were on the road again.

After two hours of laborious grinding along a surface not much better than a stream bed in the dry season, the rains hit them again. This time the downpour was more prolonged and the trucks began to slide and wallow where the water had had time to penetrate through the loose upper coating of dust. Going down a steepish incline towards the first of the river bridges, Maxwell felt the Mercedes begin to slew. There was nothing he could do either to straighten the slide or to stop the truck. The tail broke away and broadsided onto soft ground at the left of the track. By the time the remaining trucks had caught up, the Mercedes was well down and firmly bogged by the near-side rear wheel. Maxwell stood gloomily regarding the disaster, the rain streaming down his dust-powdered face and producing rivulets of mire in the wrinkles, rivulets which closely resembled the streams of muddy water that were beginning to flow down the hill.

When Ryan came up all he could find to say was 'What did you want to go and do that for?'

Maxwell wiped the rain from his face. 'We'll have to get her out quick before she sinks any further.'

'Better wait until this lot blows itself out.'

'By that time,' Maxwell said, 'you won't even see the tops of the rhino crates. The whole lot will have sunk without trace.'

'You could have tried to keep on the road.'

'Don't be bleeding silly. Which is the three-tonner with the winch on?'

'Mine.'

'Get it up here at once and we'll try and pull her out of it.'

It was the sort of job which Webb would have relished. He would have known instinctively the best means of purchase and leverage, the exact direction from which the pull should be made, the precise moment at which the shove should be given. Maxwell was not bad at these things himself, but it took him three and a half drenching hours before he had the Mercedes back on the road again. The two women had remained in their cabs all this time. Everyone else, the two white men and all the Africans, were plastered with red mud as if with war paint. Only the rhinos appeared to relish the situation, snorting and tossing their heads with pleasure as the cloudburst streamed off their gleaming hides.

The rain stopped as the convoy began to move forward again. When they reached the bridge, the coffee-coloured water, speckled with creamy flood foam and already bearing along with it torn papyrus roots, branches of trees, and thick islands of water weed, was pounding by barely a foot below the level of the roadway.

They reached high ground some five miles further on where, despite the rain, the surface of the bush was still firm and where there was cover in the form of several large acacias. Maxwell dismounted and felt out the ground on foot, then he eased the Mercedes cautiously off the road, signalling the others to follow him.

The time was close on seven o'clock and darkness was not far off. The speedometer showed that they had covered just one hundred and thirty miles in a little under fourteen hours.

Maxwell was not too displeased with the progress. He had not yet met what he thought of as real trouble, though that, he conceded, might still lie ahead. The onset of the rains was something he had hoped to avoid. On the other hand he had unexpectedly found reserves of petrol. The best thing that the rains had brought was a marked liveliness among the rhinos. Even the king was looking less depressed, and, when Maxwell poked a bunch of reeds through the planks of his crate, he champed on them greedily and with enthusiasm.

The boys had already built a large log fire. In its light he saw that Ryan and the girl were rigging a lean-to shelter with a fly-sheet alongside Ryan's three-tonner. Maxwell walked over to the fire and gratefully took the pint mug of steaming tea that Zakari held out to him. Then he stood watching the steam rise from his saturated clothes, almost enjoying both the situation and the sensation.

They were too tired to do anything beyond eat and sleep. Maxwell gave orders for the camp to be roused at four thirty. They would move out, he said, one hour after that.

During the night he woke to hear the rain beating on the roof of his shelter. He rolled off his safari bed and crawled outside into the hissing darkness to inspect the lorries. To his relief he saw that the wheels were not sinking in the surface of the bush. He climbed up into the back of each truck and found the rhinos quiet but apparently happy. When he came to Ryan's truck he could not resist the urge to peer in under the fly-sheet shelter. Inside he saw the forms of Ryan and the girl asleep, each on a safari bed, the beds pulled close together. Ryan had his arm flung across the girl. In the last lorry of all Nguru was wide awake in his cab. He grinned as Maxwell came up to him.

'Everything okay?' Maxwell asked.

Nguru said 'Yes, but half an hour ago, before the rain began, I saw quite a large fire in the sky away towards the south.'

'Bush fire?'

'Perhaps so, *bwana*.'

They got off in good time next morning. The sky was clear and the night's rain had already been swallowed by the parched bush. The lorries pulled back onto the track without much difficulty. Within an hour they discovered that what Nguru had seen in the night had not been a bush fire.

Maxwell spotted the circling vultures a long way off, and smelt the familiar smell of burning long before they reached the scene of what had been a small, bloody battle.

The place was a Magunga police post, or rather had been. The five huts were now simply blackened rings of ashes on the surface of the compound. Twenty or thirty vultures rose as they approached. The body they had been tearing at was that of a police corporal wearing police uniform on which were pinned the same badges Maxwell had seen in the sikh's garage. The corporal had a spear wound in his chest. There were six other police corpses, five of them too incinerated to be attractive even to the vultures. The revolting sweet smell of charred human flesh stuck dreadful probing claws of nausea right down into the stomachs of everyone in the convoy. The Magunga had fought for their lives, as a scattering of empty cartridge cases showed. Of the weapons that had fired these there was nothing to be seen. They had presumably been taken by the victors. Evidence of the damage that these rifles had inflicted before fire and spear had silenced them lay in the long grass on the fringe of the compound. Four non-uniformed Africans lay close together where a burst of automatic fire had caught them. The vultures had not yet paid attention to these bodies but the flies had found the edges of the bullet wounds. One man lay with his face turned up to the sky. Already his features were swelling. The Ashota were an ebony-complexioned people but the corpse's skin was now greenish. Against this background, the tribal scars stood out like grey streaks of ash.

Maxwell had seen enough. He did not want to talk or explain. There was no object in staying another second. There were no survivors. He wanted simply to be gone. He climbed in beside his wife and said 'Well, it's their private fight, not ours.'

'Let's hope they don't make it a public one.'

'They've got no quarrel with us.'

'Do they need one to attack us?'

'No,' he said. 'So we've just got to keep going.'

For the next four hours the road ran through hilly country. Long dragging climbs were followed by steep rough-surfaced descents. They made even less distance in the hour than they had on the previous day. The road they were now travelling was little more than a bush track and would become impassable once the rainy season got well under way. For one hundred and fifty miles it did not pass through even the smallest town and this perhaps accounted for the fact that, though they saw several columns of smoke on the horizon and once or twice heard bursts of distant firing, they did not come across further signs of civil war, local tribal fighting, or whatever it was that had now taken hold of the country. The thing that most troubled Maxwell as he ground along at a steady eighteen miles per hour was that he was quite unable to assess the nature and scope of the fighting. If it was simply a local paying-off of old scores, then the chances of avoiding serious trouble remained pretty good. But if it was the sort of fighting that had taken place in the Congo, then anything could happen. The convoy might be stopped, turned back, or attacked, and this sort of threat could come from the so-called organized forces of either side, for nothing was more irresponsible, high-handed or downright murderous than a self-appointed, self-constituted, utterly unrecognized African military force fighting for a principal which in the end boiled down to nothing more than a demand for tribal ascendancy at all costs. Such periods were ideal for avenging old grievances and there must be many, real or imagined, which both Magunga and Ashota held against their European ex-masters. Maxwell was fully aware that he and his party would do very well as substitutes. Nor was he able to console himself that the cargo he carried was of little interest to looters, for the rhinos bore on the end of their noses enough horn to make a number of Africans rich for life.

The rain gave them a break that day and by evening they had covered one hundred and fifty miles. Maxwell found a camp site just above a stream. When he walked back to check the vehicles and their loads he learnt that Nguru in the last three-tonner had not yet caught up with them. This did not immediately worry him since the trucks had been travelling all day with wide and irregular spaces between them as each driver settled to his most economical and comfortable pace. However, when darkness had fallen and food was nearly ready, Nguru was still missing.

Maxwell called Ryan over. 'Got a rifle?'

'Sure.'

'Just one?'

'Yes. I'm the only one who carries arms in my party.'

'Get it. We're going back to look for Nguru.'

'Do you think he's had a breakdown?'

'I hope so.'

Jen stepped out of the firelight.

'I'll come, too.'

'No,' said Maxwell. 'You'll stay.'

The girl looked towards Ryan who shook his head and said 'You stay here, bush baby, and turn the bed down.'

Maxwell spat.

'What truck'll we take?' Ryan asked.

'Take your three-tonner: the one with the winch. If he has broken down he may need a tow.'

In a wooded section of the road, about ten miles back, they came round a bend and there was the three-tonner. A tree-trunk had been felled neatly across the road in front of it and a second tree dropped behind. Two bodies lay beside the truck. Ten yards away in the bush two more lay where bullets had stopped them in their flight.

Maxwell switched off his lights and turned the three-tonner in case he needed to make a quick getaway. Then he backed up to the first tree-trunk, saying to Ryan as he did so, 'Climb on top of the crates and cover me if necessary. Keep the engine running.'

Maxwell jumped down and ran, crouching, to the shelter of Nguru's three-tonner. Nothing happened. The attackers had left. Maxwell's first action was to tear open the door of the cab. Nguru was not there. There were, however, blood marks on the seat.

Maxwell climbed up on the rhino crates. The big cow was down on her knees, jammed against one side of the crate where she had fallen when the bullets had hit her. She had been shot with an automatic weapon at point-blank range. Two great red blooms on her skull showed where her horns had been hurriedly hacked off. The little female calf had had no horn worth speaking about. Just the same she had been speared and her tiny knob of horn taken.

Maxwell heard Ryan shout a warning. He heard an answering shout from the bush and recognized the voice: Nguru's. Maxwell bawled to Ryan not to shoot and ran towards the figure coming slowly towards him out of the darkness.

Nguru fell down when he reached Maxwell. He had a deep spear gash in his shoulder. Maxwell picked him up and carried him towards the three-tonner.

The raiders had been a part of about twenty Magunga, some of them in uniform. They had been led by a big police sergeant. The ambush had been well planned and carried out with military precision. Nguru told them all this as Maxwell put a rough dressing on his wound. The raiding party had seemed to know very well what the lorry contained. Their first objective had been Ryan's eight Ashota. Four had tried to run for it and had been shot down or speared. The remaining four had huddled, terrified, among the crates. These had been dragged out, tied together and led away. Nguru himself had been speared while trying to get out of the cab in the first stages of the attack. Afterwards the raiders had been so busy dealing with the Ashota and killing the rhinos that he had managed to crawl away into the bush.

Maxwell inspected the lorry and saw that there was little he could do about it even had he time or men. All four tyres had been slashed with spears and the petrol tank had been lacerated with *pangas*. The only thing the raiders had missed were the drums of petrol on the back of the lorry. There were five five-gallon drums. He heaved these down to Ryan and together they loaded them on their own truck.

'Let's get going,' Maxwell said at last.

'And leave my lorry?'

'Any alternatives?'

'No.'

'Then get moving. They may be back when they've chopped up their prisoners.'

'Think they'll do that?'

'I dunno. I don't want to think about it because I know there's absolutely nothing I can do about it. What I do know is that those bastards have killed two female rhinos.'

'I suppose they count more than eight men?'

'To me, yes. There are bags more Ashota and Magunga but there are bloody few rhino.'

'What about Nguru?'

'There are bloody few of him, too.'

After Nancy Maxwell had inspected and dressed Nguru's wound she called Maxwell to her.

'It's a deep wound,' she said. 'He may die.'

Maxwell said 'I don't see what we can do about that. We aren't exactly overloaded with hospitals hereabouts.'

'No, but tomorrow we'll cross a main road. We could send him in the Land-Rover to Makole.'

'How far to Makole?'

'When we reach the main road: two-eighty miles.'

'That would be saying goodbye to the Land-Rover and we've no guarantee that we could get him help in Makole. From what the sikh said they're fighting in the streets there.'

'The sikh didn't know for certain.'

'When's the crisis likely to be with Nguru?'

'In the next twenty-four hours. Like most Africans he'll have made up his mind by then whether to live or die.'

'How far is that main road?'

'Ninety miles from here.'

'Will moving that far kill him?'

'No. It'll be damn uncomfortable to say the least, but if he's going to try and live he'll probably survive it.'

'I can't risk those remaining rhinos.'

'No,' she said, 'I didn't suppose you could.'

'I'll make up my mind about Nguru when we get to that main road.'

'You've made it up, I reckon,' she said.

After that Ryan had a go at Maxwell. 'What about my rhinos, now?' he demanded.

'You've had 'em.'

'You double-crossing bleeding bastard.'

Maxwell looked at him without heat. 'Look,' he said, 'I haven't the energy to spare to get really angry with you. We made a bargain. Six rhinos into the park or you get nothing. We've got just six left now.'

Ryan shouted 'You may not have the energy, you bloody faker, but I have. When we made that agreement we didn't expect to find ourselves taking part in an African civil war. I didn't expect to have a truck wrecked either.'

Maxwell said wearily 'Look, Ryan, my job is to get them there. Get all six there and we'll talk. We've got an awful long way to go yet.'

Maxwell posted guards that night. He armed his tracker and three fairly responsible Kikuyu. The fate of the Ashota had made the rest of the Africans extremely jittery. Maxwell explained to them that the ambush had only taken place because of the rhino aboard the lorry but he knew that he had convinced none of them. Maxwell stood the first watch with two of the boys and Ryan the second. Nancy Maxwell had Nguru placed in a shelter alongside her tent. The girl moved in beside her. But nothing happened during the night. They had a late breakfast in order to give both Maxwell and Ryan a few hours' sleep. As soon as Maxwell was awake and dressed he went to see his wife.

'How is he?'

'Nguru?'

'Well, I didn't mean Ryan.'

'Don't say you've come to look at him *before* you visit the rhinos.'

'Oh Christ,' Maxwell said, 'spare me. How is he?'

'He's alive.'

'Any worse?'

'Hard to tell. He's holding on so far.'

'Supposing I did send him to Makole in the Land-Rover. Mgulu is the only driver I can spare. He's as likely to kill him as anything else.'

'It's your decision,' his wife said.

'Sure. They're all my decisions.'

'You expect me to feel sorry for you? You've driven and pushed everyone for the sake of these bloody animals, and other bloody animals before this lot, and now for the good of what's left of your immortal soul it's right that you have to make this sort of choice. Don't ask me to make it for you.'

'No,' he said, 'I wouldn't. The heart died in you a long time ago.'

'About the time I got chucked out of a catching truck, you mean?'

Maxwell turned away. 'Get Nguru loaded in the front of Jen's truck,' he said.

'Loaded! Loaded is what you do with rhinos and cans of petrol. This is a dying man.'

Maxwell turned away disgustedly. 'Get him aboard then. We'll move in an hour.'

When they pulled out of camp, the day was already hot and clear. A bateleur eagle, Maxwell's favourite bird, was coasting in the sky overhead.

When six hours later they came down the escarpment that led to the main road, another bateleur was riding the up-currents along the rocky edge of the hillside. Maxwell watched it as he eased the Mercedes into the first hairpin and then lost sight of the eagle when he began to negotiate the sharp turn. The hairpin was a double one, so that when he found himself facing the original direction again he immediately searched the sky for the eagle. At first he thought that he had found it, then he saw that he had been mistaken. The dot in the sky was moving far too quickly.

The 'plane was flying low along the main road far below. Maxwell recognized it from its outline and engine-note as an obsolete piston-engined fighter of just post-war vintage. He saw that it carried wing and fuselage insignia but he was too far away to make out what these were. The pilot's attention was closely focused on the road so that he did not apparently spot the crawling convoy still high up on the ridge. The engine-note blared and then died away into a hum and the plane was gone.

It took them half an hour to inch down the escarpment road.

'Well?' Nancy Maxwell said.

'How far do we have to travel on this main road?'

'Half a mile to the left. Then we pick up the track again and turn off right on the far side. We carry on about a hundred miles until we reach the park.'

'And the river with the bridge that gets washed out in bad rains?'

'About fifty miles after we turn off the main road.'

'I want to get off that main road as soon as possible.'

'Because of the 'plane?'

'Yes.'

'What about Nguru now?'

'We'll get over that stretch of main road and turn off towards the park. Then we'll see.'

'Oh sure,' Nancy Maxwell said with sarcasm.

'I mean it.'

'You mean you'll think about it, not necessarily do anything about it.'

'I'll decide. Now let's get this bit of main road behind us. I don't know what that 'plane is up to. They can't have many of them. He's probably the only one. If he's patrolling, he'll very likely land in Makole, which means he isn't likely to be back for half an hour.'

'Probably never be back at all.'

'Maybe, but remember what Ryan heard. The colonials were supposed to be givng the Magunga a few 'planes to aid them in their great struggle for freedom. They might even have left them a pilot or two.'

'So?'

'So, I'll get off this road before I make my mind up what to do about Nguru.'

The main road would not have been a main road in any other country. It had been roughly surfaced at some time in its past life. Now the tarmacadam survived in isolated patches and streaks like the fossilized remains of a large creature temporarily preserved in a crumbling and less durable stone. It made progress slightly easier, but, in terms of speed, scarcely noticeably so. Down off the escarpment the heat was smothering and bounced up to meet you off the road. Long lagoons and fjords of mirage filled the craggy outlines of the broken tarmac with pools of magical water that evaporated as the lorry closed on them. To Maxwell it was a long half mile. In fact, had he checked against his speedometer he would have found that it was more like a mile and a half before the turning came up. Maps in this part of the world often encouraged their users by contracting actual distances. When the park road at last appeared on their right, it was no better nor worse than the road by which they had descended from the escarpment. Almost immediately it began to climb the hills on the far side. Maxwell kept going. He wanted to be as far from the main road as possible in case the 'plane came back. He had reached a long, straight, fairly level pull overhung by a rocky cliff before he had a good view of the main highway again. Behind him the other lorries were labouring, hidden in a cloud of dust.

Nancy Maxwell said peevishly 'So you're not going to stop.'

'I told you I wanted to be clear of that road. We're making a hell of a lot of dust.'

'Well, you'd better stop soon, Nguru or not. The fifteen hundred-weight's not with us.'

'Why the hell didn't you say so?'

'I'm only just certain. I've been watching in the mirror. At first I couldn't be sure for the dust.'

'That bloody girl. Why doesn't she keep up?'

Maxwell signalled to the truck behind him and pulled in close to the overhanging rock face on his left. He stopped his engine. The Land-Rover and Ryan's three-tonner came up close on his tail and stopped also.

Maxwell had climbed out on the roof of his cab. He put his binoculars on the road below, sweeping back along the way they had travelled.

'There she is,' he said at last, 'they must have had some trouble. They're just turning on to the main road now.'

Somewhere in his mind Maxwell had registered that a foreign sound had entered his consciousness. At first it was so distant as to be the sort of noise which only an animal might have registered, but faint as it was, it was obtrusive enough for Maxwell to be able to isolate it as something alien to the atmosphere. Then he had it. Far off yet, the 'plane was coming.

Maxwell's first thought was to look back at their own dust-cloud. It was settling fast and being dispersed and borne away by the air currents of the ridge. The fifteen hundredweight's dust-plume down on the main road was as blatant and revealing as the smoke-cloud of an old-fashioned coal burning ship. Maxwell knew nothing that positively suggested to him that the 'plane was a source of danger, but the whole nightmare progress of the last few days—or was it perhaps weeks?—was beginning to fill him with a sense of overwhelming dread, made worse by the fact that he did not know the real situation in this or any other part of the country. He did not know who was fighting whom, with what forces, in what numbers, in what areas: who was winning, losing, retreating, advancing; whether there were fronts, outposts, territories, or just isolated, unplanned, local battles, as unpredictable in occurrence as the eruption of sores on a diseased body. He just felt with certainty that almost any manifestation of power or militance by either Ashota or Magunga, or for that matter by parties whose identity he could not even begin to guess at, were essentially deadly dangerous.

The 'plane's engine was now a growing hum. The fifteen hundredweight below had covered perhaps a third of the distance along the main road. Through the glasses he could see the girl at the wheel, Mbagi perched on top of the rhino crates behind her, and, on the far side of the cab, a dark shape that was Nguru. In the jolting of the truck and the turbulence of dust and heat he could not see whether Nguru showed signs of life.

The 'plane came flipping over the hills like a silver fish jumping brightly in the sun. It put its nose down and came straight for the road, levelling off at telegraph-pole height. The distance between 'plane and truck was now under half a mile. Maxwell had time to register the fact that the slipstream of the 'plane was creating its own dust wake and then he saw a line of dust devils leap from the road ahead of the truck. The sound of the burst of machine-gun fire reached him a split-second later. The burst was so short, so puny-sounding at a distance that it was like a jumping cracker thrown in a bonfire, expelling all its venom at one puff. It did not seem possible that it could have done real damage to anything as substantial as the truck.

The fifteen hundredweight was slowing down, steam rising in a geyser from its radiator. Through the glasses Maxwell saw the girl leap down onto the road. He saw Mbagi running to the door on Nguru's side of the cab. He heard his wife shout 'It's coming back.'

Maxwell did not need glasses now. He heard the 'plane's engine change its note as the pilot peeled off at the top of a long steep turn and came down again for another run at the truck. Both the girl and the African were no longer to be seen. The 'plane made no mistake this time. The pilot opened fire earlier. The dust path of his bullets began fifty yards behind the fifteen hundredweight, passed over it like a wave and rushed on ahead up the road for another fifty yards before the pilot took his finger off the firing button.

Maxwell saw the black smoke as the bullets hit, then the bright flower of the explosion as the petrol tank went up. A few seconds later the flower was smothered by the base of an oily column of smoke that quickly rose hundreds of feet above the shimmering road.

The noise of the 'plane's engine died away. Maxwell stayed watching. At last he saw what he prayed for. The girl had crawled out from behind the rocks where she had taken shelter. On the other side of the road, Mbagi was doing the same. He was aware that Ryan had started the engine of his three-tonner and was beginning to turn the lorry on the narrow, precipitous road.

Maxwell ran towards him, shouting 'The Land-Rover. Take the Land-Rover. You've got maybe half an hour before he can come back.'

Ryan stopped his manoeuvre with the three-tonner and began to shunt it back again into the shelter of the cliff.

'Leave that,' Maxwell screamed at him.

'That bloody 'plane's not going to get my rhinos.'

'He's damn sight less likely to get any rhinos if you leave them up here. His job is to keep that main road clear.'

Ryan was running towards the Land-Rover. He pushed Mgulu out of the driving-seat so hard that he fell out on the road on the other side. As he started the engine, Ryan yelled 'You're not coming?'

'No, I'm going to move the Merc into a safer place.'

'Trust you. Look after your own bloody animals. Not mine.'

'Get going,' Maxwell said harshly. 'You don't have any animals but she's your bush baby.'

When Ryan got down to the girl he found her untouched except for a glass cut on the neck. Mbagi had escaped, too. When the 'plane had taken its first run, the tracker had been sitting on the rhino crates directly behind the girl. The pilot had made his first attack at a slight angle which had not been discernible from high up on the hill. His first burst had raked the near-side of the truck. It had killed instantly both Nguru and the young bull rhino. By the time Ryan reached in, the frame of the fifteen hundredweight was incandescent and glowing with a pink fire that even the blaze of the sun could not diminish. The stench of burnt flesh, animal and human, made Ryan retch. He did not even stop his engine. He pulled the shivering girl into the cab beside him and did not object when Mbagi climbed in, too. He was away up the road before the door of the Land-Rover had slammed shut. He drove as fast as the diesel would take him. All the time he listened beyond the thudding of its motor for the sound of the 'plane's engine. But the 'plane did not come again.

When he reached the three-tonner high on the hillside below the cliff, Maxwell was long gone. Mgulu sat on the ground almost exactly where he had fallen when Ryan had pushed him out of the Land-Rover. His eyes appeared to roll with terror but it was impossible to judge the cause because this was his habitual expression. Ryan put his arm round Jen and led her to the three-tonner. Without waiting for Mgulu he started its engine and pulled off in the tracks of the Mercedes.

After ten miles, he found Maxwell on the edge of a wood. The Mercedes was close in under a tall tree where the eyes of an aircraft were unlikely to find it. As he drove up, Maxwell was feeding the big bull rhino by hand. Maxwell looked up and took in the situation.

'Nguru?' he asked.

'Dead. The first burst killed him.'

'The rhinos?'

'Well, we didn't bring the bits with us if that's what you mean.'

'Were they killed by the 'plane?'

Ryan said 'Everything was killed by the 'plane.'

'I mean did they burn?'

'What's the flaming odds?' said Ryan. 'One way or another, they're dead. We're down to four and two of them are mine.'

Maxwell didn't answer.

Nancy Maxwell looked at him as he came over to the cab. She still sat strapped to her seat. There was no Nguru now to release her when they reached camp for the night.

'Nguru's dead,' he told her.

'Well at least that saves you an awkward decision.'

'Yes, doesn't it?' He paused and said 'Why the hell can't you get off my back?'

'Just for the record, what *would* you have done. Would you have sent Nguru in to Makole?'

'I don't know. How the hell can I tell? The 'plane altered everything.'

'Did it? *Did* it? Wouldn't you have let him die rather than risk a single piece of your blessed transport, even a thing as clapped out as the Land-Rover?'

'Don't ride me,' he repeated wearily. 'How can I tell what I'd have done? The 'plane altered everything. Everything alters from second to second.'

'Except your blind bloody determination to get these rhinos to where they're going, even if it means killing the lot of us.'

'Any other suggestions?'

'Yes,' she said, 'as a matter of fact I have. I've been looking at these maps fairly closely. If we turned east from here, in about sixty miles we'd be out of this damn country. We'd be over the border where there's no fighting. If you still insist we could turn the rhinos loose there. Is there anything against that?'

'Anything against it?' he repeated slowly. 'To start with, over the border they've got no game policy.'

'Unlike here,' she said bitterly. 'Here they kill people on sight as well.'

'The rhinos wouldn't last ten minutes over there. Even government officials buy and sell rhino horn.'

'And here, here in this glorious, well-administered paradise?'

'Whatever's happened so far, I believe the parks have a fair chance of surviving. Whatever happens, I'm going to get the king and queen there.'

'The *what?*' she said.

'King and queen. The pair on the Merc.'

'Oh no,' she said, 'not a poetic soul under that rugged exterior.'

'You've turned bloody sour over the years,' he said.

'I've had plenty to curdle me.'

'That's right,' he said, 'blame me for an accident that took place fifteen years ago. Blame me for everything that's happened after that.'

'Not you. Not you particularly, but the whole damn lot of you with your khaki-coloured hair shirts and your damn nobility about saving the world's wildlife. You're a lot of bloody freebooters having a hell of a good time in a man's world. You're really not much different from Ryan.'

'That's your right to think so, or think any other damn thing you like.'

She changed her tack. 'Anyway, what's Ryan going to say? He's lost half his transport and he'll probably lose the rest. Surely you owe him something.'

Maxwell said 'We'll settle that when we reach the park.'

'Like you settled the business about Nguru.'

'If you like. Nguru didn't make it. The rhinos may not make it. I'm going to see that they get the best possible chance.'

'And the girl. What about the girl? Don't you owe her something?'

'She's with Ryan. She's made her choice.'

'Don't you owe anybody anything except the damn rhinos?'

'Yes, Webb,' said Maxwell surprisingly. 'The big bull killed Webb. And that's another reason why the king and queen are going to get there. They were bought with a man's life.'

'What about Nguru?'

'Nguru's too, if you like.'

When darkness came a thunderstorm struck the countryside with the intensity and pyrotechnic frequency of a thousand-gun barrage. They snatched what sleep they could in the cabs of the three remaining vehicles, leaving the Africans to find and rig what shelter they could beneath and alongside the trucks.

Maxwell stayed awake most of the night. He had gone beyond fatigue now. He just wanted to be finished with the job.

The rain stopped a little before dawn. Maxwell got down and walked through the mire to Ryan's vehicle. He found Ryan and the girl sleeping unhappily and untidily in opposite corners of the cab. He shook Ryan, who jumped, his hand leaping out for the rifle that stood in the rack beside him.

'Relax,' Maxwell told him. 'You can keep watch now. I've been on all night. Not that I think anything will happen up here, but I won't take any chances.'

Before Maxwell rolled himself up in his blanket in his own lorry he had a look at the king and queen. Both had their heads well up, their magnificent front horns sticking up through the gaps in the crate. They were scenting the morning air. Reassured, he climbed back into the cab and slept for three hours. When he awoke it was raining again.

Zakari cooked them breakfast. In the stress of the moment he had reverted to frying the beans and boiling the bacon. Maxwell ate without noticing this. After he had eaten, he said to his wife 'How far to the river, the one with the bad crossing?'

'Forty miles.'

'And how far on the other side to the park?'

'Fifty.'

'Think that bridge will be there?'

'After last night, I should think it's an even-money bet that it's been washed out.'

'And if it has?'

'Then we do forty miles to the north-west to find the permanent crossing and another forty miles back to get on the park track again.'

'Is the second crossing certain?'

'It says so here, but then by now it may have been blown up or anything.'

'What about petrol?'

'With the seventy gallons we got from the sikh, both lorries should make it to the park but we'll be pretty short after that.'

'I'm not worried after that.'

'What's the plan? Do you aim to bash straight through?'

'I'd like to,' Maxwell said, 'but that bridge worries me. If that's okay then we might make it today. But if it's gone, then we'll camp short of the permanent bridge and go over in darkness. If anyone's watching that bridge we'll have a better chance of getting over it in the dark. We'll move straight away.'

But they didn't move straight away. Even up on the high ground the bush was becoming soggy. The Land-Rover came out straight away in four-wheel drive, but both the Mercedes and Ryan's three-tonner began to wheel-spin and dig themselves in.

It was after midday when they got both lorries back on the road. During the inch by inch progress they had made across the hundred yards of wet ground separating the wood from the road they had torn down two large trees which had made short-lived anchors for their winch ropes; they had also sacrificed most of their loose gear in an effort to give the wheels something on which to grip. Tents, fly-sheets, planks, cans, part of one of the cooking stoves, tarpaulins, bedding, all lay mashed and mired behind them in the ruts torn by their floundering wheels. Black and white were scarcely distinguishable from each other. The girl, plastered with mud flung from the wheels, was detectable as a woman only by the outline of her breasts which stuck to her soaking shirt. Even Ryan was too tired to look at these.

As they started off it began to rain hard again.

Maxwell could see that the bridge had gone long before he got to it. It was a temporary affair across a small, deep *wadi* which was bone dry for nine-tenths of the year but which fluctuated during the remainder of the period between a stream trickling along a stony bed and a torrent that rose in a few hours to climb up over its banks. It was over its banks now. The bridge, an affair of tree-trunks and heavy planking, lay across the stream, the far end submerged in the rushing water.

Maxwell said 'So that's that.'

'It's probably only just gone.'

'What's the odds? It's gone. What do we do now?'

'We passed a track on the right two miles back. We take that up to the other bridge. It's forty miles but according to the map it's a proper permanent bridge when we get there.'

'What's the track like?'

'Can't be any worse than the one we've been on.'

The track was, if anything, slightly better, for it ran along a ridge of high ground. Maxwell felt a slight rise in spirits at the sight of game. He spotted a small herd of eland in the distance among some zebra. Impala and Thompson's gazelle were down on the plain below, too. He felt almost happy again and not only because of the animals but also because their presence meant that this was a largely unpopulated area. The rain stopped towards late afternoon and at last, when coming round the shoulder of a hill, he saw the bridge ahead and far below. He took out his glasses and examined the situation. Muddy water swept high round the piles of the bridge but these were concrete, as was the stout span that crossed the flooded river. He looked for signs of militia but could see none. Then he spotted a convoy of three military lorries, moving fast towards the bridge from his own side. They clattered over and disappeared.

Ryan came up to the cab. 'What are we waiting for? Is it guarded?'

'I can't see anyone on the bridge but there's a convoy just gone over. Look. There's another truck now.'

A jeep crossed the bridge and disappeared in the same direction as the lorries.

'Well,' said Ryan, 'what's keeping us? They got over, whoever they are.'

'It may be their bridge.'

'Which way do we go once we're across?'

'We take a track to the left after a quarter of a mile. It takes us back down the far bank towards the park.'

'Did those lorries go that way?'

'No. They went straight on, along the main road.'

'We're okay then.'

'We'll wait until dark.'

'Oh, for Christ's sake,' said Ryan. 'Let's get it over with.'

Four distant explosions echoed against the hillside.

Maxwell said 'Hear those? They were mortars. We'll wait.'

'Where? Here?'

'No, a little further on. On the shoulder of this hill. There's a small wood there. The trees come right down to the roadside. From there it looks a straight run down to the bridge. We could coast down there in the darkness and be practically on the bridge before we have to start our engines.'

'What the hell you're so jittery about,' Ryan said, 'I don't know.'

'Then you're bloody unobservant,' Maxwell told him.

Maxwell picked a good hard standing, just off the road and under the trees. Mgulu pulled the Land-Rover in behind him. Ryan, however, could not find space and had to go on past the Mercedes. Eventually he got off the road one hundred yards ahead of Maxwell and just at the point where the gradient towards the bridge, still a mile away down the hill, began to steepen.

They got water from a hill stream and washed the mud from their bodies. Maxwell fed the rhinos, the king and the queen, as well as the cow and bull calf which Ryan now constantly referred to as 'my rhinos'.

Over supper, Ryan used a variation of this phrase which was too much for Maxwell.

'Maxwell,' he said, 'we'll call it a day now. We'll take our rhinos and get out of it.'

'We?' Maxwell shouted. 'Our? Who the hell is we and what the hell makes you think you've got any rhinos. Our deal . . .'

'We,' said Ryan quietly, 'is Jen and I. We're getting out of here together. You must know that.'

'Then start walking because you're not taking any rhinos.'

'You're an amazing bastard,' said Ryan. 'You've used me. You've used up my bloody trucks. Now I suppose because I'm taking your girl away you think you can do me out of the payment you owe me.

213

My bargain was for two rhinos. What would you do if I just got in my truck and drove off? You couldn't stop me.'

Maxwell said 'If you stole those animals, Ryan, you'd never get down that road. I can see you clear for five hundred yards of the way. I'd stop you if I had to shoot you.'

'Even if you hit Jen instead?'

'She'd have to take her chance.'

'Once,' said Ryan, 'I told you that you were a sentimentalist. You're not. You're something much worse than that. You're a fanatic. I thought you were one of these softheads who cared about man's great heritage and saving the animals for posterity. To me this argued that, however tough you acted, you were really just an old fuddy-duddy who cared for people more even than you do about our pals up there in the boxes with the horns stuck on the end of their snouts. I've heard people talking about you as though you were some kind of a mystical bastard and even a sort of St Francis of what's-it. But you're not, Maxwell. You really are a self-centered maniac who's just determined to show everyone concerned that he can do what he says. That's why you want to get these bloody animals into the park. Just because you said you'd do it. They haven't got a cat in hell's chance of surviving, let alone breeding there, but that doesn't matter to you.'

'Go on, talk, Ryan. Talk's your line.'

'Is it? Well, I've got plenty to say at the end of this charming excursion. *I'm* not trying to prove anything to anybody. Nor am I doing it for the good of humanity if that's what you still insist you're doing. Thank God I'm just in it for the money. And I want my ten thousand quids' worth.'

'When we get to the park we'll talk about that,' Maxwell said.

'I could take my rhinos now and be out of the bloody country and across the border with them in fifty miles and my two would be safe, which is more than you'll ever be able to say for your flaming king and queen . . . *king* and *queen*,' he sneered.

'Ryan, of all the men who've died not one of them could have been you. It had to be Webb and Nguru.'

Ryan said 'I'll tell you one thing. I'm damn glad no one jabbed me with a spear. I wouldn't have cared to rely on your idea of the humanities. I'd have got even less of a chance than poor old Nguru.'

Maxwell said slowly 'You're raving. This is my last word. If we

214

get all four rhinos to the park we'll talk about your claims. But not until then. You're right about one thing. I *am* determined the king and queen will make it. Apart from anything else, Webb paid for them. But if they don't, I want something to turn loose, even if it's your cow and calf.'

'Oh, so you admit they're mine.'

'No. I don't. And I'll tell you another thing. If you try to drive away with them I'll stop you with a rifle bullet.'

Throughout the late afternoon and early evening there were occasional and distant sounds of fighting. Once Maxwell heard a 'plane droning high in the sky. He could not tell whether it was a transport, a high-flying airliner on a normal route, or a fighter flown by god-knows-who fighting for god-knows-what cause. The pilot was probably a mercenary, just as Ryan was a mercenary: all mercenaries had only one cause and fought under one flag—their own. When full darkness came and with it a clear, dry night, the sounds died away. Not even the noise of an occasional lorry engine came up from the road. After checking the rhinos about midnight and before he turned in for a couple of hours' sleep, Maxwell stood on the edge of the hill and watched a great glow in the sky far to the south, the way they must head tomorrow. Perhaps this was a bush fire; it could be, even at this time of the year. Periodical flashes on the horizon might have been gunfire but were more likely to be caused by heat lightning.

Maxwell stayed on watch until midnight when Ryan was to take over until three. It had been arranged that they would move out down the hill and over the bridge at four. Just after twelve, Maxwell turned in. He was asleep almost before he had settled his body behind the wheel of the Mercedes.

He seemed to wake immediately with Mbagi shaking him. It was still dark. Mbagi was pointing frantically up the road ahead. Maxwell looked and saw that Ryan's three-tonner had gone.

'The engine,' he shouted at the tracker. 'Why didn't you hear the engine? You useless sleeping bastard, you deserve to be shot.'

'They did not start the engine, *bwana*. Not even the boys sleeping close by the truck heard them go. They simply rolled away.'

'How long have they been gone?'

'One hour. Two hours. Three?'

'Get everyone on the trucks. We're going, too.'

Five minutes later the Mercedes was coasting down the hill, gathering speed silently just as Ryan had done. When they reached the straight leading to the bridge, Maxwell switched on and let out his clutch. The engine fired and they roared over the bridge with no one to see or stop them.

Mbagi rode on the step alongside Maxwell. But it did not take an African tracker to tell which way Ryan had gone. The tyre marks of the three-tonner stood out clearly in the softened ground where they had turned off on the park track.

'If you were Ryan,' Maxwell asked his wife, 'which way would you have gone?'

'Never mind Ryan. If I were you,' she told him, 'I'd just let him go, whichever way he's gone. You can't stop him now.'

'Unless he has a breakdown or runs into trouble. Last night there were flashes on the horizon towards the border. He's obviously making for the border.'

'If he is,' said his wife, 'his best course is to carry on down this track to the washed-out bridge then turn back onto the road towards the park for a bit. That's the way we're going: it's the road we'd be on now if the bridge hadn't been down. Then, after a few miles, there's a fork. The left-hand track is ours, the one towards the park. But the right fork will take Ryan to the border inside thirty miles.'

It was long after daylight by the time they reached the broken bridge. This time they were on the park side of its wrecked span. Ryan's tyre marks were still with them. He had turned onto the park road where it led away from the bridge, just as Nancy Maxwell had forecast.

Now, too, it was becoming plain that something like a major, if sporadic, battle was being fought up ahead of them. Smudges of smoke rose in the sky in the direction of the border. They heard explosions every now and again and once a 'plane went whining low across the bush far behind. Half a minute after it had passed, the flattened blast of a single bomb reached them from far off.

They came to the point at which the road forked and Maxwell pulled up. Mbagi pointed to the right-hand track, indicating that Ryan's three-tonner had taken that road.

Nancy Maxwell said 'The left fork should have us inside the park boundaries within thirty miles. According to Richie and the map he marked, the release area is about five miles from the point at which this track enters the park.'

'But Ryan took the right fork.'

'Then let him go. You'll get your flaming king and queen to the park now.'

Maxwell gestured towards the distant smoke. 'With this lot going on? Looks to me like a pitched bloody battle.'

'So what? The fighting doesn't appear to be towards the park. It's all up the right fork towards the border.'

'Ryan went that way.'

'That's his bloody funeral. It'll be our bloody funeral, too, if we try to follow him, not to mention the rhinos'.'

'He stole those two rhino.'

'You owe them to him.'

Maxwell ignored this. He let in his clutch and turned the Mercedes down the park track.

'Thank God you're showing some sense at last,' his wife said.

But after five miles, Maxwell found a small patch of forest with a firm surface leading to it across the bush. He took the big lorry off the track and drove it in among the trees until it was completely enveloped in branches and hanging creepers.

'What now?'

'I'm going back to settle with Ryan.'

'Settle with him! You'll never catch up with him.'

'Wait here. Take the rifle. You won't need it, but still. No one will spot you here. I'll take Mbagi but I'll leave you the other boys.'

'And if you succeed in killing yourself?'

'Then you'll have to make that idiot Mgulu get you the rest of the way to the park.'

'And if I do get there?'

'Get the king and queen out.'

'And after that?'

'Get yourself out.'

Maxwell tipped the last five gallons of diesel fuel into the Land-Rover and started back the way he had come.

At the fork Mbagi picked up Ryan's tracks without difficulty. Soon they began to come on signs of the fighting. They passed the bomb crater made by the 'plane, a shallow depression in the hard surface of the bush, its torn sides still stained yellow, the stink of explosive poisoning the air. From the shallowness of its crater Maxwell judged that it had been an anti-personnel bomb, but there were no victims to be seen. A little further up the track they came to a burned, deserted village: a dead dog lay in the middle of the charred huts with two kites picking at it. But the occasional sounds of small arms, the rare bursts of automatic fire and the crump of mortar bombs was always far ahead. The battle seemed to be a phantom, scarcely capable of being believed in, except for the few tangible relics of its passing.

After ten miles, Mbagi spotted that the three-tonner had turned off across the bush. The going was good here for there had evidently been little rain. Once the tracker called for Maxwell to stop while he got down and examined the ground all around them.

'Well?' Maxwell demanded.

'Many men as well as the lorry.'

'How many?'

'Perhaps twenty.'

'Soldiers?'

'They did not wear boots.'

'How long ago?'

'Just now. One hour. Two hours.'

They drove on and, rounding a large outcrop of rock, came suddenly upon the three-tonner.

Maxwell saw at once that the lids of the rhino crate had been wrenched off and that both rhinos had been speared for their horn. He found the girl on a flat rock nearby. She was naked and lacerated and had been violated, probably many times. She was dead. Ryan lay under the lorry. He was unconscious. His face was caked with blood. He had not been speared but they had clubbed him. It looked as though his skull might be fractured. He was still breathing.

Maxwell no longer felt that he knew what he was doing. He put Ryan in the front of the Land-Rover. He found two full petrol drums on the three-tonner. One of these he opened, pouring its contents over the front seats and inside of the three-tonner's cab. The other he lifted into the back of the Land-Rover. Then he took the girl's body and placed it gently behind the wheel. Finally he backed the Land-Rover away and lit the grass upwind of the lorry. By the time the fire reached the petrol-laden air around the three-tonner he was in his own vehicle and backing away. The explosion rocked the Land-Rover on its wheels, the heat of the burning lorry becoming almost instantly unbearable. He waited to see that the funeral pyre really meant to destroy the lorry and its victims utterly, then he began to drive without being aware that he drove.

They stayed in the little forest for several hours. At first Nancy Maxwell had stared at him as if she did not understand what he was telling her. Then she had begun to cry, shouting and screaming as she sobbed, beating at the windscreen with her fists, then becoming silent and just sitting upright and unmoving. Maxwell left her at last and walked away into the trees, too tired to care what he bumped into or what hit him. When finally he came back to the truck, his face was bleeding where the thorns had torn it. He found that Mbagi had lifted his wife out of the cab and that she was cleaning the blood from Ryan's face.

It was the first time Maxwell had thought of Ryan. He looked at his unconscious features without emotion of any sort. At last he said 'Will he die soon?'

His wife said 'I don't know. He has a chance. His heart sounds strong. It's hard to say what damage they've done to his skull. It's like Nguru. If we could get him somewhere.'

'Some hopes.'

'Some hopes,' she echoed.

A 'plane droned across the sky again.

'Twenty miles to go,' he said. 'They've cost a lot, these two, my flaming king and queen.'

'I hope you think it's all been worth it.'

'Worth it? I dunno. I didn't bring it all on.'

'Why not just turn the rhinos loose here?'

'I haven't come this far . . .'

'No, I suppose not. Well, what's one more life or two even if it's your own.'

'It's a question of keeping a bargain,' he began.

'Oh don't give me that,' she said tiredly. 'It's like Ryan told you: you've said all along you'll do it, so you'll do it. What's the difference whether you let the bastards go here or anywhere else? Here they'd have as much chance as in the park. Probably more. Poachers know there's rhino horn in the park.'

'I've thought about that,' he said.

'Oh, hooray,' she said. 'Thank God you've thought about something.'

'We'll start in half an hour.'

'And Ryan? Is he coming with us, because if he does he'll probably die.'

'No. We'll leave him with Mbagi. I'll want the rest of the boys to get the rhinos off.'

'Mbagi tells me they won't go any further. They're half dead with fear.'

'Then leave the bastards. I'll go myself.'

'How will you get the rhinos off?'

'Richie swore they built a ramp. It's marked on the map. We should be able to find it.'

'We?'

'Please yourself, Nance.'

'We,' she said. 'It's we.'

They were not attacked as they drove on alone, though, again, there were sights and sounds of the phantom war all round them.

'This is Ashota territory,' Maxwell said. 'The Magunga must be trying to crush them here.'

'Just our luck.'

'Let's hope our luck turns soon.'

'If we get the rhinos off,' she said, 'what next?'

'Then we'll lie low in the forest and try to get out over the border when things quieten down.'

'And Ryan?'

'He can come,' said Maxwell drily.

'Then we can't afford to lie low for long.'

'Let's get the rhinos off first.'

They crossed the park border an hour later. A notice-board announced the fact. But there were bullet holes in the metal of the board and a thatched hut which usually housed a smartly dressed game guard was burned to the ground. There was no game guard.

Nancy Maxwell said 'We're risking our necks for nothing.'

'Speak for yourself.'

'I am. For my neck.'

'Read the map and shut up. We've got to find that ramp first time.'

As they drove, game became more plentiful. A great herd of hartebeeste ran across their bows, lolloping with rocking-horse gait and reflecting the sun from their polished coats so that they looked like bronze unicorns. An old lion skulked in the grass. Further on there were elephant delicately reaching down the juiciest shoots from the upper shelves of the trees. Two giraffe broke into a slow-motion gallop at their approach, and a family of baboons, loping through the grass, stopped to stare at them. On a grassy flat by a stream a black rhino was rolling in a mud wallow.

Maxwell said 'They haven't got *him* yet.'

Nancy Maxwell said 'Don't let this Garden of Eden touch fool you. The battle hasn't reached here yet, that's all. It will and then see how long he lasts.'

A 'plane droned across the sky. Its passing, somewhere to the west of them between the park and the border, was followed by a long burst of machine-gun fire.

By following a stream bed they came at last to the ramp. It had been built in the centre of an amphitheatre of rich green grass so that it looked like a stage deliberately set in the middle of an arena.

'That will do them,' Maxwell said. 'The king and queen.'

'They'll have a short reign, I'm thinking.'

Maxwell backed the lorry up against the ramp so that one crate door faced it. Then he dropped the tailboard. As he did so the 'plane came quartering back from the west, closer this time.

'He's looking for a target,' his wife yelled. 'For God's sake get those rhino out.'

'Wait,' Maxwell told her.

'Just remember that if that 'plane spots us I can't get out of this thing.'

'Wait, I said.'

Maxwell opened the cab door, undid the straps and picked his wife up. He carried her fifty yards clear and set her down in the grass high on one of the sides of the amphitheatre.

Then Maxwell went back to the truck and took Webb's gleaming hacksaw from its wallet. He climbed up on top of the king's crate and, reaching down through the slats, began to saw at the rhino's insensitive horn close to the point at which it joined the skull. The front horn took him a long time because the rhino repeatedly jabbed his head up and down in protest. As he started on the slightly shorter rear horn, the 'plane came again, closer and lower this time, but still a good five miles away. The second horn was easier because the rhino could not move his head at this point through such a large angle. The 'plane made a third pass but further away still.

Maxwell found that he was streaming with sweat.

When it came to the cow's turn, Maxwell gave himself more room to work by first levering off the centre plank on top of the crate. Though he could now reach the horns more easily, he found himself constantly having to avoid the lunges of the cow who appeared to sense that the removal of the plank had given her more attacking space above her head.

The 'plane made a fourth pass somewhere over in the direction from which they had come. There was a long burst of machine-gun fire and, from the top of the crate, Maxwell could see fresh smoke rising in the air.

He got the rear horn off at last and lay panting on top of the cow's box. When he had caught his breath he took a ring spanner from his pocket and went to work on the rear door of the king's crate. The four nuts came away easily and the door fell open, but the big rhino seemed quite content to stay inside. Maxwell began to work on the door of the cow's crate, hoping all the time that the bull would decide to walk out onto the ramp, but he stayed obstinately put. Finally he drove the bull out by lying on top of his crate and kicking his backside hard and repeatedly. Maxwell was just getting down to move the lorry so that the cow's exit was more squarely against the end of the ramp when he heard the 'plane coming again. This time the engine-note seemed unmistakably aimed at him, and when the fighter burst at him above the tree-tops, he saw that this was actually so. He did not have time to take cover. He saw every detail of the 'plane as it roared straight towards him. He saw the torn patches over the gun ports, blasted away and blackened by firing. He saw the leopard-skin insignia hastily painted on the undersurfaces of the wings and then his mind dimly registered that, since he had seen these as the 'plane passed over him, it could not have opened fire. Already it was becoming a dot in the sky, climbing away behind him.

Maxwell felt the sweat pouring off him afresh. He climbed into the lorry, and, grating the gears, shunted it so that the cow's crate was against the ramp.

The cow came out without a moment's pause. She stood there pawing the ground alongside the bull and tossing her head, just as if she still had a horn on the end of it.

Maxwell ran to where his wife lay in the grass.

'The 'plane?' she began to ask.

'He'll be back. He was out of ammunition.'

Maxwell stood looking at the rhinos. They had now mooched down off the ramp and were moving away together into the grass.

'The king and queen,' he said. 'They've lost their bleeding crowns but they'll do. There's nothing to kill them for now.'

He lifted his wife into the cab and started the engine.

Then he began to drive back towards the smoke-clouds and the place where Ryan lay among the trees.